Also by Susan Sink

The Way of All the Earth (poems)

Habits: 100-word stories

H is for Harry (poems)

available at susansinkblog.com/books

Officer Down

By Susan Sink

for Steve

On my honor, I will never betray my badge, my integrity, my character or the public trust. I will always have the courage to hold myself and others accountable for our actions. I will always uphold the constitution, my community, and the agency I serve.

Law Enforcement Oath of Honor

Sometimes, like that night in the shit field, the difference between courage and cowardice was something small and stupid.

Tim O'Brien, *The Things They Carried*

Chapter One

Most people never have to find out whether they'd act heroically in a time of crisis. They go along day to day believing that they would, if necessary, step up. But I know. I am not a hero.

In fact, I am a coward. I am worse than a coward. I was in a police squad, wearing a uniform and in possession of a firearm. When my partner was shot, I threw the squad into reverse and flew backwards out of the alley as fast as I could.

I did not see who did it. I did not see a vehicle. I called for backup from the safety of the post office parking lot, a block from the scene, and the man who shot and killed Officer Chris Miller disappeared into the night. That is what happened. I am clear about it now.

In fact, I wasn't even paying attention. It was our last call, a favor really, for worried parents who wanted the police to check on their son. They hadn't been able to get in touch with him for a couple days, so called the station and asked if we would stop by and make sure he was OK. He lived in an apartment over Arnold's Bar. The entrance was up a flight of stairs in the back, off the alley.

We went in sloppy. This guy wasn't trouble. At least, he wasn't on our radar. He was just a drunk twenty-something, or maybe using drugs, but not in a way that got him into our system. He didn't want to talk to his parents. We could understand that. All we were going to do was ring the guy's doorbell, confirm he was alive and breathing, tell him to contact his parents, and we would be done for the night.

I put the vehicle in Park and sent a quick text to my girlfriend, Julie. While Chris got out on the passenger side and crossed in front of the squad, I was typing: "r u awake? shd I come by?"

Texting. Jeez. A coward and a loser. The shot sounded at the same time I pushed Send. And I didn't think, just dropped the phone and threw the squad into reverse. I sort of remember the flash of it—the flash maybe in the driver's side window. But I didn't see anything. Not really.

I can say that now. Now that I know what happened. Though we'll never really know all of the story. The people who could tell us the whole truth, they're dead. The people charged with finding it out aren't interested. If I've learned one thing from all this, it's that sometimes the story is more important than the truth. When people get a story they like, especially in a small town like Maurus, they stick with it, even if it doesn't totally add up.

In the moment, though, my heart was racing and my adrenaline pushed me in the wrong direction. I'm sure for most guys, maybe all other officers in the world, adrenaline pushes you into

2

the scene, toward the action. But not for me. Once I reached the end of the alley, I backed into a parking space beside the post office. I started swearing up a storm, banging my hands on the steering wheel. Everything was dead silent.

Maurus is a one-stoplight town, and only the bars were open. It was 10:18 p.m. I remember seeing that time on the dashboard clock. It was really quiet. You'd think I would have heard a vehicle leaving the scene, but I didn't hear anything. No footsteps. No shouts. Just the idling of the squad. I pulled slowly back into the alley, but I didn't return all the way to the scene, not yet. I put in the call: "Officer down, send backup and an ambulance. Alley at 210 Main, behind Arnold's Bar. Maurus. Officer down."

The calm, female voice of dispatch came over the radio, and immediate responses, from Castor, from St. Albans, even Badenberg. Sheriff. A trooper. Emergency response was four minutes out. Then Nicole's voice came over the radio, louder and closer. The only one asking questions, not using numbers. "Chris? Paul? What officer?"

"Nicole," I said, "get off the line." I had forgotten she was at the station.

"Paul? Is it Chris? Is Chris hurt? Is Chris shot?" She was getting hysterical, so I tried to calm her. I guess that was when I started to feel like a cop. Talking to people at the scene, people in bad situations, that was my forte. Up to that point I thought that was what police work was.

"Nicole. It's OK. It's going to be OK. Turn off your radio."

In the silences between the brief, clipped chatter, the logistics of people calmly responding, there was Nicole's voice. "Is he dead, Paul? Is Chris dead?"

"Is the scene secure? Should we stage?" This from the Accucare ambulance. I didn't know. I didn't know the answer to either question.

I put the squad in Drive and moved forward. With purpose, and with the protection of the vehicle that always felt so substantial. There's nothing like a police vehicle—I don't know what it is. I've been in them after they've been sold and stripped of their decals and lights and they aren't the same, they're just gas-guzzling sedans and SUVs then, but a real police vehicle, a squad, well, it has authority. Moving forward or in reverse, it has purpose.

I arrived at the scene. I could see Chris on the ground at the edge of the alley, near the back stairs, in the deep area behind the bar. Even sitting in the car I drew my gun, though I knew the incident was over. I looked up at the apartment, but the window was dark. The shot didn't seem to have woken anyone up—the whole thing was surreal. Nicole was still talking over the radio, but I focused on Dispatch. An efficient woman's voice in Castor. I touched the mic at my shoulder and said, "Securing the scene." Later that would be used, to my shame, to establish the time line.

I left the car idling in Park, the radio chattering, got out, and shut the door with a loud click. It was so quiet, just a low rumble from the bar. I approached the back door. Everything seemed fully illuminated. The sky was clear and cold and there was a moon. In addition to the light over the bar door, there was a

4

streetlight in the alley. There was no hiding place, nothing obscuring the area. Two dumpsters, rear door with bare yellow lightbulb above it, wooden stairs like a fire escape to the upstairs apartment. I kept my weapon drawn and made sure the area was clear. It was completely clear.

And there was Chris Miller. The unmoving body of Chris Miller. He was lying flat on his back. Wearing his heavy jacket and blue trousers and boots. Unmoving.

I holstered my gun. Again I tapped on my mobile, bringing it to life. "All clear. Respond directly to the scene." The thumping bass from the bar felt like my heart beating, and there was that high static of people talking. It was a good night at Arnold's. Just my luck. The squad sat idling, and I could smell the exhaust. I went over to Chris to check for a pulse. But I felt oddly distracted, nervous about the alley. I just sort of stood guard, I guess. I didn't kneel down beside the body—maybe I just couldn't face what I'd done. I drew my gun again and checked behind the dumpster, over by the apartment stairs. I went back to the squad then, for the defibrillator, for the emergency response equipment. But then the EMTs arrived.

I needed to get my shit together. I wasn't attending to Chris. They would think that was strange. I was thinking about what I should be doing. But I didn't know. I was in shock; I know that now. I needed help.

Rick and Karen jumped out of the ambulance, lights still spinning, and went to Chris's side. They weren't tentative at all. Medics at war are like that, too, right? They calmly go onto the battlefield, in the middle of a battle, focused just on the person

5

they need to attend to, saving a life. It's their training. But I had training, too, and it all left me the second I heard the gunshot and saw the flash.

Karen unzipped Chris's coat and Rick started reporting immediately: "Male, early thirties, gunshot wound to the chest. Not breathing, no pulse. Appears to be large caliber, or a slug." He looked up at me. "What kind of gun was it?"

I, of course, didn't know. In fact I'd assumed it was a handgun, a large caliber handgun. But I was saved from answering because the back door opened.

It was Ashley Keegan coming out for a smoke. I moved quickly to the door, arms out, to stop her from coming closer and to block her view of Chris. Ashley looked surprised, the cigarette hanging out of her mouth, lighter in her hand. I've known Ashley a long time. She's a hard drinker, which makes her look older than her forty years. She's small and thin, with a voice marked by smoking. Her husband, Carl, has had plenty of trouble. Seeing a cop is never good news for Ashley.

"Ashley," I said. "Ashley, it's Paul."

"Jesus, Paul, you scared me." She took the cigarette from her mouth.

"Is Jim inside?"

Ashley nodded, looking over at the EMTs. "What's going on?"

"Listen. I need you to go back inside and get Jim for me."

"Someone have a heart attack or something?" she asked, looking past me. Not moving from the door.

"Ashley, listen to me. I need you to get Jim for me. Don't say anything to anyone else."

"Jesus, is it a cop?"

I put my hands lightly on her shoulders, to focus her attention. "Ashley, look at me. It's all under control. The EMTs are taking care of him. I just need you to get Jim for me. And not say anything. Can you do that?"

Ashley's face seemed unusually large, concentrating on the instructions, serious. She turned and went back inside without saying anything. When the door opened, there was a rush of music and voices and laughter.

Jim came out next: "Shit," he said. Jim is a big guy, mid-fifties, a beer drinker, and not very agile. He pushed his glasses up his nose and shuffled out, looking back at the door closing behind him as if he'd rather be on the other side of it.

"We have a situation," I said.

"Is that guy dead?" Jim asked.

"Don't worry about that. We have to make sure no one comes out this door." It didn't occur to me that the killer could be in the bar, though of course it would have made good cover. But I was sure the killer was long gone.

"Can you lock this door?"

"Yeah, but, uh, that's against fire code," Jim said.

"This is a crime scene," I said, using my cop voice. "I need this area secured."

"A crime scene?" Jim said. "Aw shit." He looked around nervously. "I got a lot of people in there, Paul. We got a meat raffle tonight."

"OK," I said. "Stay calm. Don't alarm anyone." I wasn't sure what to do. In the scenarios there are always multiple cops on the scene. Should I try to keep people calm by going on as usual? Or should I try, just me, to clear the place. Maybe, though it seemed unlikely, there was a witness in there. A witness waiting for the meat raffle to start? There was still chatter on the radio. Backup was coming. Lots of backup. I just wanted to focus on what was on the alley side of the bar door. Later, everything was excused by the shock. That's what they said, though never with full confidence, never like they really believed it. I wasn't sure I believed it either. But I couldn't have cleared that bar myself. And I was numb. I felt like sound was echoing in my head, and it was hard to . . . not see exactly, but focus my eyes on anything. Mostly, though, I just had no clue what to do.

"Lock this door, Jim," I said. "Now."

"I have to go to the office and get the keys," he said.

"Yeah, OK. Do it." Jim ducked back inside and shut the door hard.

I turned and stood guard. Rick and Karen were still working on the body, pumping oxygen, shocking the heart with a portable defibrillator.

That's when the red Malibu came flying down the alley. "Fuck," I said, reaching for my gun and moving toward the car. I saw the cloud of blond hair through the windshield.

"Nicole, no," I said, wishing I could make her disappear. I kept moving toward her. Everything seemed to be in a sort of slow motion. She'd barely stopped the car and she was out. "Chris!" she shrieked. I got to her and restrained her, held her close. She felt so tiny in my arms, and warm, like a small animal. I was between her and Chris, and she was wild, trying to get through me more than around, trying to propel us both toward the body.

"Nicole, no," I said. "You can't go over there."

She wasn't hearing me, still pushing against me while I held her.

"It's Chris. Chris, oh God."

"Nicole, let them do their job. They're helping Chris. You have to let them do their job."

She let out a loud screech, and I glanced over and saw what she did, a bloody compression bandage beside the body. In the half-light of the alley it appeared black, not red, but we both knew it was covered in Chris's blood.

"Nicole, I need you to come with me," I said. "Nicole, I need you to come sit in the squad." She collapsed in my arms, and I guided her to the back of the vehicle. I almost had to prop her up while I opened the door. And once opened, we were flooded with a blast of heat. I noted again how cold it was, as I eased her into the backseat, where it was warm and safe. I could hear the voices on the radio, and I could hear sirens approaching.

"You're OK, Nicole. Everything's going to be OK. Chief is on the way. It's going to be fine."

She looked at me, but she didn't see me. "Chris," she said, in a high voice, wavering. "Chris," she said, at almost a whisper.

"Hear that siren, Nicole? Backup is on the way."

"Backup," she repeated.

9

"Stay here, Nicole. Just stay in the squad and listen for the backup. Do you hear those sirens?"

She nodded, staring blankly at me.

"Listen for the sheriff for me. Listen for the chief."

The alley was getting crowded with vehicles. The Malibu was sprawled across it, the driver's door open. The ambulance was behind the car, off to the side. I needed the Malibu to move from the alley. Out of the way. I moved to the door and saw the large keychain and keys dangling from the ignition. But I didn't move the car. I just closed the door.

That's when the chief's car pulled into the alley. He had a red light on the roof of his Taurus but no siren.

And that's when it started going bad for me. That's when I know the shock started setting in. Maybe I could just let go, once the chief was there to take over. A sheriff's deputy was close behind, the sirens coming from more than one direction now, getting louder. I started to feel like I was choking, like I was going to suffocate, there were so many cars in the alley. I couldn't control them or make them do what I wanted. My arms and legs were numb. I heard the car door open behind me—Nicole. Chief Kramer was walking toward me and I couldn't move.

Nicole flew past me and into his arms. He stopped, holding her with one arm, clutched to his shoulder, but his gaze stayed on me.

He didn't look angry. He didn't look any particular way. He looked official, but it didn't calm me the way I thought his arrival would.

"Are you OK?" he asked. I don't know why, but the question surprised me. I still couldn't move, but I nodded. I was OK.

It felt like I was holding everything in place by staying still—the EMTs, the body of Chris Miller, the locked back door, the cars, all three vehicles and the ambulance, everything but the revolving lights, which made it seem like we were all spinning. The scene was secure, but not really. No yellow tape, just my consciousness, my will. If I stayed in place and didn't move, I could hold it all that way for a few more moments.

The chief moved forward first. And already the deputies were slamming their car doors, one walking to the body, the other to the chief. "Is the scene secured?" the chief asked, still holding my gaze.

"The back door is locked, no one's coming out of the bar," I said.

Then it passed. My responsibility, my authority, whatever claim I had to the scene and what had happened. "OK," Chief Kramer said. "I want you to go sit in the back of the ambulance. I'll come talk to you in a minute."

I was so relieved to have someone tell me what to do. I did as he said. I saw the chief hand Nicole over to one of the deputies. I saw Tim Lang, not in uniform, running up the alley toward us. He must have heard it on his scanner. He looked at me, his lips a thin line, and slowed to a walk. One of the sheriff's deputies came up beside me. "I have EMT training," he said. We all did, but I guess he meant some kind of special trauma training. Other cars were arriving now—from Castor and Badenberg. The whole area was bathed in revolving lights. The alley and First Street behind it were blocked by cruisers. In the ambulance I couldn't hear anything but police radios and chatter, but I learned later they were clearing the bar, taking everyone's name and sending them on their way. The peepers with their cellphone cameras were blocked by cruisers and officers. A deputy I didn't recognize was unspooling yellow crime scene tape.

That's when someone finally went upstairs. I heard the boots on the steps up to the apartment, the door being forced open, and then the boots coming back down. The windows in the apartment were dark and empty. Nobody. Nothing. The guy wasn't even home.

Chief Kramer came back then, again asked me how I was doing. Tim Lang was with him, his coat unzipped and hanging open. He was wearing a Wild hockey sweatshirt and looked so ordinary, so out of place, that it threw me. I said I was all right. "Do you need any help?" I asked, and they looked at me blankly.

"We've got it under control," Chief Kramer said. "You did good, Paul."

Tim helped me down from the ambulance and led me over to one of the Will County sheriff's vehicles. I told him I could drive my squad, but he didn't want me to. "We need that to stay where it is," he said. Of course. It was part of the crime scene. Tim opened the car's back door and even lightly touched my head as I ducked in and took a seat. I realized then that I had moved to a different side of the crime. I was part of the crime scene, too. I could see them loading Chris's body on a gurney, wheeling him to the ambulance, closing the doors on him.

There were a lot of people, all sorts of uniforms, and I couldn't tell if Chris's face was covered or not. They left the ambulance lights on, but they didn't turn on the siren, even after they left the alley. There was no rush. I knew then for sure he was dead. He'd been dead before I put the squad in Reverse, before I whizzed backward in the same direction the ambulance was now headed, toward the post office and safety.

Or at least that's what I tell myself. And that's what Tim told me in that backseat, where he joined me. That I shouldn't feel bad, because there was nothing I could have done. Chris died within seconds, Tim said. It was a shotgun, he told me, loaded with a large slug. How could you hope to survive a shotgun wound at close range like that?

I wish he hadn't told me those things. Once I knew a few facts, my imagination filled in the rest. Or maybe it wouldn't have mattered. I should have known more, because I was there— except I wasn't. All I saw was a flash, but then it got mixed up with what Tim told me. When he talked to me, I could see it, a man with a shotgun shooting at Chris Miller, then turning the gun on me.

"Who was it?" Tim asked.

I shook my head. "I didn't see him."

Tim didn't seem to get this, not the way I meant it. "Were you still in the car?"

"Yeah."

"So you, what, ducked? I mean, did you see his back— where he went? What he did with the gun?"

I shook my head. "No, I didn't see him," I said.

He looked at me, but kept going without a pause. "I'm sure I wouldn't have been able to recognize the guy either, not in those circumstances." I didn't bother to say it again—*I didn't see him. I wasn't even there.*

One of the things the chief took heat for later was the way things happened at the scene. They should have removed me sooner, or at least kept me isolated, so as not to taint my testimony. As it was, I sat in that sheriff's car for almost an hour, sometimes with Tim, Kenny Streator, a couple other guys checking in, always asking me how I was doing. They all said the same thing: What kind of person would shoot a cop? They were already calling it an ambush. The guy, they said, had been waiting for us, maybe even made the call to get us out there. Cop killer, is what they said. They seemed to know all about it, and because I was one of them still, because I of course must have known these things even better than they did, they said them to me. So I guess I had as good a picture of the crime as anyone by the time we got to the station.

Chapter Two

Asheriff's deputy named Pat drove the car I was in. He also shook his head and repeated the story. "Bad situation," he said. "Certainly don't expect that in a town like Maurus. Cop killers ambushing uniformed cops in an alley—behind a bar filled with people. That is gutsy. We're gonna get the son of a bitch, you can bet on that."

The station was busy. Tim Lang was already there, setting up a command center. Larry Peterson was writing a media response on a yellow legal pad, and Shelly had been called in to work the phones. Word was getting out already and both phone lines were ringing. Pat took me into the break room and had me sit there. When we came in, I had started to my desk, the one I shared with Kenny, another part-timer. But Pat said no, I should come back and have a cup of coffee. He was sitting with me, both of us with our coffee, when Chief Kramer arrived.

Chief Bill Kramer was always a comforting presence. His family has lived in Maurus for generations, and there were lots of Kramers in the area. Chief Kramer was in his early sixties, and he never seemed to get rattled. He was like a high school coach or one of your parents' friends who would come and sit around the fire pit telling stories. He was a fisherman, summer and winter. He was a member of the Knights of Columbus and joined in with the other men of the parish to serve the monthly pancake breakfast or sell brats outside the meat market. He wasn't funny, not a guy who told jokes.

I've seen police chiefs who are uncomfortable with their position and want to put you at ease by joking around. That wasn't Chief Kramer. He was a natural father figure, not intimidating but with no need to prove himself either. He was solid, a fixture. They said all sorts of terrible things about him afterward, about incompetence and mistakes that were made. By June he retired, said he wanted to spend more time with the grandkids. I felt pretty miserable when I heard. Everybody knew he was leaving because of the Chris Miller case. Whether he was forced out is not clear. Most of the days of the year, most of the years, he was exactly the right guy to be the police chief in Maurus. As for me and my behavior all around, it certainly didn't help him.

The chief took a chair next to me at the small, round table. His steel gray hair was exactly as always, like he just came from the barbershop, and he set his feet solidly on the floor, slapping his knees with his hands. He'd taken the time to change into his uniform, I noticed, though at the scene he'd just had on his jacket, zipped up, over street clothes. In that first interview, he was on my side. We were in this together. And he asked the question I knew was coming. The question that, surprisingly, no one had asked me yet.

"What happened, Paul?"

I didn't know where to begin. It seemed absurd to say, *A guy shot Chris.* The chief wanted to hear what he didn't already know. And I didn't have anything to tell him. He sat looking at me, serious but also concerned. He looked tired, or maybe sad. He'd just lost an officer, after all. I shook my head.

"Start with the call," he said. "Why were you in the alley?"

"It was a welfare check. Parents wanted us to check on their son."

"The apartment upstairs?" He was helping me out. Beginning with the easy part.

"Yes. The stairs to the apartment are in back. That's why we were in the alley."

"OK, good," Chief Kramer said. He put his hand on the table. The sight of his thick fingers, his plain gold wedding band, reassured me. "Then what happened?"

"Chris got out of the vehicle first." I know how strange it is to say this, but when I was telling the chief, I actually thought: *Why didn't I get out, too?* I'd forgotten about the phone, the text. Maybe you shouldn't question a person in shock. But there was urgency. I understand that. Still, it felt like I was figuring out the story as I talked. The story already seemed like a memory from a long time before, although of course it was the same night. I felt like I was trying to remember and recount a movie, or a story someone else had told me, not an event I had just witnessed.

"Chris crossed in front of the squad and headed toward the bar—the apartment. He had just cleared the front of the vehicle and was moving to the stairs. Then he was shot."

"From where? Where did the shot come from?"

And like remembering a movie, I saw, then, what happened. Not just Chris seen through the windshield, but the whole thing. Like I was watching a re-creation on a cop show. I answered the question. "The guy stepped out from behind the dumpster, to the left. And he fired."

"OK." Chief Kramer tapped his hand on the table. Maybe I was going too fast. Next question. "Did you see anyone else? Was he alone?"

"I didn't see anyone else," I said.

"OK. Can you describe him? The shooter?"

"He . . ." I struggled to remember—to see what he looked like, this man in my story. "It was dark," I said, though it was not. There was a light right there, over the bar door, and the streetlight in the alley. Enough light for Rick and Karen to work on Chris. Enough for me to see and identify Ashley from the same distance. I brought up the light on my picture of what happened. And I saw—I know I imagined, but I saw it then, in my mind, and I just knew it in my bones: "He pointed the gun at me."

"He pointed the gun at you." The chief's mouth turned down. He shook his head and said it again. "After he shot Chris, he pointed the gun at you."

"Yes." I could feel it, the fear, the sound of my heart beating in my ears, the shotgun pointed directly at me. The man, a dark figure. Tall, clutching the gun. "I couldn't see his face. It happened very fast. I backed up."

Now there was surprise on the chief's face. "What do you mean?"

And then the shame, but much less than I felt later. In that moment, I was justified. The killer was pointing a gun at me. "It was reflex. He had a shotgun pointed at me. I backed out of the alley."

"You left the scene," he said.

I guess if there was a time I could have come clean, that was it. To hear what I'd done laid straight out like that, I recoiled. I looked down and said, softly, "I'm sorry."

The chief sighed and took a moment. I noticed that Pat, who was taking notes, didn't seem to know what to put on his yellow pad. The chief nodded to him, and he wrote something, though I couldn't see the words.

"But you saw the gun," Chief Kramer said, with that same calm, direct voice. "Before you backed up you saw the gun," he said. "A shotgun."

"Yes, a shotgun. He held it low, kind of at his waist." It seems so absurd to me now, though for a long time I believed this was what happened. It must be something I saw in a movie. A Western. In the nightmares I had later, the guy was even wearing one of those long coats that cowboys wear, a duster. But not this guy. I told the chief he was wearing a hoodie. I know that's unimaginative. It's what everyone says, right? It's what they said about the Unabomber that was so wrong. But I believed it. To this day, actually, although I know I didn't see anything, when I think about the murder I still picture that guy with a shotgun in a hoodie. Sometimes he's wearing a jacket over it, a leather jacket or a windbreaker. Other times not. But I always see him, zipped into that hood, that shotgun held in both hands at his waist, the way no one ever holds one.

Maybe I made up the description because I wanted so much to know, wanted to help. I wanted so much to have done the right thing. And everyone was so nice to me—that night I was still a brother, still one of the partners. We didn't have assigned partners in the department—we referred to all the guys as our partners, and even guys from other departments when we worked a scene. What I'd done was unimaginable. And here was the chief giving me a way to do my duty. Here he was making it easy for me to fill in the blanks.

I'm not a liar, I'm really not. Even as a kid, aside from the normal stuff, stealing candy, misleading my parents, I told the truth. Anyone will tell you I'm a straight-up guy. I can't explain, but in that moment I felt I really did know. We were ambushed in the alley by a cop killer. The rest of the story just kind of followed. Anyone could tell it. I couldn't see his face because of the hoodie. It had to be true.

"And then what did you see? Where did he go?"

"I didn't see anything. I didn't see him leave the alley."

"Do you think he went inside the bar?"

"I don't know. Could have."

The chief paused again, and Pat with his pen hovering over the pad. They needed a story just as much as I did. He didn't write that down. "So you didn't see him leave the alley, but that was because you had backed up. Yet you were still . . . you were still facing the alley, lights on?"

I shook my head. I knew this part. "I backed into a spot at the post office," I said. The chief paused to take this in. I could see what he was thinking, though he didn't say it. *All the way to the post office? You didn't keep an eye on the scene at all?*

"OK. Let's go back to when you arrived. Before the shooting. Any vehicles when you entered the alley?"

I shook my head. "It was empty. No parked vehicles."

"And when you returned to the scene. Was that after you called it in?"

"Yes, right then."

"How long would you say?"

"A minute. Or less. Thirty seconds, maybe. The dash clock read 10:18."

Pat wrote it down: 10:18. Of course, I was wrong about that, too. That was when the text was sent. Later we learned I called dispatch at 10:20. Two minutes. One hundred and twenty seconds of pure cowardice. Of course, it hadn't felt that long. Maybe it was almost 10:19 when the text was sent, and just barely 10:20 when I called dispatch. Maybe it was sixty-one seconds. At my lowest, I sat and watched the second hand of a clock go around that long. It's a long time.

"And when you returned," the chief said. "There were no cars then either? No car down the street? The sound of a vehicle—a truck, a car?"

I remembered the silence. Just the sounds of the bar. I hadn't heard a thing. "I'm sorry, chief. Nothing."

21

"OK," he said. But it wasn't OK. He took another approach. "How tall was this guy? What was he wearing? Besides the hooded sweatshirt."

The figure, the man I now believed I had seen, came easily to me. "He was tall—I don't know, six feet, maybe a couple inches more. On the thin side."

"You didn't see his face? White? Mexican?"

"White. Maybe work pants. Dark ones. Gray sweatshirt. Zipped up. Heavy, with pockets. And I don't know how I know this, but he was white. A white guy."

I saw that Pat wrote down "white" with a question mark. Then: "No positive ID."

I shook my head. Chief sighed. He was working at it, but I knew he stilled maintained sympathy for me. He was in my corner.

"So you think this guy was there specifically to shoot cops?"

"I don't know."

"He wasn't coming out of the bar or anything? He was waiting there for you?"

"He was there. He didn't come out of the bar."

"And he was alone? You're sure he wasn't with anyone else?"

"He was alone."

"He would have seen the squad? He would have known Chris was a cop?"

"Oh, yeah. Definitely. He had time to aim at Chris. Chris walked around in front of the vehicle—he knew. He knew it was cops."

"You didn't get out of the squad," he said.

I felt my face go hot. "No," I said. I wanted to say again that the guy had a gun pointed at me, but I didn't.

Chief Kramer bent toward me then and looked me in the eye. His hand stayed on the table but moved toward me, as though he was patting me on the knee, or the shoulder. I looked from his hand up into his face. He was calm. He was serious. "Paul, listen. I'm glad I'm not going to tell two families they lost their sons tonight," he said. "It'll be hard enough going to Chris's family. I understand how you feel, but you have to know this was not your fault. You couldn't have done anything for Chris."

I couldn't take him looking at me like that. I looked down at his hand on the table again and fought back tears. The chief straightened in his chair and raised his coffee cup. We paused while he took a sip and I pulled myself together. Pat put down his pen to give me a moment. Then the chief continued.

"What about the guy upstairs. The welfare check. Did you see him?"

I was confused by that question. "You mean afterward?"

He shrugged. "Any time. Did you see him?"

"His lights were off. We didn't get that far. He wasn't home, though, right?"

The chief just looked at me. "I just want to know what you saw. Everything you saw."

Then I went on, moving beyond the crime itself. "I only saw two people—Ashley Keegan came out for a smoke. I sent her inside to get Jim. And Jim locked the door so no one else would come out. I didn't see anyone else."

"Except the shooter," Chief Kramer said.

I nodded, but without conviction. I looked over at Pat's yellow pad. He wrote down the names: "Ashley Keegan, Jim— bar owner?"

That's when Larry Peterson stuck his head around the corner and gestured for the chief. They both left the break room, the chief saying to me, "You just sit tight."

Pat put down his pen, but he didn't say anything to me. I could tell he was uncomfortable with my story. He was judging me. He got up and went over to make a cup of tea, just to have something to do. In my mind's eye I saw the shooter again, the gun aimed my way. And I was overcome by emotion. I shook my head and the vision was gone.

Of course, by then I'd moved from coward to liar. And criminal. Misdirecting an investigation, providing a false statement. That's ignoring the initial crimes: leaving the scene of a crime and dereliction of duty. The list was getting very long. But I didn't feel like a criminal or a liar. My discomfort was due to leaving the scene even though there was a gun pointed at me.

But mostly I felt OK. I felt like a cop. I told them what happened. I made my report, like I'd made so many reports before, complete and believable. It made sense. Pat didn't have to like what I said or did. Sometimes I think this is the way police work, the way life works. We come up with the only story that could be true and we tell that story to ourselves and to one another. I believed then that what I'd told Chief Kramer was the absolute truth. I wasn't trying to cover up for myself or lie. I was trying to help.

Word got out very quickly. People at the bar started making calls and sharing the news before they even got in their cars, no doubt with primary information coming from Ashley Keegan and Jim. The local media were arriving, metro media on their way.

Our station shares space with city hall and the public library, all in a converted bank building. City hall was just a series of cubicles with a counter, and across from that was our window, where Nicole or Sherry—the administrator on duty—sat. The door to the station area was locked, but there was no room for people to congregate in that hallway.

We'd practiced this kind of scenario annually, in crisis drills, though they had never been about an officer shooting. The scenario was always a disaster in town, a tornado or major fire, even a terrorist attack of some kind, like an attack on the water supply, ricin sent through the mail, an outbreak of deadly bird flu. The crisis plan called for the library, just a single long room, to be used as the communication center. I knew from the drills that Larry had set up a folding table there and pulled over the librarian's phone. He had a bunch of prepared press packets with town demographics, information on city officials, basic stuff, and some assistant was no doubt circling the location of the crime scene on the map in each packet. By now staff would have pulled together some chairs from the city offices and from the library computer area and moved aside the kids' tables and chairs. Larry would be ready for the media.

When I left the break room to see what was going on, I noticed the printer on Sherry's desk was spitting out copies of the press release. I wanted to see one, but Pat intercepted me before I could get to the desk. The chief was in his office speaking to the Will County sheriff. Then I saw my parents, through the front window. My mother was wearing her glasses, after being awakened, not bothering to put in her contacts, and pushing the glasses up with her hands to wipe away tears. There were other people out there, Kelly Otrushko from the *Castor Standard,* the daily, and Larry, and maybe radio people, who knows. Kenny went over and opened the door to let my parents in, and then he shut the door behind them and locked it again, and sort of herded us all toward the break room, away from the window.

I received my mother's tearful hug. "Oh Paul, thank God, Paul," she said. She wasn't usually this sloppy and her hug crushed against my uniform and badge. I wasn't used to having people hug me while I was in uniform and was conscious of my holster and gun. I had taken off my portable radio in the back of the squad, but I still felt stiff and bulky.

My dad hung back with Kenny, talking. They went off together, and it was decided that I should leave before more press arrived. When my dad came back he was all business: "I'll bring the truck around." He drove his pickup into the old drive-thru for the bank, and Kenny led my mother and me through the back door. There were two SUV squads in the drive-thru, motors running to protect all the equipment. I could see past them to First Avenue, where a news van from KSTP in the Twin Cities was just pulling up.

I wanted to stay and see what would happen next. I wanted to speak to the chief. I asked my dad as I slipped into the backseat, "Does the chief know I'm leaving?"

He nodded. My mother got in front and shut the door. As we drove out, a female reporter and a cameraman were heading inside. I sat back more deeply in the seat, glad to disappear into the truck. My mother turned to my father and whispered loudly, "Was it Chris?"

He nodded.

"Dead?" she asked.

He kept looking straight ahead and nodded again.

Chapter Three

There was one cop who wasn't there that night. Trey Schleper was hunting deer up north, and he got a call late Friday night at his buddy's cabin. I'm sure they were drunk, but that didn't stop Trey from getting in his truck, leaving the six-point buck he'd shot that day hanging from the porch for the other guys to deal with, and hightailing it down to Maurus. He got back to town about five a.m., and when he didn't find me at the station, he came looking for me. He took a piss on my back door (or so I suspect when I discovered it later) before heading to my parents' house and nearly breaking down their back door.

I was groggy. I can't say I'd really slept. Between nightmares and the strangeness of my childhood room, I didn't fully register whether the pounding was real or in my imagination. But the loud voices in the kitchen brought me to my senses real quick.

"What the hell do you think you're doing?" It was my dad.

"Is Paul here? Tell that motherfucker I want to see him, now."

"You're not seeing anyone," my dad said. "Go home, Trey."

I pulled on a sweatshirt and sweatpants and went out to help my dad. My mother was in her bathrobe in the hallway, and she put out her arm to hold me back.

"I got this, Dad," I said, pushing past her into the kitchen.

"No, Paul, go back to your room," he said. That's my dad, always in charge.

"Paul, you son of a bitch," Trey yelled.

"You don't know what you're talking about," my dad said. "Now get off our property."

"Paul! You gonna make your dad fight for you now? Come out here, you little bitch!"

"I *got it*," I said to my dad, pushing lightly on his chest, stepping in front of him. But he didn't move. He grabbed my shoulder as I slid out onto the top concrete step. I was barefoot, but the cold barely registered.

Trey's the same height as me, six-one, but with a very different build. He's apelike, with big shoulders and ropy arms, a long torso and short, powerful legs. He's got a wrestler's build. He has curly hair that he wears pretty shaggy. Without any product, having taken off his knit cap in the truck, he had sort of a mullet going. My dad had switched on the light—it was just before dawn—that made Trey's blaze orange coat even brighter, and his face, too, vivid against the dark yard.

"Trey," I said, but that was as far as I got. He stepped up and grabbed me, pulling me down to his level. My dad was yelling, holding the storm door open but not coming out.

"You miserable little faggot," Trey said. I couldn't do anything but take it. He clutched the front of my sweatshirt and kept his face right in mine; I could feel his hot breath. His nostrils flared and his eyes flashed hatred.

When I didn't respond, he pushed me onto the ground. My mother was yelling now, and my father was out on the steps. "Think about what you're doing," my dad said.

I stood up and just held out my hands at chest level. I wasn't going to fight him. He came at me and wound up to punch me, but halted his fist an inch from my face. I turned my head—the worst was not quite being able to see anything, and he backed off, then spit on the ground. "You miserable pussy," he said. "You left your partner to die! There's a cop killer out there because of *you*!"

He made another little run at me, and I stood my ground, not flinching, even though he made three little punches in the air, grunting each time. He was wound up like a boxer, light on his feet, oddly controlled. "You . . . you—should be locked up," he said. "Cowardice in the first degree." He turned and spat again. Looking up at my dad, he said, "I hope you're very proud of your son." He turned and pointed at me, "You're the one who should be dead. You!" and stormed off. We heard his truck door slam, his engine revving up. I looked over and saw Mrs. Kretschner in her robe and slippers standing on her step, her porch light on, watching the whole scene.

I went back inside. My mother was at the kitchen table crying softly, her head in her hands, her glasses in front of her on the table, and my dad grabbed my shoulder as I walked past, this time trying to be reassuring. I just kept on down the hall to the bathroom. I looked in the mirror, not sure what I thought I'd see, then threw some water on my face. I could hear my parents talking low in the kitchen as I went back into my old room and shut the door. I put some socks on my freezing, damp feet and sat on the edge of the bed, tuned in to the pins and needles as they thawed.

Sitting in that room, I was surprised at the distance I felt from Chris Miller. The distance I had felt right away, even at the scene. Distance from the body of Chris Miller, really. Maybe I didn't want to think about that part of it. I had barely even looked at the body.

But it's strange, because I'd just been talking to him. I was the last one to see him alive. Still, I had to keep reminding myself that I was actually there. The last one he said anything to before he died. Usually that means something, right? But the truth is that I just thought about myself. Clearly. What was supposed to happen—I was supposed to focus on the shooter. I see it over and over again in cop shows on TV, what I was supposed to do.

I was supposed to draw my weapon and shoot back. Even one shot anywhere, out into the alley, would have given me time to move, to move into the scene. When I replay it, I have to work to figure out the logistics—I am always exposed when I leave the vehicle. He can get a shot off, too. I have to shoot first. Or I just stay behind the door of my squad as he flees, and turn and get a shot off. As I work it out, his body falls next to Chris Miller's. I shoot him and become a hero.

I can play out the scenarios. I could draw them for you on a whiteboard like football plays. When the shooter hears my door open, he drops his weapon. He's not a professional. He's a guy with a shotgun. He has to move fast and a shotgun is clumsy. He drops the weapon and moves away from me. I see the weapon fall, lying there by the dumpster, and I have time to aim and shoot at the man in dark pants and a hoodie. I shoot him and he falls.

Hindsight is 20/20, right? How many people that winter—hell, even now—are sitting in bars and restaurants in Maurus, gathered around tables or in front of their televisions on Sunday afternoons watching the Vikings, in hunting blinds or ice-fishing shelters, in hair salons, even, playing it out for themselves? What they would have done. What I should have done.

I wonder, too, if they were surprised.

"I never woulda expected that from Paul Thielen."

"He seemed like such a solid young man."

"You never know how you'll react at a time like that."

"Yeah, but you'd think the police, they're trained for that situation."

"They take an oath. It's in their oath to have courage."

"Not sure you can make someone have courage, just by saying the word."

"Paul was just a kid, whaddaya want from him."

"No he wasn't, isn't, not a kid. He's thirty-one. Kids much younger than him are off in Afghanistan and Iraq."

"That's true. But there you expect people shooting at you. Not in Maurus."

"If you're a police officer, you always expect it. Cops get killed at traffic stops."

"He had a gun and knew how to use it. There's no excuse, really."

"Yeah, you're right. No excuse."

"I wouldn't want to be his partner, that's for sure."

"Me neither. Wouldn't want to be paired up with a guy like that."

"He'll have to leave the department now."

"Yeah, he'll have to. Nobody's gonna trust him."

"I don't think he should even be allowed to have a gun."

"Definitely not. If I did that, if I left my partner to die like that, well, I hope someone would take all my guns away—for my own protection. I don't know what I'd do to myself."

These conversations played out in my head. They were going on in Lynn's coffee shop. Down at the Blue Line, the Staghorn, even Arnold's, which closed until after the funeral, but filled immediately when it reopened. In the living rooms. And then they moved on to the other question: "Who do you think coulda done something like that? Shoot a cop in cold blood?"

In those early days, there were all kinds of theories. We had to find some way to answer the evil that had come into town.

Until the night Chris Miller was killed, I never had a sense of harm lurking in Maurus for me, a peace officer in the community. Then there it was, in what had before been the simple darkness of our hometown. I knew that town so well, it was like I had a kind of night vision. Even the streets where I didn't know many people, like Quarry Trails, were familiar to me. I knew the stars in the sky and the houses with their garage doors and lawn ornaments and trees. I knew the tragedies: the fires and the car accidents and the trees blown down. I knew the drunks and the domestics and the defectives and the demented and their caregivers. Even Edgewood Estates, the local trailer park, filled with Mexican immigrants, workers at the chicken processing plant, alive with mariachi music and children, was a place I went without fear. Chris Miller's shooting was like that movie *No Country for Old Men*. It felt like that kind of evil, from some other place or other world. Evil that didn't respect basic rules or recognize any authority. Who could kill a cop? In Maurus? In a place where everything was known, the unknown was terrifying.

People treated the amateur videos made at the scene like evidence. People had made them on their phones as the officers were directing them to their cars, and they were all over YouTube. The audio was on the radio the next day, people talking about how everything was normal and then the police came in and started taking down everyone's name. How they thought it was a raid, though Arnold's always checked IDs. They talked about how there might have been a murderer, a cop killer, in the bar. "Someone said a cop was shot," they said, "We didn't hear anything—the music was pretty loud, but you'd of thought we'd a heard something." They sounded drunk and sort of excited, and they had absolutely nothing to contribute.

One guy was shown on the news holding up the three-pound package of pork chops wrapped in white paper he'd won in the raffle. He said he was about to head home anyway to get it in the freezer when the police arrived. Another guy wondered if they'd get their money back since they never got to the beef bundle and the prime rib. They weren't helping out the town's reputation as backward, that's for sure. One television reporter explained what a meat raffle was, gave its history in Minnesota, as if that was important background for understanding the murder.

Amid all the speculation and drunk talk, those cellphone videos introduced two vehicle descriptions. Many people who had been in Arnold's that night said they'd seen a white pickup or a black sedan. The descriptions of the black sedan were especially varied. People said they saw a car full of people "from Minneapolis," though no one could say the exact make or model or the license plate number or even how they knew the people were from the Cities. It was, of course, code for "black." Maybe people looking for drugs, they said. People who were not from around here. Young. Maybe Somali. Maybe Hmong. Black guys. Street-gang-looking guys. Driving around, not coming into the bar. Two guys, four guys, maybe five.

As for the white pickup, everyone agreed that had been parked at Staley's and no one knew who it belonged to. It came from out in the country, everyone said, though no one could say how they knew that either. Some deranged farmer with a grudge against the government. We didn't want to believe that.

The Minneapolis gang made much more sense to the town. A lot of time and energy was wasted looking for them. Databases were searched. State officials came up here to look around. Narcotics squads with open cases. Gang task forces. Two more

35

meth houses were raided, one in the country and one in Badenberg. But they couldn't make any ties to anyone in the Twin Cities. And of course, there wasn't any black sedan or black guys or Hmong gang members in Maurus that night. That was just a story that moved the danger away from us and let us sleep. Gang violence made sense of the senseless and let us look away from ourselves and at outsiders for our trouble.

I wasn't involved in any of these conversations. I read about the vehicles people thought they saw and the made-up perpetrators on the Chris Miller Facebook page or in the online comments on articles in the *Castor Standard*. No one asked me about the shooting. Not what it was like to be the last person to talk to Chris Miller. Not what I was thinking or feeling. No one but the investigators.

When I went back into the kitchen, my parents were still sitting at the table. "Don't listen to Trey, Paul," my mother said.

I just nodded.

"You should tell Chief Kramer about it," she said. "Trey had no right coming over here and threatening you like that."

I shrugged. "He's just upset."

"We're all upset," my mother said, her voice cracking. "All of us! That's no reason to threaten someone, someone who's been traumatized by—"

"I'm not traumatized," I said. "And he didn't threaten me. He's right. I should of done something."

"No, Paul, no," my mother said. "I'm glad you're levelheaded. I'm glad you didn't get yourself shot, too."

"In what world would you call what I did levelheaded?" I said.

"Paul, you did the right thing, getting out of there. You were under God's protection."

I looked at my dad, but he didn't say anything. I was kind of glad he didn't come to my defense. My mother saw me look at him and frowned. "You want some coffee, Paul?"

"I can get it," I said, walking toward the counter. But she jumped up in front of me and pushed me out of the way.

"Just sit down, I'll get it," she said. She unhooked one of the brown stoneware mugs that hung under the cabinet and poured the coffee while I went to the fridge for milk. It was the second pot of the morning, I realized, and she turned and poured more into my father's mug, too. It must have been just after six, because that's when people started hearing the story on the radio, and that's when the phone started ringing.

My mother answered, the first call of many from relatives wanting to know if I was OK. My father turned on the Castor AM station, where they were doing weather. Then came the story of the shooting. It was the top story, and though they didn't have much information, they kept repeating what I recognized as the core of Larry's press release.

"A police officer was shot and killed in Maurus last night. It happened in an alley behind Arnold's Bar around ten p.m. No suspects have been arrested and the officer's name has not been released, pending family notification."

They didn't mention me, or that I'd left the alley. In the extended version they mentioned the officer was on a welfare check and it was not clear if he had been targeted or walked into a crime in progress. That last part was pure speculation, and I could imagine the press conference and badgering that Larry must be taking at the station. It was also the first suggestion that Chris could have been targeted. That seemed as unlikely to me as the second scenario—what crime could have been in progress in that empty alley?

I wished they'd just release Chris's name. His parents were in town, easy to notify, and Nicole, and Kelsey, and the kids. But he was from a big family. Maybe they wanted time for his family to notify people personally. But I had family, too, and so did everyone else on the force, and I could only imagine the panic from the number of calls we were getting. All my aunts and uncles, early-risers. Which was good for my mom, because she needed to talk. She needed to say again and again that I was all right. But I couldn't help but notice that after her first conversation with her sister, Aunt Jeanette, who was probably already finished with the morning farm chores, she sounded more defensive about my being there. She said she didn't know what had happened, just that I had gotten out safely, and the murderer had gotten away.

I sat at the table and drank coffee with my dad. He lifted his head and said, "Trey was out of line."

I nodded. "It's OK. That's just Trey."

"It might not just be Trey," my father said.

I nodded. I was having trouble swallowing the coffee, so I gulped it and it burned my throat. We both knew what people would say about me, about this. For a moment, with my mother talking low and fast into the phone to one of the aunts, I wondered if I could lose him as well.

"I'm sorry," I said.

"We'll stand by you, Paul," he said. "We'll always stand by you." But he was looking at his coffee, not at me. This was a new way of feeling sick for what I'd done. I'd put my dad in a bad spot, both of my parents. They'd been disappointed in me probably in the past, but nothing like this.

I set down the coffee mug but still held it with both hands. I needed a glass of water but couldn't rise to get it and was afraid I might choke, from the coffee, from my dad. I didn't want to get emotional. Not then. I just nodded. My mother hung up the phone but it rang again immediately. I went to the sink for the glass of water.

When the doorbell rang, and I saw Kenny Streator at the door, I half expected him to arrest me. I was surprised they would send Kenny and not someone more senior. Kenny and I were the closest in rank. We were both part-timers and he had started just two weeks before I did, gaining only that much seniority and a badge number one lower than mine. We didn't work together often, because usually we alternated shifts. A tall, redheaded farm kid, Kenny looked especially young that morning.

I invited him in, but he stood just inside the door. He seemed rooted to the doormat in the entry, though there was no snow or mud to track through the house, no reason he couldn't come all the way inside. My father had come into the room, too, and said hello.

"Hello, Mr. Thielen," he said. "Sorry to bother you." We were all nervous. He didn't say anything else, so I prompted him.

"Trey was over here this morning," I said.

Kenny looked surprised and a little worried. "He was pretty agitated at the station," he said. "What did he do?"

"Oh, nothing really. Just letting off steam."

"He and Chris were pretty close," Kenny said. I nodded, though it wasn't exactly true. No one on the force was close to Trey. He was a loose cannon, a problem for the chief and all of us. He was too aggressive, would hassle people. He was a "step outside of the vehicle" cop, overusing the Breathalyzer. He always gave tickets, never a warning, and tried to turn it into some kind of competition with the rest of us, even though we didn't have quotas. As Larry Peterson said, he was bad for public relations. Chris probably came closest to sympathizing with Trey, but he wasn't the same.

Kenny told me I was being put on administrative leave, just a formality, and they should have taken my gun and badge the night before. I went to get them, and Kenny was still there on the doormat when I came back. My mother had joined my father, standing back by the couch and looking awkward. As I went down the hall I heard my mother offering Kenny coffee, and his overly polite response, saying he'd already had too much at the station. Kenny tried to be cool about the situation, apologized as he received the items. I felt a part of my identity leaving me. I felt a change when the weight of the gun left my hand. I must have looked pale. Kenny asked if I was OK. I shrugged. I asked him how long administrative leave lasted.

"I don't know. There's a lot going on. I guess it depends on how quickly we catch the son of a bitch who did this, and what happens next. The scene was pretty clean. There's not much to work from." He seemed embarrassed, but I couldn't be sure. I didn't know how I was supposed to be with him.

"So I don't go back to work? Not until the guy is caught?"

"I don't really know how it works. I'm sure they'll send you paperwork about it, right? You'll still get paid. I just think they don't want you working until things get a little quieter." It turned out I couldn't work even a desk job. I couldn't even be at the station my twenty hours a week. I couldn't work more than twenty hours on any other job while I was on leave if I wanted to retain my status and keep getting paid. Though of course I don't know what I would have done for work, or who would have hired me.

Later, HR offered me therapy, but it was a vague suggestion and I didn't want to talk to anyone. I don't know what I'd have said, or what kind of help that was supposed to be, anyway. I also thought it would make me look weak, and in those months that was not an impression I wanted to reinforce.

After he took my badge and sidearm, Kenny backed out of the door, saying goodbye, nodding to my parents. It struck me again that this was what it felt like to be on the opposite side of the law. How many times had I backed out of a home after engaging someone on a call? How often had I felt like Kenny, defined and safe in my uniform, yet still mindful, trying to be courteous and respectful of the space I was intruding upon? But was I a suspect of some kind? Or a victim? A person of interest? One thing I definitely was not: a cop.

My mother went off to answer the phone again, but my father looked embarrassed, maybe even ashamed. I wasn't prepared for that, for Kenny Streator being able to make my dad feel ashamed. I'd only seen that look a few times before, on the faces of older men at Edgewood Estates or job sites, the ones who couldn't speak English. They needed to answer questions and they couldn't, and they were frustrated. Especially when their kids, daughters, had to translate for them. My dad had that kind of pride, and I had struck a blow to it by my actions. Of course, he was the opposite of the Mexicans at Edgewood Estates. He spoke the language of this place thoroughly. And here he was, reduced to speechlessness. It was demeaning for both of us. We just stood there in the living room, alone. This was before the media figured out I was at my parents' house, while they were most likely staking out my own.

Kenny also brought me back my cell. I'd dropped it in the squad and now I looked at it more closely. The battery had gone dead, which was lucky, because they couldn't check the messages or see my texts. Not that they couldn't get them from the phone company or something. First thing I did was plug in the phone and check my messages. Julie had said yes, for me to come over, and then she'd gotten pissed that I didn't. She must have turned off her phone and gone to bed, because she didn't hear the story until the next morning, on her way to work a Saturday morning shift at the dental office. She heard the story on the radio and pulled over. I should have called her, but the phone was charging, and the landline was ringing off the hook. To tell the truth, I didn't think about calling her. I should have let her know I was OK, but it honestly didn't occur to me.

She called from the side of the road, hysterical. "Oh Paul, it's not you, oh, no, who was it? Were you there?"

"Yes," I said. "It was Chris Miller."

"Oh my God, oh God, sweetie, how awful, how terrible for you! Are you all right? Were you shot at, too?"

"I'm fine, I'm just fine."

"Are you home?"

"At my parents'. Why don't you just go to work. There's nothing we can do."

"Yeah, right. I'm coming over now. I'll call in."

Frank showed up too, shortly after Kenny left. He came in through the back door and gave me a bear hug in the kitchen. "Little brother," he said. I can't really explain how he said it—in a way I had never heard before. And that was the first time tears came to my eyes. In those hours after the murder I'd felt all sorts of things, but I hadn't really felt what it would mean if I'd been shot until Frank said that "little brother" to me. Or maybe I just hadn't realized what my death would have meant for my family. We're not big on emotions. My mother had cried, but that was to be expected. But to see Frank—well, I owe Frank a lot, and I know he loves me, but of course we never talk about our feelings. That morning I saw our relationship in a different way.

Once Julie was there, and Frank, our little circle, we got some breakfast together. Everyone was quiet, and when we were all seated in front of the cereal boxes and sliced oranges and bananas, I told them what happened. My mother disconnected the phone and sat down. Julie sat next to me and cried softly as I told the story. She held my hand in hers and her hand was cold. I tried to warm it in mine, to little effect. Eventually she had to let go of my hand to wipe her eyes, and then her hand was both cold and wet. I know it's not nice to say, but that annoyed the hell out of me.

My mother cried, too. My father had a deep frown on his face, which was probably concern but I could only read as disapproval, and Frank kept rubbing his hands on his pants legs. As though they knew I was only going to say this once, no one said a word to interrupt me. And so I told them about the welfare check, about the ambush, about the shooter pointing the gun at me and me backing the car out of the alley. I stopped there, letting it sink in. My father's frown was as deep as it could be, but I still saw it shift to disappointment. "It was a reflex," I said guiltily.

"Oh, thank God," my mother said. "Thank God you did that, Paul. That was the archangel Saint Michael putting his protective wings around you. That was my prayers for your safety."

I looked at her blankly. I looked at Frank.

"That was the right thing to do," he said. "That was all you could do."

My father said nothing.

I told them how I called Dispatch, and about Nicole, and Julie said, with a sob in her voice, "Poor Nicole." Like they were friends. She looked at me with her big, wet eyes, but her tears also bugged me. "They haven't even been married six months," she said. It wouldn't have surprised me if she knew how many days and hours as well.

I told them how the others arrived and secured the scene. And that was all there was, really, to tell them.

The doorbell rang, and it was the first reporter. Later we found out they were at Frank's house, too. They were relentless, one after the other ringing the bell, on the street waiting for one of us to emerge. I wasn't the real story, so there weren't cameras, just reporters, interns maybe, hoping to get a statement from the person who was there—"the partner," as I would be called.

People imagined our partnership like they saw in cop movies, but it was nothing like that. I hardly ever rode with Chris. He had his own squad, but I just happened to be on duty and he came with me on the last stop. He was *my* backup that day. I had followed protocol at least far enough not to do a welfare check alone. We never knocked on doors alone. On a small force like ours, we were all responsible for one another. But most of the time, all the time really until that night, we just felt like two guys in uniforms checking things out.

I think it was when they heard at the station about the media showing up at my house that they decided to bring me back in. I was following texts on my phone, mostly people just wanting to know if I was OK. My friend Ty had left several texts, and I texted him back that I was OK. No details. When he followed up with a call, I didn't pick up. I wish I had, though I'm not sure it would have made any difference. I just would have liked to talk to him one more time before he heard what I'd done.

I took the call from Tim Lang, who said Kenny was coming back to get me. They wanted to talk more about what happened.

Chapter Four

When I got to the station, the mood had definitely shifted. There were all kinds of cops there, from the state police, the sheriff's office, the state BCA. People nodded, acknowledged me, but didn't come over to talk. I'd asked Kenny on the way over if Trey was there, and he said the chief had sent him home. I was relieved, but it seemed Trey had had an effect on some of the other guys. Maybe I should have expected everyone to be serious—it was a serious situation. But they were decidedly different. Not friendly.

This time, Kenny took me into the small office, which we used to interview suspects. The whole station was shifted around and full of people. The state's Bureau of Criminal Apprehension's investigator, Jelinek, was in charge, and he had set up shop in the chief's office, right inside the entrance. He looked at me through the glass as I went by. I was escorted, actually, Kenny directing me. I wasn't a fellow cop on the case anymore. I wasn't the lucky survivor. I was a witness. For some of the people crowding the office, I was even a suspect. A number of people wanted to question me, which was understandable. I was all they had, in a way. They hadn't found a weapon at the scene. My description of the guy was vague. There were lots of questions.

In that interrogation room, where I was for the next sixteen hours, most of the time sitting alone, I started to get used to my terrible new reality. The first person to come in the room was Chief Kramer. He didn't have a guy with a yellow pad with him anymore, though there was another officer present, a sheriff's deputy named Jim from Castor. We had met on a joint training, but he didn't say hello. Jim sat by the door and Chief Kramer walked by me to the other side of the table. I stood up out of respect, but he didn't acknowledge me, just took a seat. He was focused on a a little digital recorder he brought with him. He had to find the socket and I pointed to the wall behind him. He fumbled to get it working, and I reached over to help him, but he shot me a look and sat back, out of reach. Once he saw the numbers rolling, he set it between us and spoke, formally, naming the people in the room, the time and purpose of the interview. "Once more for the record," he said, addressing me for the first time.

His manner had changed. I could understand he was tired—I don't know if the guy got any sleep that night, or even that week. But that wasn't it. The night before he had taken care of me, but now he didn't. Our relationship had changed.

It took me awhile to figure that out. I'd been thinking about the scene, and what didn't add up to me was the call from the parents, the thing that got us to that alley in the first place.

"I've been thinking about the call, Chief," I said. "The welfare check. Do you think that was a hoax? Do you think someone was trying to lure us in?"

Chief Kramer just looked at me.

"Did it come from the home phone? Do they know who made the call?"

"We're looking into that," he said.

"Have you talked to the guy? The welfare check?"

He wasn't giving me anything. He rubbed his eyes, and then he stonewalled me: "Paul, you don't have to worry about the investigation."

"OK, but I thought maybe—"

"I'm here to interview you, Paul, not the other way around. Your only job now is to remember whatever you can to help us find this killer. And tell it to us straight. You're the only witness we have, at least for now. We're looking into everything."

I'm not an idiot. I know "shut up" when I hear it. I sat back in my chair. I tried to look as open as possible. "Absolutely, I want to help. I wish I remembered more, Chief. I wish . . . well, you know, I wish I'd seen him better."

"Let's go through it again. Tell me what happened."

We were just getting started. He had a series of questions, all quite standard, and I told him what I'd told him the night before. I didn't remember anything else. I stuck to the basics and didn't embellish. The story was hardening into truth for me. I knew enough to tell it simple and straight. The crazy thing is, I was telling myself that I didn't want to lie. I was actually telling myself those exact words: *Don't lie*. And maybe there is a difference between misremembering and lying, but I'm not sure.

Then they left me in the room a while, and Deputy Jim brought me a can of Mountain Dew, though I hadn't asked for one and would have preferred water. He left me alone—so I guess he wasn't guarding me. The next person to come in was a professional investigator from the state. He was in his fifties and wore a suit. He exuded professionalism and confidence, and he didn't act like a cop. He was more like a Twin Cities businessman, a guy who would be at home in a boardroom. He was good-looking, with salt-and-pepper hair and wrinkles where they should be, at the corners of his eyes and on his forehead. You could tell he smiled a lot, though he didn't smile at me. He seemed like a "just the facts" kind of guy, a bureaucrat with a report to make.

He had a black leatherette folder with papers inside, and he referred to these sheets as he talked to me. He had his own recorder, and he used it with confidence. He made a tipi of his fingers on the leatherette folder and spoke his name and mine, the date and time, for the record. He wanted me to go through my story again for him—maybe he would hear something different. He'd been to the scene, been all over it. He told me they hadn't found a gun there. They hadn't even found a shell casing. "Did the shooter pick up the shell?"

I guess it was a fair question, but I couldn't give him an answer. "I don't know," I said.

"Did you see him bend over and pick up anything from the ground?"

My frustration came through. "He easily could've picked it up after I left the alley. I only saw him pointing the gun at me. It must have had two shells. The one he used to shoot Chris, and the one for me."

His face kind of fell. Had he not been told about my retreat? "What do you mean 'when I left the alley'? How long were you out of the alley?" he asked. I didn't answer.

"How long," he said, more slowly this time, "was your partner lying there, dead or dying, while you were away from the scene?"

I just looked at him. The blood rushed to my head as he talked and I felt off balance. I looked down at my lap to compose myself, and when I looked up he was still waiting for an answer, and he couldn't hide his anger, which was pulsing in his jaw. "Less than a minute," I said. "But enough time for him to pick up the shell and exit to the east to his car or truck."

He just looked at me, his neck pulsing.

"I'm sorry," I said. "I know. I know what I did."

"Did you hear a vehicle leaving the scene?"

I shook my head. My ears were ringing, but I tried to keep it together. "I'm sorry but I didn't hear anything—they say I was in shock."

His head cocked to one side, a slight smile on his lips. I knew it was weak—to mention shock. He rifled through his papers, opening and shutting the black folder. That seemed to help him regain his composure. But if he was no longer angry, he was also no longer particularly interested in what I had to say. I was discredited in his book. When he continued, his questions were about the scene after the shooting. We went smoothly through the story. He remembered his reports and their blank spaces that needed filling. He wanted something to put in those spaces. He asked about the dumpster, about my movements, about Ashley and her cigarette. He had me draw everything on a piece of paper. I made that drawing several times for several people that day.

When he left me in the room I was hungry, and jumpy from the Dew. Every now and again I'd feel this rush, caffeine or adrenaline or blood to my head, kind of realizing what I'd done, what it meant, and where I was now. I needed to walk around. It was a small room and there wasn't space to pace. A few times I stood at the door with my hand on the knob, but I couldn't turn it. People were talking out there, the day passing, and I just wanted to look out a window, but I didn't want to face the people on the other side of that door. I stood against the corner and tapped my heel against the baseboard, like a caged animal. I wanted to know what was going on out there. It was the same as the night before in the ambulance. I was sealed off but also under the bright light. I didn't know what to do. I just knew I had to tell them everything I knew. I had to fully cooperate.

The guy from the state returned with more routine questions. He had Jim bring me a sandwich and a bag of chips, which I ate. The whole room smelled like ham and mayonnaise, which made me feel slightly sick. I was able to go out and use the bathroom, and I kept my head down. No one said anything to me. The whole station was buzzing with activity. I'd never seen the place so crammed with people or so busy. I threw water on my face and Deputy Jim accompanied me back to the little office, like it was his station and not mine. I sat in there and the afternoon dragged on.

It was with Steve Jelinek that things got bad for me. Jelinek was the guy who had taken over chief's office. He was the lead investigator for the Bureau of Criminal Apprehension down in St. Paul. He was dressed like a golfer, in khaki pants and a polo shirt with a windbreaker he never took off. Very much out of season. He had blondish hair, a little thin on top, and was tall and lanky except for a little middle-aged spread, which gave him some heft and presence. His face was long and he always seemed to be squinting. It made him look impatient and a little frustrated, like he was straining to see and you were making it harder for him, making him stand with the sun in his eyes.

He didn't like me. I was clear about that from the moment he walked into the room. He didn't try to hide his dislike. He slammed down a folder on the table and sat. A young guy slid in behind him and closed the door. Not Jim. A requisite witness. Jelinek had a mini tape recorder, too, and he sort of muttered into it as if he didn't want me to hear what he was saying. Just the identifying information: "Interview with Paul Thielen, partner of Officer Christopher Miller, who was shot and killed on Friday, November 9, 2012." When he said that last part he looked at me, sideways and squinting, as if he expected me to contradict him. He started with some routine questions, and I instinctively addressed him as "sir." He wasn't even as old as chief Chief Kramer or the last guy who interviewed me, but he had that kind of presence, just kind of military. This was the first time I felt interrogated more than interviewed.

He asked me about all my movements the day before, not just once I reported for work. He wanted to know what other calls I had. It had been quiet, and I had spent some time visiting with Nicole at the station. I did some paperwork. We had a call of a drive-off at the Holiday, just a local who thought he'd paid with his credit card and drove away after pumping his gas. I went to his house and had him go back and pay. After that I drove around through some of the neighborhoods and made a loop through the high school parking lot, where I came across a couple of kids making out in a car. I sent them on their way.

I was at the station visiting with Chris and Nicole when dispatch called about the welfare check. Chris offered to come with me if I would drop him at home afterward. Nicole had another two hours of work.

Jelinek had a follow-up for everything. How did Chris seem? What was he like at the station? Did he have any reaction to the welfare check call? Did I think there was anything unusual about the call? Did I remember what the dispatcher said exactly? How was Chris in the car?

I expected that we would go through the scene in the alley again, but he stopped me when Chris got out of the car.

"Did he say anything?"

"When?"

"When he got out of the car? Did Chris Miller say anything to you?"

I paused. I didn't really want to tell him, but I knew I didn't have any choice. "Uh, he said I was pussy whipped, sir."

Jelinek raised his eyebrows. He was still sitting sideways, his head at an angle, squinting up at me. "What?"

"He said I was pussy whipped. It was a joke."

He looked at me for several long seconds, as though he was processing this, trying to decide what it might say about me, then he tapped the manila folder edge on the table a few times. "Was it usual for him to joke like this?"

I wasn't sure what to say. "Chris liked to bust people's balls. He didn't mean anything."

"But why would he say that? What was the joke?"

I told him the truth, though it cost me. It felt as bad as leaving the scene, at least to me. I told him I was checking my phone. He opened the folder and wrote that down. Oh, yes, he wrote that down, even though the whole thing was being recorded. And then I told him the rest—that I was texting. He wrote that down, too.

"Texting your girlfriend?" I nodded. He added that, then he closed the folder.

"Did you respond?" he said. "When he said you were pussy whipped?" He seemed to enjoy repeating the phrase, calling me that.

"I didn't think anything of it. It wasn't a big deal." I didn't want it to be a big deal. Not what Chris said, and not the texting. I wanted Jelinek to see it wasn't important and open the folder and erase it. "I'm—I'm not comfortable telling people that part. I don't want to make Chris look bad."

He shook his head then, and zeroed in on me, his head low, looking up into my eyes. *"You,"* he said, "don't have to worry about making *him* look bad." I felt my face flush. I wished I could take it back. I would do anything not to have said that. I was only just starting to realize what I'd done. And I knew I was in trouble, much bigger trouble than I was prepared for.

It was my text that established the exact time of the incident. And, of course, the time between the text and the officer-down call was noted and repeated again and again. But that little piece of information also sealed my fate. After that interview, everyone in the station knew about the text, and so did everyone they told. Out there in the busy station a picture of me was forming. I was the bad cop. I was the sloppy, lazy, texting, head-not-in-the-game guy, the scared asshole who left his partner to die in the alley. That was the story, and I couldn't change it. I couldn't defend it. I just sort of collapsed into it then. I just let it take me over.

Jelinek also knew the interview had changed. He had one more angle to play out. One more road to go down.

"What was your relationship with Chris Miller?"

"What do you mean?"

"How well did you know him?"

"I've known Chris since we were kids. We were in school together. We played sports together."

"Did you like him?"

"I guess so," I said.

"Were you friends? Growing up? Were you friends?"

"We didn't hang out together—I didn't have any problems with Chris."

"I didn't ask if you had a problem with him. Would you say you had a rapport?"

"As kids?"

"As fellow officers."

"Chris was kind of responsible for me joining the force. He encouraged me to join."

"That's not what I'm asking. Once you were on the force. As partners. Would you say you had a camaraderie?"

I knew the answer to that one. We all had the answer memorized. "On the force we're all partners. My partners are my brothers."

He paused. Opened and closed the file. "What does that mean to you?"

My ears were ringing again, the beige walls of that room closing in on me. I guess maybe I was having a panic attack. I knew the answer but I couldn't say it. It wouldn't sound true, not from me at that moment, not in this context. We were together in an ambush, not a usual situation. But of course, that situation is when camaraderie, brotherhood, is supposed to work for you the most. It's supposed to push you into action, give you the adrenaline, the drive, to protect, to avenge, to do whatever is necessary.

I didn't have an answer for Jelinek. I couldn't spit out those words, about brothers in blue and standing strong in battle. "I know I failed Chris last night. I was not a good partner."

Jelinek just looked at me, waiting for more.

"But I didn't have anything against Chris. I sure as hell didn't want that to happen to him, or to anyone." I looked Jelinek in the eye, giving the only thing like a defense I could: "If I could go back—if I could change my behavior and be more alert, do anything to stop it, or get a better ID, maybe even get a shot off at the guy, you know I would."

Jelinek opened the file again. He wrote something down.

"What do you think about Chris's relationship with Nicole Rogers?"

"It's terrible for her, of course," I said. "They were just married."

"I know that. But what did you think about them getting married?"

"I didn't think anything about it," I said. But the truth might have showed on my face. The question took me by surprise. For the first time it occurred to me that maybe I should ask for a lawyer. But I couldn't think why that question would make me want a lawyer. I just didn't like it when the questioning got too far out, or personal. That made me nervous.

"Seems like everyone around here has an opinion. Surely you must have an opinion about their relationship, too."

"Hey, you know, you can't help who you love."

"Yeah, but he was married."

"It happens," I said. "He got married young."

"You're friends with Kelsey Miller, though, aren't you?" Again, that one threw me. I only hope my paranoia didn't show on my face. Who had this guy been talking to? What had they said about me? What the hell were they saying about me?

"I grew up with her, too," I said. "I wouldn't say we're friends." I hadn't seen Kelsey since the summer, and even then I had just run into her at the bakery. It was pretty soon after Chris and Nicole got married. I asked her how she was doing—she had the youngest kid with her, and she looked disheveled, tense, with her hair in a loopy ponytail that flopped on her head. She was picking up buns for a barbecue at her mom's house. She seemed grateful I came up and talked to her.

"But you were on her side, during the divorce."

That was a really odd thing for him to say. "Hey, listen, I don't know what people have been saying. I like Kelsey. She's a good person. I don't take sides, but I do think she got a raw deal in all this."

"What do you mean by *a raw deal*?"

I took a breath and tried to calm down. I wasn't sure what he was after. I only knew that everything I said sounded illogical and wrong. "Her husband had an affair with someone at work. He left her with three kids, one of them just out of diapers. In my book, that's a raw deal."

He seemed to be waiting for me to say more. "Shit happens. Love is messy. I like Nicole, too. I went to the wedding. I sat with Tim Lang and Larry Peterson. I went with my girlfriend, Julie."

He asked other questions about Chris. He wanted to find a source of conflict between us, or get me to criticize Chris. I wasn't going to give it to him. You don't badmouth the dead. That's a pretty basic rule. And if he was looking for a motive for *me* to have killed Chris Miller, well, he wasn't going to find one.

59

Would he really think I would shoot a cop in cold blood, my partner—with a shotgun, for God's sake—in a public alley, because I thought he was a cocky asshole?

"Are you sad that Chris Miller is dead?"

"Of course I am," I said. He didn't say anything, just let me sit with the response. "I think maybe I'm more shocked, though. The whole thing doesn't seem real." I wasn't sure how he thought I was supposed to respond. Would he think better of me if I broke down and cried there in the interview room, expressed deep remorse that it was Chris Miller who died, said I wished it was me? Of all the emotions I was feeling, none of them were particularly about Chris Miller. I was pretty worried about myself—the consequences of leaving the alley. I wasn't quite sure what had happened or would happen to *me*. Maybe Jelinek thought I should have been the one killed because I didn't have a wife and kids, or because I was such a wuss at the scene. Or that somehow I'd been involved. Surely other people thought that.

I didn't feel like crying. Never for Chris Miller. And maybe that's a problem. I'm a selfish bastard for saving my own skin, for running. I thought of myself, not my partner. Even afterward, I thought of my guilt, of my failure, of my cowardice. But I didn't really think about Chris Miller, not in the way people were suggesting, like we had some special bond. Not like he was a hero. That makes me a very bad cop. But does it make me a bad person? Or just an ordinary person.

Jelinek interrogated me the entire afternoon. The shadow officer left and another came in. Jelinek had a bunch of zingers for me, interspersed with questions meant to get at details. "If you had been paying attention, let's say not texting, not looking at your phone, do you think you would have seen the shooter before he shot Chris Miller?"

"Why didn't the killer shoot you first, since you were in the driver's seat, on the side facing the alley?"

"That time you were in the post office parking lot, were you thinking about Chris? About the shooter? Or about yourself?"

"What do you think Chris Miller was thinking about in his last moments? Do you think he heard the squad shift into reverse? Do you think he died alone? Was that right for a police officer? Is that the kind of death your partners can expect?"

How could I explain anything to him? Chris and I, we didn't expect an ambush, weren't looking out for one, weren't prepared when it happened.

But during a pause in the questioning, one of the long periods they left me alone, I did think of another incident, another call I'd answered with Chris. It started with a 911 call from the Kwik Trip. It's only two blocks from the station, on the corner of Highway 41, so I said I'd respond. Someone was acting suspiciously at one of the pumps, just sitting there in a car and not getting gas. It was nine o'clock on a Saturday night, but it was July so it was just dusk. When I got there, Chris had already arrived, pulled up right behind the car, and had his lights on. He even had his spot on—I never used my spot—and I guess I understand that, because you don't know who you're dealing with.

"Step out of the car," he said through the loudspeaker.

There were two other cars at pumps, but their owners were inside with the clerks, pressed against the window, watching to see what was going to happen.

I pulled up next to Chris and asked him if he knew who the driver was. He had run the plates and said the car was registered to a woman from Maurus, fifty-four years old.

"Do you think it could be a medical?" I asked.

"Well, if it is, she should get out of the goddamn car," he said. Then he said through the loudspeaker again, angrier this time: "Step out of the car!"

I drove over to the front of the gas station and got out, the car between me and the pumps. The clerks have binoculars they use to record license plates when people drive off, and I wanted a closer look. I went inside and asked the kid, "Is it a man or woman?"

"It's a woman," he said.

"What is she doing?"

"She's not doing anything. She's just sitting there. But, like, for a long time."

"Lemme see," I said, gesturing for the binoculars. He handed them to me and I went and stood just outside the door. It was strange. She was too still. She wasn't moving at all. I got closer. No one is that still, especially with a police car behind them and a spotlight through their back window.

There wasn't a woman in the car. It was a prank. It was a manikin, from God knows where, placed in the driver's seat. I started walking to the car, waving my arms to call off Chris.

But instead, Chris got out of his car with his gun drawn. "Forget it, Chris," I said. "It's a doll."

But he had already sprung forward, in a crouch, moving to the driver's side window. I stopped. He pulled open the driver's side door and then, gun still drawn, reached in and pulled the manikin out onto the ground. I thought he was going to shoot. Instead he kicked the manikin, right in the head. He kicked it so hard the arm came off and skidded across the parking lot. I looked back and saw the people standing in the window. If they had been laughing, they weren't now. They were stunned.

Chris walked over and picked up the arm, then got the rest of the manikin and turned back to his squad.

"What are you doing?" I asked.

"I'm going to find the fucker who did this," he said. "This is evidence."

I walked over to the station to give back the binoculars. I figured we'd use the plates to find the car's owner, and I guessed some kids had probably taken the car for a joyride. That's what I planned to tell the clerk. Chris was behind me, the manikin safely stowed in his squad. While I was basically chuckling with the other patrons, who said you just never knew what kids would get into, Chris came inside. He was not amused.

"I'm going to need to see that tape," he said, pointing to the security monitor.

"Oh, that doesn't work," said the kid.

"Don't be a wiseass," Chris said. "I can see the picture on the screen right there."

"Well, it works in giving surveillance, but it doesn't record."

Chris paused at that. "Let me see your ID," he said.

"Mine?" asked the kid.

"You're the one who called it in, right?" Chris said. "You telling me you didn't see who left the car here?"

I didn't like this at all, and neither did the other patrons.

"I didn't see nothin'," he said. "I thought it was a lady in the car."

"You want me to believe someone could put a manikin in the driver's seat, set it up like that, and leave the car, leave the whole area, and you didn't see it?"

"I had customers then, sir."

I really didn't know what to do. I couldn't interfere with another officer's questioning, but it was clear this kid wasn't involved. And Chris was freaking out the other patrons. They seemed afraid to leave, since that might make them look guilty.

"Chris," I said. "How about we start by finding the owner of the car."

Chris looked at me, then back at the clerk. "I'm going to need your name," he said. He pulled a notebook out of his breast pocket and took a pen from the counter.

"Ryan Peters," the kid said. Joe Peters is a local doctor, and this must have been one of his sons. I thought Chris would see then how silly he was being, but he wrote down the kid's name.

"And what about you, did you see anything?" he asked, gesturing with his pen at the two men and a woman standing by the door.

"No, we didn't see anything. We thought it was a person, too," said one of the men. Chris looked out and, seeing the two cars and three people we did, I could tell he was concluding that at least one of them was involved. But it was just a couple and then a guy on his own, and after Chris got their names and phone numbers, he let them go.

When we were outside again, I wanted to ask if all that was really necessary. But Chris had seniority, was full time—and anyway, it was over and no one got hurt.

Still, Chris followed that case for over a week, until the chief ordered him to let it go. Larry, who wrote up the reports for the police blotter in the *Maurus Record,* wrote a playful entry, which Chris didn't appreciate. I could have made a big deal over Chris's overreaction, but I didn't. As suspected, the woman's car had been taken from in front of her house that evening. She had a hidden key in one of those metal containers up in the front wheel well, and some teenagers had found it, so they didn't even tamper with the ignition. Truth is, plenty of people around here leave their keys under their seat mats or in their glove compartments and their cars unlocked. This woman didn't have kids at home, but there was one next door. Chris wanted to dust for prints. Dust for prints! Everyone moved on pretty quickly except for Chris.

I'm not sure why this was what I thought about during questioning. I wondered why Chris hadn't been prepared this time. Why hadn't he thought this could be dangerous? Why had we both taken it so lightly? All that fuss for a manikin, all those times Chris had gone by the book, and then seemingly without warning, for no reason at all, behind Arnold's Bar, with a meat raffle going on inside, the worst thing that can happen.

But it wasn't the first time Chris showed this kind of inconsistency. I don't know why it didn't occur to me then, except that I hadn't been part of the Lisa Hawkins inquiry. Chris had been put on the Lisa Hawkins case, and at the time he dismissed it without any consideration at all. He hadn't dogged it down. He hadn't dusted for any prints, or even looked for her car. He turned it over to the Welker Police Department without, as far as I know, even driving out to the Agamis and conducting a few interviews. That hadn't seemed unusual when it was reported at the weekly meeting. But it should have. A missing person is a significant case. There was even a drug angle, which usually was right up his alley. I should have noticed when it was jettisoned so quickly—what case was more important? And what would have happened if Chief Kramer, or any of us, had spoken up and said maybe it was not someone else's problem, but ours?

Chapter Five

I can't remember a time I didn't know Chris Miller. We went to preschool together. He always stood out, but not exactly for good reasons. What I remember about him from preschool is that he jumped off the bottom of a seesaw and Jennifer Weller fell off the other end and broke her arm. It wasn't Chris's fault. That seesaw was dangerous, and at four years old, who could understand how a seesaw worked? He just decided he was done and so when it lowered he got off. They got rid of the seesaw after that.

Chris was one of those guys who people say are "all boy." If you told him not to do something, like don't climb that tree, he'd run right over and climb it. If you yelled at him instead of applauding his good tree climbing, he'd look confused like he thought you wanted to see him climb a tree. Or he'd fall off the branch you knew was weak and then he'd cry, like how did that happen, and you'd end up taking care of him.

He wasn't a bully. He would never hurt anyone on purpose. He was just ADHD or ADD, you know? He had a little too much energy. On a field trip, he'd go off and not be on the bus when the rest of us were sitting there all paired off. You had to pity his buddy, who found himself without a seatmate and couldn't explain where Chris had gone. We would sit there sweating on the bus while the teachers and parents went out calling his name. He'd come back crying, saying he was scared and his buddy had left him somewhere.

It was predictable. Even if he was supposed to stay with one of the chaperones, he'd somehow get away. One time we went to the nature preserve in St. Albans to see a maple syrup demonstration. That was a little bit wild as field trips went, to this big forest. Still, there were specific things we were supposed to do in groups. Stations we moved to with one another.

First was to tap a tree, pounding in the stile with a hammer and hanging a bag on it. We got to empty sap from full bags hanging on trees into large collection bins. Then we went to the sugar shack where they were boiling down the sap and saw the evaporator. That was when someone noticed Chris was missing. The chaperone went back to see if he was still emptying bags, but he was gone.

That forest went on and on. The wide path through the trees made me think of the flying monkeys in *The Wizard of Oz*. The parents and teachers were all worried and had no idea where to look. The staff at the preserve said they hadn't lost a child all season. Usually kids found the syrup demonstration really interesting and they stuck with the plan. The anxiety spread to us kids and all I could think of was those flying monkeys and the scarecrow with his stuffing all pulled out.

It's funny how adults seem to think that once one child is missing the others might also try to escape. They herded us into the room the staff used to give nature lectures, even though they didn't have anything more to tell us. One girl, she was probably a college student, was in charge of us, while all the other adults went looking down the paths where the maple syrup bags were hanging. They told us there were two thousand taps. That was a number like a million to me. They went on forever, and Chris could be anywhere.

Finally, he came out on his own, walking down the path, completely covered in mud. He'd fallen in some swamp and lost his shoes. He was crying and said the mud sucked off his shoes and he couldn't get them. His mud-covered coat made him look like a turtle. We just couldn't believe it. He did get in trouble for that one, but again, mostly the adults were relieved. They hurried us onto the bus so we could get back. I remember Pat Carson loaned Chris his jacket, even though it got all muddy and I knew he'd get in trouble at home. Chris had to be prompted to thank Pat, and he still sat with the teacher shivering.

Despite all the trouble he caused, Chris was a charmer in grade school, and most of the teachers had a soft spot for him. In junior high something happened, his star dimmed briefly, and he had to work to get back that attention. Mostly, we thought he was obnoxious, but he was clearly trying so hard that you couldn't help but just tolerate it, humor him, and roll your eyes.

But Jelinek was right if he thought I was angry about what happened with Chris and Kelsey. Chris got the big prize, Kelsey O'Neal, and he just threw her away. I didn't know if there was more to the story—the affair alone was enough to take Chris down a few notches in my book. And he hadn't been all that high up to start with.

In a town like Maurus, you learn to let things go. That's part of the culture, what the parents and the teachers and your neighbors and everyone tells you. Things aren't going to be fair. Things aren't going to go your way. People don't do what they're supposed to, but you have to live with them. You have to get along. I went to Chris and Nicole's wedding because I was invited, and what was it to me? I worked with Chris and was expected to attend. I didn't even really know Kelsey anymore. I saw Nicole all the time at the station.

I'll never forget the first time I saw Kelsey. The summer before high school started, I did a lot of fishing in the Mikinak River. I would ride my bike down to Frogtown Park with my pole in back and my tackle box slung over the handlebars. One day I caught a quick glimpse of a girl walking down Third Street as I coasted past. I barely even saw her. But a wholly new thought popped into my head: *Hey, a pretty girl.*

I don't ever remember having had that thought before. It was surprising and I knew it was important. So even though I was almost at Frogtown, I made a long, slow loop on my bike and headed back up the street. When I got to Third, there she was. She was wearing cut-off shorts and a white T-shirt, and was she ever pretty. She was barefoot, standing at the edge of the road, which didn't have sidewalks, just grass and gravel, doing something with her foot. I stayed back and watched her. She nudged something with her foot. Then she picked it up, still with her foot, balancing on one leg with her arms outstretched, and moved it over like a crane, or more like a dance movement, and dropped it in the grass. She was fully concentrating, and she held her curly hair off the side of her face with one hand.

I was totally thrown by this girl. The white T-shirt with a low neck showed her tanned skin and her long arms, one raised to her hair, the other out at her side for balance, and then her leg lifted like that, her foot curled around whatever it was. It was like that pose from *The Matrix,* like she might all of a sudden rise into the air. I know that sounds silly. I felt embarrassed then, confused by what I was watching and my own response.

Once she dropped her leg, she bent down to look at the thing again. She scrambled around and found a stick to nudge it with. I had pulled up on my bike by then.

"What is it?"

I surprised her, although I thought she had to know I was riding right up to her. There wasn't anyone else on the street.

"Oh!" She jumped back and then laughed at herself at being surprised. She looked around to see if she'd embarrassed herself in front of anyone else. Then she returned her attention to the curious object. "It's a frog," she said. "I think it's sick."

"Did you pick it up with your foot?"

She scrunched up her nose and looked at me. "Yeah. I didn't want to touch it."

"Why not?"

"Because of warts."

"Oh." I stepped off my bike and unhooked the tackle box. I let the bike fall to the grassy edge of the road. I set down the tackle box and walked up next to her.

"Maybe it has heat exhaustion," she said.

"Maybe." I looked down. It was a large frog, more gray than green, squatting in the grass. The frog was definitely breathing, gills pulsating, eyes open, but it wasn't going anywhere. I've seen lots of frogs, and this one didn't seem interesting. But the girl was.

"It should probably be near the river," I said. "I can take it. I'm going there anyway." I opened my tackle box and the top tray accordioned out. Without a thought I reached down and picked up the frog and put it in there, snug against the container of bait, beneath the rack of hooks, bobbers, and sinkers. The frog's skin was papery and dry and it didn't try to jump at all. I closed the tackle box.

Kelsey was smiling at me, the sweetest smile, wide open and easy, honest. Her hair fell over one eye. She had a sprinkling of freckles across her nose. Her hair was permed, I guess, because she doesn't have curly hair now. She seemed really happy that I was helping the frog. "Thank you," she said.

I shrugged. "Sure." There wasn't anything else to say, not at least anything that occurred to me at fourteen, though I suppose asking her name and where she went to school, where she lived, what she was doing there, would have been a good start.

But I picked up my bike and rode away, and although I thought about those questions and had a nice little imaginary conversation with her while I was fishing that day, I didn't think about her again until the next time I saw her, once school started back up in September.

Maurus is a Catholic town. In fact, it didn't have a public school until 1968. The public grade school, Kennedy, named after JFK, was built on the edge of town, out past the brewery, as if the townspeople couldn't quite stand, even then, to have a public school. Like my old German farmer uncle Jerome would say, if it was at least named after a Catholic, he could "let it." Before that there was just St. Willibald and everyone for generations went there to be taught by the nuns. All the kids I knew in Maurus went to St. Willibald. After eighth grade, all the kids were funneled into Maurus High School, except the few Catholic kids whose parents were willing to drive them every day to the Catholic high school in Castor. Kelsey O'Neal was in the new mix of kids from the surrounding small towns feeding into Maurus Senior High School.

Maurus High is around a curve in the road on the far east side of town, across the street from the municipal golf course and a bunch of retirement houses—kids call them the Monopoly houses, perfectly matching green patio homes—that block the golf course from the road. When we ditched French class in late fall sophomore year, we'd go hang out on the golf course. The Horst River runs through it and we'd smoke cigarettes and climb on trees along the bank before heading back for last period. By junior year John Wendinger had a car and we weren't interested in hanging out by the river. When we ditched, which wasn't often, we'd go into Castor for fast food or a matinee at the Cineplex.

On the south side of Maurus High is an older neighborhood of homes. There's one more row of houses by the athletic fields and then the unincorporated part of Maurus, all small farms south and east until you get to the interstate and, on the other side of that, St. Albans.

There is a small Lutheran church in Maurus, too. It's on the south side of Highway 41, back where Fraser Lake and the Agamis are, the lakes with cottages and summer homes owned mostly by people from the Twin Cities. I guess that's where the Lutherans live, though occasionally you meet one in town, too. I'm always surprised when I find out someone is a Lutheran. I know Minnesota is famous for its Lutherans, but not around here. The only Lutherans I know converted when they married Catholics.

The second time in my life I saw Kelsey O'Neal, she was in the hall with her cousin, Ellen Fridley, who lived right off Third Street near Frogtown. That solved the mystery of why Kelsey was on Third Street. Kelsey lived in Dasso, a farming town southwest of Maurus. Her stepfather worked at the Co-op, where farmers rented large equipment in spring and fall and where people got seed and feed for their chickens if they had any.

Most people in Maurus don't have chickens. They get their eggs from relatives on the farm or they don't want farm eggs. These days, I know people want to have chickens, but not in Maurus. It is seen as backward or just too country. My mother brings home fresh brown eggs from family visits and complains that my cousin doesn't clean them properly and there is grass and hay stuck to the eggs. She prefers white eggs from Staley's, but I like the ones from the farm. Uncle Jerome and Aunt Jeanette are dairy farmers, but not in Dasso. I never gave much thought to the place, or any of those towns south of Maurus, until those kids joined us at the high school. We wanted to get to Castor, not farther out into farm country.

Wearing school clothes, and in a group that included that big mouth Ellen, Kelsey didn't have the same effect on me. I knew she was the girl—the curls gave her away, and the sweetness of her face, her cheeks and mouth and chin like a series of hearts, one inside the other. But she looked like just another girl. She already had friends, Ellen's friends, and when I saw her in the hallway the first time she didn't even look my way. And that was fine. I was more interested in sports than girls.

It's probably truer to say we guys were powerless about the girls. They sorted everything out themselves, what guy could be interested in what girl, who could call somebody on the phone. They kind of pushed us around into the groups and couples they wanted us in. As I say, we couldn't do much but say yes or no. We got their notes and phone calls. We showed up at the parties and did what we were told with spinning bottles and visits to the closet or laundry room. We endured the giggles and dramas that unfolded around us. Which isn't to say we didn't get something out of it. You never knew how it was going to turn out and sometimes you got thrown together with a cute girl. Those first two years of high school, nothing really developed of any seriousness. We went to dances in groups, not as couples. We danced in large circles of boys and girls, singing along to the popular songs. Except for the few who were hooked up early, we stood around on the dance floor chatting during the slow numbers.

Kelsey turned out to be not much different than the other girls. She giggled a lot and after football games she sat at the Dairy Queen with a table of girls shooting straws and flirting with exactly who you would expect girls to flirt with. Of course, she was under the sway of Ellen, which was too bad.

She did remember that day with the frog. At a large party in the fall of freshman year when Colby Meyers's parents were out of town, we got close enough to talk, and she said, "Hey, do you think that frog lived?"

I felt my face flush. She caught me off guard, and was just so direct. I guess I thought she didn't remember, or at least that it was just between the two of us, and here she was just blurting it out.

"What frog?" Ellen asked.

"Paul and I found this sick frog, and he took it to the river for me." That wasn't how I would have described the scene, and my face got even redder.

"You and Paul?" Ellen said. "When?"

"Last summer," Kelsey said. "On your street. I was walking around and Paul came over on his bike."

Ellen gave Kelsey a look like she knew there was more to the story. I felt a need to defend myself.

"I didn't find it. Kelsey did. I came over because she was picking up this frog with her foot," I said.

"What?" Ellen looked at Kelsey. Kelsey burst out laughing. Then Ellen laughed, too. They put their arms around each other, like it was an inside joke, and continued to laugh. Maybe they were drunk. I stood there, not sure what to do.

Then Kelsey broke away and asked, looking me right in the eye: "So what happened to my frog?"

I shrugged. "I put him by the river. When I was done fishing, he was still there."

"So he was still alive when you left him?" she asked.

I nodded, but I didn't join in the fun. I was losing interest in this whole thing. I wanted to get out of there.

"Did you give him water or anything?" Kelsey asked.

"I poured a little water on him. He was in a shady place, a damp place."

Ellen laughed so hard she snorted, and things went downhill from there. I held up my hand, *whatever,* and walked away from them, to a group of guys on the other side of the room. When I looked back, Kelsey was taking a swig of beer from a red plastic cup and looking at me. But she didn't come over and talk to me anymore, and I didn't go over to her.

I was an athlete, but not someone who stood out. I guess some people thought I was shy, but I just didn't have much to say. Why talk when you don't have something to say?

I liked football well enough. I played on the defensive line —I was really skinny but at least I was a little taller than some of the other guys. My brother got me some protein powder and showed me how to make shakes, and although I don't think it made much of a difference, I gained some weight and could hold my own.

In high school, the defense is sort of a big crowd of guys throwing themselves at whoever is across from them. I had my guy and I made my tackles. When I messed up, maybe a few fathers noticed, and my coaches. But no one else could tell exactly why the other team scored; they just generally complained about "the defense." When my dad talked to me at home about my performance and the game, he talked about the defense as a whole. "You need to get to the guy with the ball faster." "You need to stop them from inside twenty yards, hold them to field goal tries when they get that close. Most kickers in high school can't kick that far." "The D did a great job of stopping them out there today." Jimmy Wilson got a few sacks so I guess you could say he was our star defensive player. But we rose and fell as an entire defense squad. We were a single unit. You'd think that would help me later as a police officer, where we were also a sort of defensive unit, defending the town.

Freshman and sophomore year playing on the JV team, Chris Miller was a wide receiver. He wasn't a good receiver, but he did make a few catches and even ran one in for a touchdown. He was easy to cover, because he drew attention to himself. Even if he was covered, he'd be angry when the QB wouldn't throw the ball to him, or if the coach didn't run enough plays to get him the ball. He liked to go long, but our quarterback couldn't throw distances. That wasn't Chris's fault, he'd let you know, and he blamed the quarterback. He was scrappy and people loved him. When he dropped the ball, everyone in the stands groaned, and when he caught a pass, they all went nuts. He thought the groans showed people had faith in him—that they expected him to catch the ball every time, like he did himself.

Junior year, he was moved to cornerback. He seemed to think he was still playing offense. He was less concerned with the guy he was supposed to be guarding and focused on getting an interception. He followed the guy he thought would get the pass. This just meant he was never defending his own man, who then ended up being wide open and getting the pass instead.

The coaches told Chris, "Your job is to stay with your guy, no matter what you think the quarterback is going to do." "But they never throw to my guy when I'm covering him," he'd say. "That's right," the coaches said. "That's the idea." He wondered then how he was ever supposed to get an interception. "If you'd put me back on offense, we wouldn't need to have this discussion," Chris said. But we had better receivers, another concept he couldn't grasp. Still, Chris wasn't a guy who moped around or said the coaches were idiots or anything. We always had a good team, always took the conference, though we were beat by powerhouse teams from the western part of the state in the early rounds of the playoffs. Chris just couldn't understand why the coaches didn't see him the way he saw himself—as a really good receiver who could score touchdowns if they'd only give him a chance.

And no one was surprised he was one of the guys that Kelsey flirted with. At the Dairy Queen and in the halls at school, Chris was in the middle of things. He caught on to the girl thing before the rest of us, and in the spring of sophomore year, Chris and Kelsey became a couple. And for the next two years, all her sweet smiles were for him. They were joined at the hip, and she'd stand looking up at him as he pressed her against her locker between classes. At the Dairy Queen she still shot straws across the table, but now she only shot them at Chris.

I don't think it mattered to many people to be popular—it didn't matter to me and my best friends, John Wendinger and Ty Schillingham. But Chris wanted to be liked. That was the most important thing. He wanted to be class president, so he'd get up every year and give those stupid speeches in the gym with the other candidates. Still, we always elected some girl who was smart and in band or spent years in student government.

Chris lobbied hard for Kelsey and him to be prom queen and king, telling everyone to vote for them, saying it would mean a lot to Kelsey. I usually didn't go in for that stuff, but I did go over in the cafeteria and cast my vote for Chris and Kelsey.

Like so many things with Chris, he gave this run at prom king and queen his all. When they were crowned at prom, he seemed to have taken it for granted that they would win. Kelsey seemed embarrassed, though she also clearly liked the attention from the other girls and her hair was fixed so she could show off the tiara. Chris wore a little cape and stupid puffy crown like Burger King, and he had brought along his own scepter, which he twirled with his fingers like a small baton. It was funny. For that night at least, he was a player.

The court always dances to a slow song, and Chris made the DJ put on "Sweet Lady" by Tyrese, his and Kelsey's song. People thought it was hilarious to see him singing to her as they danced, and lots of people sang along. She was in the spotlight and happy.

I knew I couldn't have ever done that—the whole prom queen and king thing. I was happy for her. We all had dates for prom, but nothing serious. John and Ty and I had split the limo. Ty had an actual girlfriend, so John and I went with two of her friends. During the break in the action for the crowning ceremony we guys stood back, enjoying the performance, while the girls stood up close and talked, covering their faces with their hands and leaning into one another. I wondered if they thought Chris was some kind of romantic hero or were making fun of him. I secretly hoped they were making fun of him, because if this is what it took to get a girl, I was not going to be very successful.

Chris played the romantic hero again years later with Nicole, and maybe that was what bothered me at the time, remembering how he had been with Kelsey in high school. I saw Chris and Nicole getting together in the station, first the flirting, then him bringing her coffee in the morning or the Blizzard she liked from DQ on summer afternoons. Vanilla ice cream with caramel and Heath bar was her flavor. I finally said something to him when we were together alone, after he'd walked Nicole out to her car and was gone a bit too long.

"What is going on with you and Nicole?"

He sighed. "I know."

"You know what?"

"I know it looks bad."

"It looks like someone is going to get hurt."

He looked at me and said: "I can't help it, Paul. I'm in love with her."

"What about Kelsey?"

"Kelsey and I haven't been happy for a long time," he said. He said it like we were friends and I would understand. Like I was the guy he wanted to unburden himself to about this. I just looked steadily at him. I didn't really want to get into a discussion about his marriage. I only wanted him to know that I knew, that everyone knew. And that I didn't approve. "Maybe Kelsey and I have never been happy," he said.

"But you have three kids," I said.

He got this look on his face then, clenching his jaw, a little combative. "I love my sons," he said.

"No one doubts you're a good father," I said. "But isn't it better if they have both parents?"

"I don't know—Kelsey's a great mom, but Nicole's my soul mate. I got married too young. I've been with Kelsey since I was fifteen." He had his rationale at the ready, all the clichés. I was not enjoying this conversation at all.

"You have to do something. Everyone knows, everyone here. You can't have both of them." He didn't say anything, so I turned back to my paperwork. "I hope you know what you're doing."

When I got up to leave, he stopped me. "Thanks for your concern, Paul. But trust me, Kelsey isn't going to be sad to see me go. And I'm going to do right by her and the kids. I'm not going to stop being a father to them."

"That's good," I said. "I hope things work out."

He left Kelsey shortly after that, and six months later he and Nicole were married. It was only five months after the wedding, less than a year from that conversation, that Chris Miller was shot.

At Chris and Nicole's wedding, his three boys were all in the procession, the youngest carrying the ring on a pillow, walking with a little flower girl, and the older two, though way too young, as groomsmen, walking down the aisle with two of Nicole's friends. That was embarrassing, too. At least he hadn't made his son Shane his best man. That duty went to his brother, Gary, who was completely supportive of the new arrangement. He gave an embarrassing toast, talking about Nicole being "the love of Chris's life." I guess that's what you say at weddings, but he was over the top about it. The sense I had was of Nicole saving Chris from a whiny bitch, a loveless marriage where he was being crushed by duty. As his brother said, "Chris has not been himself these past years, until he met Nicole and light returned to his life." It was horrible. I felt really bad for Kelsey and her kids.

I wondered what Kelsey would think of the wedding. I wanted to think she'd tired of Chris's shit by then and would think it was all a stupid show. I hoped she wasn't out somewhere getting drunk and missing Chris while her son Zach was running up and wrapping himself in Nicole's giant white skirt. Tim Lang came back to the table with drinks and said he'd heard Chris telling Zach to go give "your new mommy" a hug. "That's gross," said Missy Lang. I had to agree.

Trey was in the wedding party, too, so he sat at the head table, not with the rest of us. Trey and a couple of Nicole's sisters had put together an imitation of the Michael Jackson video "Thriller" for the reception. It was a YouTube thing they'd seen. I couldn't believe how many people knew that dance and got up to join in. Julie knew better than to try to get me on the dance floor. I couldn't help but think it was prom all over again, just missing the crown and little cape. Trey egged Chris on—they were both clearly really drunk by then—when it was time for the garter belt. It was awkward, Nicole's aunts and grandmother looking on. Trey stood behind her, and Chris made this big deal out of feeling his way up her leg. Then Trey reached around the chair and grabbed Nicole's boobs—he actually groped her right there. Not that her boobs weren't mostly out of her dress anyway, but really. And there was a loud gasp. Nicole swung around in the chair and slapped him, and everyone laughed, even Chris. If they'd been in a bar, there would have been a fight.

I thought Missy Lang's eyes were going to pop out of her head. She turned around at the table and was . . . well, speechless.

"Oh, wow, look at Nicole's grandmother," Larry Peterson said. We all looked, and saw the grandmother laughing her head off. She had her hand over her mouth, but maybe just to hold in her teeth. So there you had it.

Even Julie could only shake her head at that one. Most of the time she was busy saying how nice everything was, how cute the kids were, how pretty the bridesmaids' dresses. She wanted to know what I thought of the venue, just Scherer's Hall, and the flowers, and . . . well, everything. She wanted me to propose to her and I felt the pressure.

Julie was right in there with the single women when Nicole tossed the bouquet. When she joined the fight for it, her black hair thrown back and arms clawing, her feet briefly splayed behind her as three women scrabbled on the floor, we were all kind of shocked again. Matt Foley sank back in his chair and said, "Jesus." Larry patted me on the shoulder, saying: "Be careful, my friend." Missy Lang took that opportunity to say how lucky any guy would be to be married to Julie. In the end, Julie came back to the table with a shrug, no bouquet.

"That was a little intense, honey," I said.

She laughed, and ran her hands through her hair. "Oh, that was nothing." Larry raised his eyebrows, and she said, "Bitches." Julie never talked like that. We all laughed, but it was a little bit scary.

Chapter Six

Chris's first wedding was a much smaller affair. Chris and Kelsey finished up high school with the rest of us and got jobs. Chris worked for a couple years at his uncle's auto glass business then started his two-year degree in police science at the tech college in Castor. Kelsey got a job with one of the granite retailers, processing orders and scheduling installations. She was probably good at that, because she liked people and was sharp enough to keep track of details. I heard she got pregnant, and then they were married.

In senior year of high school, people pretty much broke into two groups, those going to college and those who had offers of work, mostly through family businesses or connections. Many of those who went to college, like Ty and John, moved into apartments near Castor State or commuted to the tech college.

I wouldn't say Maurus was fully committed to the importance of a college education. Enough of the fathers had come up working in the granite quarries or on farms that they didn't really get college. College was expensive, and everyone was worried about how to pay for it. Since most of us didn't know what we wanted to do, four years of college seemed like a big, expensive gamble. Our teachers told us how important it was but didn't offer much help getting there. We tried to find schools that wouldn't cost too much but could give us a step up in life and, so, make our parents happy.

Neither of my parents had gone to a four-year college. My dad had an in with the granite company and a good union job waiting for him. My mother was from a farm family and they didn't believe in college for girls. After a couple years of work as a receptionist, she did a two-year program at the technical college and got a job doing books for a large car dealership in Castor. When Frank was born, she stopped working and hadn't gone back. She and a friend cleaned a few houses for extra money and she helped Frank and Joan by taking care of their two girls.

I was offered a baseball scholarship to North Dakota State. I applied, mostly on a whim, to Arizona State, too, because I thought it would be great to go someplace warm. But the baseball scholarship sealed the deal.

I liked football, but my sport was always baseball. And Maurus, like most Minnesota towns, is a baseball town. During the school year, the attention is on football and basketball, but spring and summer are all about baseball, even for adults. Baseball is a game our dads taught us that we played in parks in the summer, not something we learned at school from coaches. The Twins dominated our lives from spring training through October—all our dads and most of the moms, the aunts and uncles, cousins—and everyone we knew followed the Twins.

The game was on in the background, inside or out, most summer days and nights long into fall. We all grew up loving Kirby Puckett. On television, the radio, in the car or the garage or even from speakers pointed out through the kitchen window into the backyard, the sound of baseball was everywhere.

In the summer when we were young, our moms took us to watch our dads play in the men's league. Every baseball diamond in every town for miles had a game of some kind at six o'clock Monday, Tuesday, and Thursday nights and all day Saturday. Wednesday nights were for church and meetings, and Friday nights the men stayed home and grilled.

At the end of June the sun didn't set until ten o'clock. The sounds of a baseball game, the smell of grass and bug spray, running around in the yellow gravel and climbing on chain link backstops—those are some of my earliest memories.

There is also a baseball stadium in town, across the street from the house I bought when I joined the department, just past the church. The stadium is a large, concrete structure, with concessions and gates and permanent stands. You can see the floodlights driving in from any direction, before you see any other evidence of a town. It's like *Field of Dreams,* baseball in the cornfields. We all thought that, and one day, coming back late from the Cineplex in Castor, we came around the long bend near Kennedy and saw the lights like a spaceship hovering over town. It must have been a moonless night, and for some reason it struck us. We just naturally fell silent, though we didn't notice we'd stopped talking until Ty turned from the front passenger seat and said in a loud whisper: "If you build it, they will come."

We laughed at him, but then John and I joined in, quoting lines from the film.

Although it was an old movie, we'd all seen it because of the character Moonlight Graham, who was from Minnesota. Because our parents loved the movie, we hadn't let on how much we liked it. Once Ty went so far as to speak the words we all were thinking, we embraced baseball as our identity, our birthright. We became serious about our future as baseball players, practicing with one another, aspiring to hit the ball farther and make more diving catches. We all thought of that as our story, the story of baseball players from the farms, just like we all thought we were Roy Hobbs from *The Natural,* with baseball bats carved by lightning. Other high school teams used aluminum bats, but not us. Even when the coaches encouraged us to switch, we stuck to our wood bats. We were purists.

Then, the summer before sophomore year, when I was playing on a traveling team, I got on a hitting streak and my teammates started calling me "Wonderboy," the name of Roy Hobbs's bat. I loved it, of course. The nickname followed me into the school year, and I was sheepish about it, but I was also happy the name stuck. I found a poster from the Robert Redford movie on eBay and taped it to the back of my bedroom door. I got more serious about lifting and practicing. I even began to believe that I could be a great baseball player. On the traveling team, we had a bus that went around the state for weekend tournaments, and we were good.

Ty and John played, but I was the one who excelled at baseball. I thought I was really going places when I got the college scholarship. Then I arrived at NDSU. My roommate was a pitcher from North Dakota named Cooper Krekling. These guys all had great baseball names: Avery Adair, Grant Lemke, Jordie Quist. And they looked the part. They had broad shoulders, muscled arms, small waists, lean legs, and small feet. They were solid and quick, and they wore their uniforms like they were an extension of their skin, like superhero suits.

I was smart enough to leave my poster at home, and I learned pretty quickly that I wasn't going to be a professional baseball player. I lifted with them, put in my miles on the track and on the trails, but I was no match for Cooper and the other top players. I could hit and I could catch a fly ball. I did my job well enough with some clutch hits that it was worth keeping me in the outfield. Cooper lived and breathed baseball. He knew more about pro players, going way back, especially pitchers, than anyone I'd ever met. I knew about the great hitters, but really just who you would expect. Cooper had analyzed the pitching of seemingly every player who ever played the game, and pitching was all he talked about. And there was a lot to talk about, given the variety of pitches and windups and the long list of career-ending injuries. He talked a lot, always about baseball, and I mostly listened.

He'd also already taken up the baseball habit of chewing tobacco. I tried once, tucking a small wad in under my lip, trying to work saliva into it and not swallow the juice. It was harsh and burned my gums. The effects were decidedly unpleasant. I didn't know that tobacco could make you sick, but after about five minutes, I went to the bathroom and dug the foul stuff out of my mouth. I came back and announced that chewing was not for me. To show how tough I was, I chugged a bottle of beer, and some of the remaining tobacco slime washed down with it.

My heart started racing and I felt dizzy, so I excused myself from the suite where we were hanging out and went back to my room. I thought I was going to throw up, and lay in bed for hours with the room spinning before I fell asleep. After that, even the sight of those spit cups, the smell of the chaw, made me feel nauseous. Just the fact that Cooper and Jordie had a slug of chaw in their mouths by ten a.m. showed they were made of tougher stuff than I was.

Cooper's love of baseball seemed to fit perfectly with an interest in biology and kinesiology. It just gave him other ways to talk about pitching. I took the courses my counselor told me to take.

Within a semester I knew that college was not for me. The classes didn't seem much different than high school, though they met less often and required a ton of reading and writing and endless time in labs. The textbooks were boring and I managed to do the work but couldn't remember what I'd done once I'd finished. I couldn't figure out what I wanted to be or how doing this work in these classes was going to help me. When I came home at Christmas, my parents were happy about how I'd done: an A, two Bs, and a C in biology. Good enough to keep my scholarship. But I was just happy to be home, away from school. I didn't have any answers to their many questions, and I didn't want to think about going back after the break. As New Year's approached, my mood soured.

The Sunday before I had to go back we were in the kitchen, and my mother wanted to know what was wrong. I just shrugged.

Frank had come by after church to help dad repair a problem drain for the washing machine. We spent a long afternoon in a cold basement, they sent me on several trips to the hardware store, and even though I liked being down there working with Frank and my dad, I was awkward and they treated me like a little kid, kind of in the way. I didn't fit with my father and brother, who knew how to fix everything and didn't even have to talk about it.

My dad knew every pipe, board, and wire in the house. In the thirty years my parents had lived there, he'd probably completely rebuilt it from the inside out, Frank alongside him. They worked well together, speaking in gestures and half sentences, almost like they had a secret language. And they had the same hands, large but nimble. They could feel things with their rough fingers that I couldn't feel. Frank knew exactly how much pressure to apply on the wrench so as not to strip the threads of a corroded pipe. When I tried, the pipe just broke off. They could analyze rust and oil and any fluid leaking from any vehicle, appliance, pipe, or seam. They were sure of themselves in knowing these things and easy with each other and their environment. The women, my mother and Joan, depended on them.

But for some reason they had pushed me to be different, not to get my hands dirty. They didn't let me close enough or tell me their secrets. When I was younger they sent me out to play baseball, to have fun, and somehow I missed the chance to enter the higher echelons of their world. I was off playing video games and they didn't bother to interrupt me. My dad thought any time spent on a computer was good. Compared to a lot of guys, I'm handy. I'm able to take care of little things, hang pictures, fix a toilet or leaky faucet, diagnose problems, even do some drywall work. I can replace a broken window, but once I tried to glaze a window and that was a big failure. My dad came over and redid it for me. I had to call my dad or Frank, or a professional, if I needed plumbing or electric or a major repair. They had decided, together, what I should and should not be able to do. But what if I wanted to get my hands dirty?

After the drain was fixed, Frank washed at the kitchen sink, lathering up to his elbows like a surgeon, and mom worked on a pot of venison chili. My dad pushed me. "What the hell is wrong with you?"

"What? Nothing."

"That's bullshit. Just tell us what's going on."

So I told him. "I'm thinking college might not be for me."

"But why? You're doing well," my mom said, spinning around from the stove with a bag of frozen corn in her hand. "Not going to be a doctor, probably, but you're doing well."

"I just don't see the point."

"The point is to get a good job," my father said. This good job was perhaps the vaguest of all notions. I wanted someone to tell me what it was exactly you did in "a good job." I knew my dad wasn't the one to ask.

"Yeah, I don't see how sitting in classes just like the ones I had in high school are going to get me a good job."

"It's the degree," he said. "You have to have a college degree to get into management. Most jobs now require a college degree."

My brother, Frank, spoke up then. He hadn't gone to college and in three years had secured a steady job in construction. "College isn't going to help you if you want to work with your hands."

Dad shot Frank a look that said Frank's opinion on this matter wasn't welcome. "You aren't supposed to know what you want to do yet, Paul," he said. "College will show you lots of other possibilities, lots of things you can do. You'll get an interest as you go along."

"But I see other guys who are interested in what they're studying. I just don't care."

"Maybe it's because baseball hasn't started yet. Once the season starts, and you see what big-time college baseball is like, you'll enjoy school more."

"Everyone says the first year of college is hard," mom added, turning back to the stove, dumping the corn in the pot. "It will get better."

"Maybe," I said.

"It takes awhile to get used to it—it's a big change," she said. "And anyway, these classes are just the basics, not the business classes. It will get more interesting."

I nodded.

"You have a full ride, Paul, a scholarship," my dad added. "People would kill for a sports scholarship, especially at a good school like NDSU. This is your opportunity to move up, to get a good job and not have to bust your butt every day of your life in a quarry or on roofs or whatever."

I nodded again.

"Don't screw it up," he said, rising from his chair. Then he left the room.

Chapter Seven

When I became a police officer, complete with a college degree, my dad was proud of me. He insisted on helping me with the down payment to my house. And then, of course, more dramatically than anyone could have predicted, I fucked it up.

After Chris Miller's death, everything got crazy fast. I was branded a coward by the end of the first day of interrogations, but the bullet made Chris Miller an instant hero. And what struck me most in those days afterward was how little all the hero stuff matched the actual person named Chris Miller, the kid I grew up with. No one would have ever predicted Chris Miller would become a hero. Except, that is, for Chris Miller himself. This was exactly how he—and maybe Gary and Nicole—saw himself.

When a police officer is killed, there is a particular outrage and grief set aside for the event. I didn't know that before Chris Miller's death. I don't know why I didn't know it. I just didn't. My two years as a cop had been full of good things, nights at Arnold's with Tim, times I'd been able to help people. But even though everyone talked like we were all brothers, there was a strong hierarchy, and I was at the bottom of it. I was higher than

Nicole, or the other secretary, Jean. I shared a desk with Kenny Streator. But the desk had belonged to a guy named Harry Carver. Although he was retired, he still came around, did some archive work, but mostly sat around and talked. Everyone referred to the desk as "Harry's desk." They'd say: "I put that file for you on Harry's desk." I had an in-box there that was my own, a few pictures, a coffee cup.

The job itself was more or less what I'd expected. Lots of cars in ditches and fender benders. Answering calls when neighbors weren't getting along, loud parties, drunkenness, fights. Petty thefts and drive-offs at the gas station. We didn't write many tickets. We didn't harass people. Protect and serve, with the emphasis on *serve.* Chief Kramer said he saw our job as keeping the chaos in check. Not getting rid of the chaos or hoping for order—realizing the world is chaotic and we just can't let it get to a point where the chaos takes over.

That was the job, even the night we went to the alley behind Arnold's. But when Chris Miller was shot, it became clear that people thought the cops belonged to them in a very special way. It was a particularly heinous act, an affront to our sense of what it meant to be a civilized society. "Who would shoot a police officer?" Bernie Schlachter said to a reporter. "A public servant who puts his life on the line for the community. What kind of animal would shoot a cop?"

There was a vigil at St. Willibald's the Saturday night following the shooting, and a large shrine with candles, stuffed animals, and flowers at the scene. The vigil was going on less than a mile from where I was being interviewed at the station. I saw the coverage in the Sunday *Castor Standard* the next day, all these people from town, parents with their children, holding candles and crying. Chris's relatives, sure, and I felt terrible for them. I could understand that kind of grief within the family. But then there were teachers we'd had in school. Coach Philips saying, "He was a good guy, a big-hearted kid. He had a real joy for life, and he just loved his family and this community so much. He will be missed."

It isn't that I disagree with any of that—how could you? What they said is all, in its way, true. Still, how people responded seemed out of proportion. Like everything, the public grief took me by surprise.

The children were a big focus. Those three little boys: Shane, the oldest at nine; Kyle; and little Zach. He had still been a toddler when Chris took up with Nicole. But no one was noticing that now. No one was judging Chris now.

And Nicole! She threw herself entirely into the role of grieving widow. She wore Chris's tactical jacket to the vigil, and I was surprised to see the photo of her there, surrounded by friends. That big, black coat with patches on the shoulders and his name over the chest swallowed her up. She was a wreck, helpless and stranded.

Right away, the fundraisers started. Posters went up for a spaghetti dinner at the parish to raise money for the family. There was a "break-a-thon," where karate students took pledges for each board they broke during a public demonstration, and people could pay to break their own boards. Someone had wristbands made up reading "Forever a Hero" and Chris's badge number and they were for sale everywhere: at the bakery, at Staley's, on the counter at Lynn's coffee shop. There were T-shirts for sale, pins, car decals. His badge number, 2605, was like a code word for hero.

A local tanning booth gave a portion of fees from one day to the memorial fund. The local country station put on a fundraiser concert at the high school with local bands. An alum from the high school who was living in Utah, a guy who graduated long after we were gone from the school, put up a snowboarding video and pledged that if he got enough votes online to win a video contest, he would send the winnings to the Miller family. There was a massive Facebook and email campaign, and he almost won.

A trampoline and bounce house place had a fundraising event for kids. In Castor, there was even a night of extreme fighting—five cage fights, and twenty percent of the ticket price went to benefit Nicole. The fight night was put on by the Will County Police Officer Wives Association. Bouncing for the kids, cage fighting for the widow. It was surreal. Everyone wanted to pitch in and do something. All you read everywhere were the clichés: Chris Miller made the ultimate sacrifice, died like the warrior he was, paid the highest price for his community. And always, everywhere, on posters and T-shirts, the photo of him in his uniform, with his buzz cut and his goofy grin, looking like he was eighteen years old.

And there were plenty of comments that went straight to me, to my part in the event. A police officer in Iowa posted on the Facebook page, saying: "You were a true hero, Officer Chris

Miller. When others ran from danger, you ran right into the face of it, and paid the ultimate price." I know I shouldn't have even been reading this stuff. But I couldn't stay away.

And then there was Kelsey. Or, actually, there wasn't much of Kelsey at all. She stayed in the background, for the most part. Nicole was busy in the spotlight, and even Chris's parents and family circled around her. There was a short article on a Tuesday in the *Castor Standard* about what a good father Chris was, with a photo of Kelsey and the boys. The story didn't give any details of the divorce, of course, but anyone could tell it was not a good story by looking at little Zach. Kelsey was nothing but positive about Chris in the article. She said only Shane really understood what had happened. She talked about ways she would keep Chris's memory alive for the boys. Other than that piece, you hardly heard a word about her. I'm sure a lot of people thought Nicole was the boys' mother. In fact, a more prominent photo in the media showed Chris with Nicole and the boys, taken at Sears, the model family. Husband and father.

I put on my uniform and went to the funeral, along with more than a thousand other officers, the governor, one of our senators, and seemingly every man, woman, and child in a fifty-mile radius. St. Willibald's wasn't big enough, so they had the funeral at the cathedral in Castor, twenty miles away. The exits from the highway were jammed in both directions by long caravans of police cars. The roads were lined with police cruisers, parking wherever they could.

The funeral was on a bitter cold day, still no snow, and a bright blue sky. The kind of day we love in Minnesota, when the lakes start freezing and the trees are mostly bare, deer hunting season when you put on your Carhartt coveralls and boots and your blaze orange and walk through the woods before sunrise, the weeds crunching underfoot.

Instead, we were all in our dress uniforms, and the cold went right through our polished shoes and thin socks and easily penetrated our dress trousers with their perfect creases. Still, we stood at attention, in ranks. I didn't even think about Chris Miller, not in the beginning. I distracted myself by just thinking about cops, about being one of these guys. I focused on playing my part, being in line, the logistics. No one knew who I was. No one knew I was "the partner." There was a grand anonymity to that day. We were placed as we arrived, no attention to where we were from. And we marched down St. Bruno Street in Castor, a street lined with people, a solemn parade. We marched up the broad steps of the cathedral. Inside, we filed in and sat in the pews reserved for us. The large, formal nave was for police officers, dignitaries, invited friends, and family. Rows and rows of blue and tan and green uniforms. We ended up filling most of the place. I found out later there was an overflow area that was also filled, where people watched the funeral on a screen. Even more people stood outside in the cold. Of course I didn't think about Chris Miller. No way would this many people show up for his funeral. They showed up for something else.

The chief, Trey, Larry, and Tim were pallbearers. This made it easy for me to keep my distance. I knew Trey especially wouldn't want me there, but our whole squad, except for me, and many of the Castor sheriff's deputies, were up front. I was hiding. In my uniform, in with all the other uniforms, in our solemn silence, I had no trouble staying anonymous. One of the guys standing next to me, seeing the department ID on my shirt, asked why I wasn't up front. I just shook my head, didn't answer, and he didn't ask any more questions, just said, "Sorry. It's a tough loss." I nodded and kept my face turned forward.

I was surprised that Father Jonas from St. Willibald presided. He did a great job, giving directions on the parts of the Mass for the many Lutheran officers and nonpracticing Catholics in the crowd. The casket was on the altar, draped with an American flag and crowned by a huge bouquet of flowers. Nicole was there, still wearing Chris's big black coat. From where I sat, off to the side, I could watch Kelsey, in black pants and a plain black sweater, her hair long and straight, a boy sitting on each side of her and Zach on her lap. He sat for a time facing her, focused on her hair and face, and he clapped her face between his hands and pushed his face up against hers. She resettled him with a small container of Cheerios, but he wanted to feed her, too. She looked more tired, stressed, than sad. She wasn't wearing much makeup, if any, and her hair was just held back on each side by barrettes. No one could accuse her of trying to take the spotlight.

After the homily, when Father Jonas talked about loss and family in a great, simple way, in an honest way, giving us a break from the public nature of all this, there was a eulogy by Chris's older brother, Gary. It was over the top in the same way

I'd been hearing and reading since the event, full of strange, military references. I squirmed a little under the weight of it, but looking around I could tell it was striking a chord with the other cops. I did look over at Kelsey one more time, when Gary said he'd follow through on a promise "to take care of Chris's beautiful wife, Nicole." He said he'd made that promise to his brother late one night when they'd been talking about the danger of the job. He said it was as if Chris knew "he would be called upon to give this ultimate sacrifice," and his only concern was leaving behind his "soul mate," Nicole.

Kelsey's expression didn't change. She was looking steadily at Gary, stoic, or maybe just off in a different world. I hoped that was the case, because I didn't like the other option, her having to sit there and hear Gary throw in his allegiance so completely with Nicole, as though Kelsey wasn't also losing something huge, as if Kelsey didn't also require care.

Finally, we processed out. Because of the crowd, I could avoid pretty much everyone, just be in with the mass of uniforms. There was a color guard down St. Bruno Street, and I have no idea where you get these things, but there was a horse pulling an old-fashioned cart carrying the coffin. Like John Kennedy or Abraham Lincoln. Surreal, truly. And yet everyone acted like it was a normal thing to do. If anyone thought it was a bit much, they didn't say so.

For the burial, we got in our cars and the coffin was transferred to a hearse. All along the route, there were people. All the way back to Maurus, on the side of Highway 41 through Castor and St. Albans, then the stretch of farms once we'd passed under the interstate, there were groups of people with signs or just standing and waving at the long procession. I was in a car with Julie and my folks, and we quietly observed the scene. I sat up front with my father. The heat was blasting from the vents, but I couldn't get warm. I took off my leather gloves and held my hands right on the vent, where the hot plastic burned my fingers but still didn't warm me.

When we entered Maurus, there were even more people. Outside Kennedy Grade School, children and teachers lined both sides of the road. They were waving American flags and some held signs: "Officer Chris Miller, Our Hero," and "Thank You, Chris Miller" and "Never Forget 2605, Our Hero." It was so cold, and there they were, these long rows of brightly colored winter coats and knit hats with pom-poms on top. I don't think I'll ever see anything like it again. I saw Clare then, Frank's youngest, with her class, holding a flag, waving it wildly at us. It made me pull back, away from the window. I had spoken to some of these kids at an assembly about stranger danger. I was surprised to find tears in my eyes. A police officer had been killed. It was too beautiful, everyone lining the road. It was too terrible, too, what I had done, and what I was afraid was lost to me now. I tried to wipe my eyes without the others in the car noticing.

My dad put his hand on my shoulder. "We don't have to do this part," he said. "You don't need to go to the burial."

I shook my head. "It's OK." We parked in the line of cars, and I walked up to take my place with the ranks of officers, while my family mixed in with the other civilians. We were in the new part of the cemetery, where there aren't many trees. It was wide open, and there was a raw wind blowing. I leaned into it to get to the neat rows of white chairs. From a distance, they looked like the gravestones of a military cemetery, all those identical white headstones, rows and rows of them. But they were filling up with men in blue, or state troopers and sheriff's officers in tan and green, each with his hat tilted at the same angle. It was like a graduation then, a sad, solemn sending off. Except no one spoke. There was just the bare trees and the flat land, the other graves of various shapes and sizes, and the white canopy over the place where Chris Miller would be laid to rest.

Finally, the family and the hearse arrived. Although they'd led the procession, they'd stayed in the shelter of the cemetery office, or their warm cars, to give the crowd time to get settled.

They pulled out all the stops in the cemetery, too. A full military funeral, regulation for an officer killed in the line of duty. Taps and a twelve-gun salute at the gravesite. Two members of the National Guard folded the flag and presented it to Nicole, who sat crying softly, holding a rose. Father Jonas was brief with the invocation. When they lowered the coffin, Nicole really broke down, and she called out Chris's name. A shiver ran down my spine, remembering her voice over the radio the night Chris was killed. That was the worst moment, the absolute worst.

The boys went up with Kelsey and tossed in some dirt. Shane was solemn and pale, looking to his mother for guidance. The photographers were having a field day. Thank God little Zach didn't salute or anything. I couldn't have taken any more JFK reenactments. Kelsey continued to do her part, guiding the children, keeping it—unlike everything else—simple. Later people in town would make a big deal that she didn't cry. They said she was cold, didn't care that the father of her children had died. As if that were possible.

I thought she was dignified. She had to get the kids through this horrible day. Plenty of people were crying. I even saw a few cops wipe their eyes at certain moments, though mostly we were there to show strength. We were there—I guess—to show that evil couldn't bring us down. That we would come back in greater numbers. We were there to show everyone how brave we all were, that we would all pay the ultimate sacrifice, just like Chris Miller, if we were called upon to do so. And for that reason, I know, I shouldn't have been there. Maybe that's why I couldn't get warm.

In the end, it looked like Nicole was going to throw herself on the coffin, which would have really capped things off. But with Gary at her side, as promised, she managed to restrain herself just a bit. She had a teddy bear she put in the grave, and a folded sheet of paper I learned later was a poem. She muttered something while Gary held her and wiped tears from his own eyes. She had a little bottle, too, and put some dirt in it and closed it with a stopper. It was a strange souvenir, and strange that she had the presence of mind to do it. I wondered if she was confusing it with ashes. It was not hard to imagine the shrine she had started at home, and how this bottle of dirt might go in a place of honor.

When we got home, my dad brought out a bottle of Jim Beam and two juice glasses. I was so cold I thought I'd never be warm again. My mother didn't say anything about the midday whiskey, just went to the fridge and got out bags of sandwich meat and cheese. No one had even suggested we go to the church for the funeral reception. My dad poured a healthy shot into each glass and handed one to me. I poured it straight down my throat and felt the warmth, not spreading out, just pooling, burning, in my stomach. "I'm going to go change," I said.

In my childhood room I changed into sweats, a thermal, and a hoodie. I put on wool socks that hugged my feet but didn't do anything to warm me up. The uniform seemed flimsy and insubstantial in my hands. I put them in my car and when I got back to my own house later that night I boxed up the shoes, threw the black socks in the laundry basket, and hung the uniform on a wire hanger. Then I pulled all my other clothes to one side of the rack, so I could slide the uniform way into the back. Somehow I knew I wouldn't be wearing it again.

Chapter Eight

Sitting on that bed in my childhood room, with all the baseball trophies still on a shelf and the same blue plaid bedspread and curtains, made me think of summer breaks during college. That was the last time I'd lived in this room, a time I was actually happy.

Frank got me a job on his crew building houses in the Quarry Trails subdivision. I loved it, being out in the truck in the early morning, working hard all day, and especially the shower once we got home. The way the cool water warmed as it poured over my head and down my shoulders and back, until finally the heat was washed away and the cool water reached my belly. The soap, gray in my tight-skinned hands, washing the dirt of the day away.

After dinner, Frank would swing by and we'd go to the stadium and watch the Graniteers. They were the amateur team in Maurus, where I was headed, if anywhere. I could see a future—construction days and baseball at night. I could see myself doing that indefinitely. I didn't talk about leaving college, and my father knew construction was a good, short-term opportunity to raise money for school.

The Graniteers were on their way to another state championship that summer. Everybody went to the games when they played in town, and we even went to a couple games in Dasso and St. Albans. I was folded in with Frank's crowd, who were older than both of us, since he was one of the youngest guys working on the construction crew.

So we spent those nights with about a dozen people in their twenties and thirties, everybody wearing baseball caps, the women with ponytails threaded through the back and the men freshened up after working hard all day, the smell of cologne, shampoo, and aftershave in the air. Everyone threw back plastic cups of the weak swill the local brewery was famous for, cheap but potent enough in quantity.

Unlike at college, I felt totally at home with these people.

I stuck close to Jim Kastenbauer, a guy who grew up on a farm nearby and, at twenty-eight, was already divorced with three kids, living in a trailer on the family dairy farm. What I remember about him from that first summer was that he had a real sadness about him, not bitterness but just plain old sadness. I stuck by him because his sadness interested me. When he wandered off to his car at the end of the night without saying goodbye, I always thought that would be the last time he'd come out. But then there he was at the next game, with a resigned look on his face and a slow, easy walk.

Family dairy farms are fewer and fewer these days, but there's still a culture out here. The old men with their German accents and their hands—incredible hands. Sometimes fingers gone or deformed, big pads of hands like catcher's mitts, you'd swear they were swollen or something. You know even in the coldest winter those men just never wear gloves out in the barn, or pull them off so much it's as good as not wearing them at all. One guy at church, who always serves breakfast with the Knights of Columbus, Augie Bechtold, had an incredible hand. Although he only had three fingers and a thumb, his fingers had spread to fill the entire space of a regular palm. He used it as well as anyone with all five fingers. Where are you going to get work gloves for a hand like that?

Dairy farming is relentless. The families are stuck to their farms year round. They have to milk twice a day, and now there's a lot to it in terms of machinery and inspections and feed and veterinary services. Other animals need to be moved around, too, but the dairy cows demand constant care and attention. You can get a neighbor to water and feed the horses or the goats, but you can't trust your cows to anyone, even for a day.

There are dairy farms here for the same reason there are granite quarries. The land is too rocky to be good for crops. Still, the dairy farmers need pasture and they need hay, so they always have as much land as they can get. If their own property is too small, they rent or own small plots for feed corn all over the place.

Jim Kastenbauer looked like an actor playing a farmer, with a kind, intelligent face and lines on his forehead and down his dimpled cheeks. He was tall and lanky, not the usual compact German farmer. Even as a young guy his hair was thinning, which I think added to his sad look. He looked more like a cowboy, slightly bow-legged, and his clothes, especially the jeans he wore right through summer when all the other guys were wearing cargo shorts, were soft and worn. He wore plain T-shirts in soft colors and well-creased caps from feed suppliers. He never went to college, though he should have. He could have run some big agriculture project with the U of M, but instead his girlfriend got pregnant and he got married. A common story.

When I met him, he talked a lot about organic farming. This was ten years before it really took hold in our area and it sounded pretty far out there to me. There were a few wackos around who wanted to burn corncobs for fuel and had signs up on the edge of their woods denouncing oil and the government. People who ate lots of sprouts and nuts. There was Mark Schott's mom, who had officially changed her name to Cyndie Ryverlight after Mark's dad left. She made pottery and was a midwife, and Mark had been born at home. We felt sorry for Mark because his mom and her friends were so embarrassing. Once he said, "I wish she'd just quilt like other moms." None of our moms quilted, so we thought that was pretty funny. He had no idea what other moms did.

One thing about Cyndie Ryverlight, though, she could dress a deer. Once when we went over to pick up Mark for a movie there were three deer hides stretched out and drying on their front yard. Then we found out his mom was going to use them to cover her sweat lodge in the backyard. There were middle-aged, naked women out there for a whole month, and some big witchy ceremony on the shortest day of the year. Poor Mark.

Jim was not like that, but he talked like them. He had wild ideas. He had done some reading about this guy who had cows and chickens and pigs and moved them around so their manure fertilized everything. "It's symbiotic," he said. He told me about how the guy threw straw and corn into the manure the cows were dropping all winter in the barn. In the spring, instead of mucking it out with shovels, the guy just turned his pigs loose in there. They went after the corn and broke up of the layers of dried cow manure and it was ready to be spread when they were done. It did sound like genius, but I said to him: "Yeah, Jim, but then you have to take care of pigs as well as cows."

"That's what my dad said," Jim muttered, and poured more beer down his throat. "Pigs aren't a big deal. You don't need a lot of them."

I felt bad for shooting down the idea when Jim already seemed so defeated. Jim also thought maybe he'd like to start a winery. "People in the upper Midwest are starting to make some good table wines, interesting stuff," he said. "It's not about aged wines so much anymore; you don't need to put stuff in oak casks for decades or buy a lot of expensive equipment. People in this area, you know, they've always liked things sweet. You can do interesting blends with the grapes you can grow here. If it takes off, you can buy more grapes from other places."

"How do you know this stuff?"

"I read about it, books and articles. Once you get on a list, you start to get all these mailings. One thing leads to another. There's a lot of resources out there."

"You want to be a farmer?" I asked, somewhat incredulous. Most people I knew wanted to get out of farming as soon as possible.

Jim gave me his sad look, and lifted his cap to run his hand through his hair. He looked exactly like a farmer when he did that. "It's an honest way of life," he said.

I nodded. "Your dad must be happy that you want to, you know, take over."

His face hardened at that; this was clearly a sore subject. "He's not planning on giving up farming anytime soon. He's only fifty-four. And it's not clear the farm could support my folks and me." He rubbed his work boot against the edge of the bleacher in front of us, like he was scraping something off of it, though it was clean. "It's hard to change things on a farm—you end up waiting half your life or, basically, working for wages, and then you're too old when you get control to want to do anything interesting or new."

We had farm stands around, mostly where we bought corn and watermelon, and Joe Pfannenstein had U-Pick strawberries, but no one talked about organic food.

"I don't want to be a poor truck farmer like Joe Pfannenstein," Jim said, "who has all his kids out there working and has that horrible, swampy piece of land you can't get machinery through anyway. People around here, though, they don't even eat vegetables."

I couldn't say I ate many vegetables myself. We had corn and tomatoes from my uncle's farm in the summer. Mostly, though, we ate meat and potatoes. If my mother made a vegetable on the side, it was most often frozen corn or green beans. Jim looked down the row.

"Carrie," he said. "You ever been to a farmer's market?"

"A what?" she said.

"You know, like on Wednesdays in Castor, where you get fruits and vegetables right from the farmer?"

"Castor? I wouldn't go to Castor for vegetables. They have vegetables at Staley's."

Jim turned to me. "Hear that? The vegetables at Staley's are awful. They're all packaged up. Broccoli in plastic bags from Dole and, if you're lucky, green beans in a Styrofoam package. I'm sure Carrie buys those bags of iceberg lettuce if she buys lettuce at all. If she eats vegetables, they're frozen."

"Would you be growing broccoli?" I asked.

"That's not the point," Jim said, and shook his head, exasperated.

I wanted to get Jim, and really I liked him. I still do, despite everything. He lost a lot in this whole thing, too. Maybe more than me.

At the time I liked Jim because he knew exactly what he wanted to do. He cared about things and had purpose. He had dreams. I needed a guy like that to give me some direction, but I knew Jim, with his frustration and sadness, wasn't the guy. And I didn't want to be a farmer.

I didn't have anything against farmers, not at all. But growing up we didn't mix with the farm kids. They were just different from us town kids. They were hard workers, and we all admired that. But they had different interests. We wanted to get into Castor to the Cineplex or the mall or the Pizza Hut, to get road bikes and cars and go swimming in Agami lakes. We talked about music and video games and television shows.

The farm kids drove pickup trucks and there was a clear hierarchy among the trucks. In the winter, they rode snowmobiles to school. You'd hear the loud roar of them and see their headlights careening along snowbanks on trails to the parking lot. After school, on really cold days, they'd be ripping around on those snowmobiles on the athletic fields before shooting off down Highway 41, cutting down into the ditch at high speeds. There were little signs all over, miniature stop signs and yield signs, a whole trail system with intersections and merges and everything once you got out of town. A lot of town kids had snowmobiles, too, and they'd ride them, but not to school. It was recreation, not a mode of transportation. They'd take them out to the family cabins or state and county trails for an afternoon. Most of the time the shiny machines sat covered on a trailer in the driveway. That was the way with town kids. On the RV pad in the summer you'd see the trailer with two Jet Skis, and in winter the trailer with the snowmobiles. They always looked new, making you wonder if anyone ever rode them at all.

When you rode a snowmobile to school, it meant you arrived pretty much frozen and covered with snow. The snowmobile suits didn't fit in the lockers, so the school put out big racks for hanging them near the front door, where they dripped all day and had muddy, salty puddles beneath them. A special area was set aside in the school parking lot, and sometimes there would be twenty or thirty snowmobiles lined up out there like a dealership.

You could tell who snowmobiled to school because they had red, chapped faces and crazy, matted hair and looked surprised, like they couldn't adjust to the indoor light. Sometimes one of them would forget to bring a change of shoes and would be clomping around in snow boots all day. At the end of the day I was glad to get into a warm car or on a warm bus, but they'd zip up and go out to their machines. In December or early January it would be almost dark by four o'clock, and they'd look like swarming fireflies heading back out to the country with their headlights shining.

The cold didn't daunt them at all. That's the other thing about farm kids in general—they always seemed the most wide awake, even though I'm sure they got the least sleep. It was like in college when the veterans or the guys in ROTC were always wide awake even in the earliest classes. While some of us were struggling after staying up late for no good reason, the farm kids had been up for hours, out in barns doing chores.

We were superficial enough to judge the way they dressed. The farmer kids had their own sense of fashion and it was not cool. They wore cowboy boots, or work boots with brand names we'd never heard of, when the rest of us were interested only in Nike and Adidas. All of us town kids wore Carhartt, but farm kids did not, not to school. Carhartt was for working in, part of a uniform you wouldn't wear other places. They wore jackets you could get at Target or Fleet Farm. They wore a lot of Minnesota Vikings and Wolves clothing. We didn't spend a lot of money on clothes, and the farm kids clearly spent less, but somehow they always looked more dressed up. Even in T-shirts, somehow, they looked more formal.

So until Jim, I didn't really know farm kids except to sit in the classroom with them or play football with those few whose fathers cared more about football than having a son at home to help out.

Jim wasn't your usual farmer.

A few of the summer guys still called me "Wonderboy," and before I left to go back to school, Jim asked me if I'd ever read the book *The Natural*. I didn't even know there was a book, but he said I should check it out. "You might not like Roy Hobbs once you've read it," he said. "Hollywood changed things all around."

I didn't think much about the recommendation—I can't say I've ever read a book for fun. But then, lo and behold, *The Natural* showed up on the reading list for my English class in the spring of sophomore year. So I read it. And Jim was right. At the end of the movie, Roy Hobbs, the Robert Redford character, steps up to the plate in the championship game at the critical moment. He has a choice of throwing the game or swinging away and hitting the game-winning home run. However, swinging away might also kill him, rupturing the old wound from when he was shot by Barbara Hershey early in the film.

Of course, in the movie he hits a massive home run, and as he's running the bases, we see he's bleeding, but he makes it around and is a total hero.

In the book, though, Hobbs is corrupt. He agrees beforehand to throw the game. When he steps up to the plate, though, he can't go through with it. He has to get the home run and decides to win the game. So he's trying, swinging away, but he strikes out instead. He just plain strikes out like people do all the time. He's not a hero, but word gets around that he threw the game on purpose. And then at the end of the book some kids recognize him and he's disgraced. They believe he threw the game. Everybody does. And he can't prove his innocence—how can you prove you were trying? How can you show what's in your head? You can go from hero to disgrace in a moment. And also, maybe he deserves it, because he *was* going to throw the game. Although he doesn't take the money, he was going to strike out.

I turned on Wonderboy. When I came home I took down the movie poster and resolved to stop anyone from calling me that. That summer Frank got married to Joanie and the group following the Graniteers just sort of dissolved. I drove into Castor after work those next two summers and went to hear music or hang out with Ty, who had a house with a bunch of guys he knew from school. Then Ty went off to chiropractic college and I stayed in Fargo and did an internship with a bank my final summer break.

I majored in business, and I gave it a shot. The banks in South Dakota recruited recent graduates for jobs in the credit card industry. I got one of those jobs and moved to Sioux Falls. I went to an office every day and processed orders and spoke with people on the phone about their service.

It was hell. I felt like mush. I started going to a gym regularly, but I realized pretty quickly that what I missed was using my body, not to lift weights and use machines but to do work and to play sports.

I tried to get some people at work interested in going to baseball games in Sioux Falls. It turned into a big hassle, finding a night that would work for most people, someone making and putting up signs and everyone having to get their money in by a certain date so someone else could get the tickets. In the end only a half dozen of us went to one game. It was the Sioux Falls Canaries against the Gary-South Shore Rail Cats. We lost, but it didn't matter. My colleagues were more interested in the outing than the game, the beer and hot dogs and promotions, the team logo stuff they could buy just to say they'd been there. They spent a crazy amount of money on T-shirts and hats and foam fingers they'd throw away. I missed baseball, and I wanted to work very far away from these people. I wanted a job without telephones and computers and cubicles.

So I went back to Maurus to work with Frank. He was starting his own business as a landscaper. He had a lot of work at the beginning, when they were marching subdivisions out across acres and acres of farmland. He hired me and paid me well. He split the time on the machinery and doing handwork with me. We had a good rapport and I was starting to feel like he must have felt doing projects with my dad. Productive and useful. At the end of a job, the places looked great and people were happy. If something washed away in a sudden storm, we went back and made it right. My mother was supportive of both of us, but I knew my father was disappointed that I didn't stick it out in business.

"Why do you want to work so hard?"

"Being a hard worker is a good thing. You taught me that, dad. Plus, I get to be outside."

"I've worked with my hands my whole life," my dad said. "I've cut granite and engraved monuments and it's no picnic."

"It provided us with a good life," I said.

"It provided us with the basics," he said. "And I'm not saying you have to be rich. I just wanted you to make money from your smarts instead of your labor. Labor is the lowest thing to make money on. No one values it."

I didn't know what he was talking about, because he'd always made a union wage and he would have a pension with good benefits when he retired. What I was making with Frank was more than I had made in the cubicle, although it's true that it was seasonal work. Heat and bugs didn't bother me; I just loved being outside. It felt like very good working conditions to me.

I knew it was not great at the granite company. It was noisy and dusty. Still, people around here were grateful for the quarry and granite jobs. There weren't as many as there'd been in the past, but the granite had kept manufacturing pretty stable in the area. We were known for our good work ethic, and there were machine shops and other businesses that allowed another generation to stay. My dad hadn't been one to complain about his job.

"I like the work," I said. "It feels right to me."

"That's because you're young. You can't see the big picture. But you have a degree—you have so many more opportunities. And you're choosing the hardest way."

"Dad, I hated it. I don't want to work in an office, or a cubicle. I don't want to stare at a screen all day. That would be death to me."

He shook his head. "I'm fifty-two years old and I'll tell you what, I loved this work at nineteen, too. But when it was time for promotions, they brought in guys with degrees over us. I've been stuck for over thirty years."

"But you haven't been stuck. You haven't done the same thing. You've moved around."

"Yeah, but not for something better—and not because I got a change. I followed the economy up and down. When things get bad, laborers are the first ones to get cut. As things automate, fewer men are needed. When things are good, whatever is going on in your life, you forget about it, and you work the overtime and get a little ahead. And when things get slow, you look for another company that is doing better and will take you on.

"They're not always going to be building houses at the clip they are now," he continued. "You're coming in during a boom. Everybody needs a new lawn. Everybody wants a deck, a retaining wall, a little pond. That's not going to last. The economy will shift and where will you be?"

"It isn't going to drop that much, Dad. There is a lot of land out there to develop."

He stopped then. There was no reasoning with me. He patted me on the back. "You're a good kid. You're smart and you work hard. And you have the degree. They can't take that away from you. You'll use it when you need to." When I just shook my head, he added, "Parents always want something better for their kids."

That conversation put me in a funk, realizing my dad wasn't happy or hadn't been happy, thinking of all the hours he put in on the job while wanting something else. I did remember times he didn't have a job, though he always found something soon enough. I remembered, too, the scent of BENGAY, the time he crushed his finger, the time we worried he might lose his sight when a tiny sliver of granite got in one of his eyes.

Mostly, though, I didn't care about pleasing my dad. I was young and I didn't waste time worrying about my future. We worked hard and I felt good. We hauled and spread dirt, laid sod, put in rock and edging. We laid tiles to improve drainage, graded and dragged and seeded, even planted trees.

But in 2009, everything came to a stop. The economy crashed and Frank got worried. He said he wasn't going to need me that summer, not on a regular basis, because there would only be enough work for him. And he hoped there would even be that much.

Chapter Nine

Without a commitment for the landscaping season, I returned to baseball. I got a spot on the Graniteers at shortstop. I kept my winter job at Home Depot, which was flexible enough. The season ran from May to August, followed by playoffs and the state championship game the week after Labor Day.

That's when Chris Miller came back into my life, too. He and Kelsey brought their three boys to the Graniteers game once when there was a family day promotion. He was cocky as ever, this time as the proud family man. He was wearing a NYPD baseball cap, though it had been eight years and most people had stopped by then. He had on some kind of police-related T-shirt as well, from a fundraiser or something, dark blue with a white logo. His hair was short, and the two boys had shorn heads. It was easy to imagine Kelsey sitting them down one by one on a kitchen chair with a towel around their necks and going at them with a shaver set on a quarter inch. Or maybe "the boys" went to the barber together. It made Chris look like a child, I thought, no matter how hard and boisterously he was playing the role of the dad.

Seeing Kelsey made me sad. How quickly had she become another plain, Maurus woman. She still had a good figure, maybe a little too thin, but her features had become less pronounced somehow, and her hair was dull and no longer curly. She had it pulled back in a ponytail at the base of her neck, not even high on her head where it might have some spunk. She looked tired and drawn, overshadowed by the children. She sort of hid behind the baby, resting him on her hip and fiddling with the pacifier he didn't seem to want. She had a large diaper bag on the other arm, and she had that kind of wiry strength that comes from wrestling with little kids all day.

They arrived early, while we were out on the field warming up, and Chris made a big deal out of knowing me. I waved to him when he called my name, but that wasn't enough. He called me over to meet his sons, and since I was just playing catch at that point, I trotted over to them.

"Hey, Chris," I said. "Long time no see."

"Yup, you probably didn't even know I was with the Maurus Police Department," he said.

"I heard something about that," I said. Kelsey smiled, and I thought maybe she looked slightly embarrassed for him. But I might have been wrong.

"Look, Shane, this is Paul Thielen," Chris said, putting an arm on his kid's shoulder. "Shane really loves baseball. Shane, wouldn't you like to play for the Graniteers someday?"

"We went to see the Twins," Shane said. I nodded. "I got an autographed ball from Joe Mauer."

"Cool," I said. "He's having a great year."

"Yes, he's going to be MVP," said Shane.

I looked up at Kelsey, not wanting to ignore her. "Hi, Kelsey."

"Hi, Paul." She shifted the baby.

"Who's this little guy?" I asked, moving closer to touch his cheek. He kind of jerked in his mother's arms to see me better, with that kind of palsied twisting that babies do.

"This is Zachary Michael," she said.

"Hey, Zach," I said. I don't understand why people refer to babies with their full names. Who cares what the kid's middle name is.

"Can you get me an autographed ball?" Shane asked. I could see he resembled his father in more than his haircut.

"Sure," I said, turning to him. "I can sign a ball for you."

"How about the pitcher? What's the pitcher's name?"

"That's Bill Feld. I can ask him to sign it for you, too," I said. I leaned over and rubbed his stubbled head. "I'll pass it around the dugout. You can get it after the game."

"Isn't that great?" Chris said to Shane.

"What do you say to Mr. Thielen, Shane," Kelsey added.

"Tha-ank you," Shane said, in that exaggerated way kids do when you have to ask them. "I'm a pitcher," he added, getting to his real point.

Chris laughed, to emphasize how cute this all was.

"I bet you're a good pitcher, too," I said. His younger brother was standing by, not saying anything, just staring. I crouched down to his level. "Do you play baseball, too?" He shyly turned into his mother, grabbing her leg.

"He plays T-ball," Kelsey answered. "He's a little shy."

"OK," I said, standing up, looking around. The guys were taking various positions for batting practice. "Well, uh, I gotta go."

"Of course," Chris said. "And hey, have a great game." He still had that big grin. It was what always made the guy likeable, that open grin.

"My dad was a pitcher!" Shane yelled after me as I jogged out to the field. I looked back and nodded, but then I thought, *Really? Did Chris tell them he was a pitcher?*

Chris had played one year on the high school team. I didn't remember him pitching. I remembered how he'd come out to hit, confident in his abilities as always. He'd spit on his way to the plate, though our coach was opposed to spitting. He'd pull the batting helmet back and forth on his head and get in an exaggerated stance. And then he'd do the worst thing. He'd point his bat out where he was going to hit the ball.

Once, against our rival Staggerford, he actually said, "You guys might want to move back out there in left. It's coming to you." And he pointed his bat. Then he took a few more practice swings and got back in the batter's box. I was embarrassed for him, but also knew I'd be embarrassed for all of us if he failed to hit the ball. He swung and missed on the first pitch, which was high. The coach told him to settle down and wait for his pitch.

126

The pitcher wasn't very good, and Chris took the next one, a ball. Then he fouled off a nice pitch, very deep down the far left side, and looked back at the bench, smiling. It was as if he'd already hit a home run, and he pointed his bat again out at left field. No one talked like that at the plate. It was absurd. The guy had two strikes on him. The coach clapped his hands and told him again to settle down.

Chris did hit the ball on the next pitch, a glancing blow, and it did go left, but on the ground. It was easily fielded by the short stop, but then for some inexplicable reason—probably because Chris had managed to rattle him—he overthrew first.

So there Chris stood, grinning widely, on second base. There he stood, thinking he hit a double, though of course he should have been out. He scored on a legitimate hit by Phil Constance, and slid unnecessarily into home plate. No one was throwing to home.

The big man. He came back to the dugout, amid applause, rubbing the dust from his uniform. He made his way down the bench, as was our ritual, getting low fives from everyone. "I shook 'em up good, huh?" he said to the coach, holding up two fingers, signifying a double. The coach just chuckled and said, "Have a seat, Chris." He didn't even say anything about the spitting. What was the point.

I got a ball from a bag in the dugout and passed it around for autographs while we were batting. After the game was over, Chris and Shane were waiting, though Kelsey had gone to the car with the younger two. We'd won, and I'd made a couple of good, clean plays, nothing spectacular, and gotten two hits.

"Good game, Paul," Chris said, and he seemed genuinely impressed. He slapped me on the shoulder and I squatted to be on a level with Shane. I handed him the ball and he started looking it over.

"Where's Bill Feld?" he asked. I looked at the ball, but I couldn't find Bill Feld's signature either.

"I'm sorry, Shane, it doesn't look like Bill signed it."

Shane frowned. I could tell the ball had lost its value. "He had to concentrate on pitching," I said. "He doesn't like to do things while he's playing." I stood up, half apologizing to Chris.

Shane jutted out his lower lip. He was going to cry.

"Shane, stop it," Chris said. Shane looked up at him, his eyes full of tears.

Chris reached over and ripped the ball out of Shane's hands. The kid stood there, empty-handed, and then he started to whine. Big tears ran down his cheeks.

"Shane, that's enough," Chris said. "Don't be a crybaby."

I thought Chris was pretty harsh. Chris looked at Shane with disgust. Then at me, pulling me into it. "He's sensitive, like his mother," he said.

I just played with my cap, neither disagreeing or agreeing.

Chris held the ball, saying, "Stop it now, Shane. Stop it." The kid was trying to choke back his tears, which resulted in a sort of whimper. He still had his hands out where he'd been holding the ball.

I couldn't have predicted the next move. Chris turned and threw it as hard as he could. It went out into the field and rolled in the grass where we couldn't see it. I was as surprised as the kid, who stopped crying then. He looked at his dad, as if wondering if he was supposed to go get it. But Chris grabbed him by his collar and spun him around, leading him to the car.

I watched them go, thinking, *So that's how it happens. That's how you get to be a Miller.* I figured his own father had been something like this. I remembered the time he'd come home covered in mud. What had his father done? Then I looked out to the field, wondering if I should go get the ball. I knew the team would be offended if they found it, so I walked out and picked it up. I put it in my locker. I'd give the ball to some random kid at some other game.

There are three bars in Maurus. One is an old man's place, the Staghorn, a hole in the wall with lots of taxidermy, stuffed woodland animals on the walls and in cases, and Pabst Blue Ribbon on tap. It is across the street from where the quarry yard used to be. When the quarry moved to Highway 41, they tore down all the facilities and pulled up the trolley tracks that delivered the rock to waiting train cars. That lot was next to the dam on the Horst River, which supplied power to the granite company in the early part of the century. My dad talks about going down there as a kid to watch the giant slabs swinging out on cranes and stacked, and block brought into the warehouse through a giant open wall in the cutting shed to be cut into slabs. He and his friends would pick up small pieces of granite, which they traded like other kids traded marbles.

Now there's nothing on the lot but the concrete pad, gravel, and brush. The whole thing is behind chain-link fencing, marked "Property of Maurus Granite Co." The only building left standing on the block is the Staghorn, which looks a little like an old western saloon. I've seen a photo of the downtown back when the street wasn't paved and all the buildings had that Wild West feel to them. Old quarry guys still drink at the Staghorn and no doubt swap stories of the old days.

The Blue Line is where people meet up when they're visiting for the holidays, and where the fans of the Graniteers go in the summer. It's a sports bar with three pool tables and darts, which in some ways reminds me of someone's finished basement. It's kind of a halfhearted attempt at an English pub–style restaurant, with dark green carpet, wood paneling, and hanging lamps over booths along the back, and some hockey photos and sticks up on the wall to communicate the theme.

Then there's Arnold's, which is kind of a catchall. It attracts a lot of motorcycle enthusiasts for lunch on Saturdays and Sundays, but I wouldn't call them bikers. Arnold's isn't a tough bar. It's just a regular place, more for people in their forties and fifties, with drink specials every night of the week and some live music, mostly country western, some rock and roll, the meat raffle on Sunday afternoons and occasional Friday nights, and good chicken wings and potato skins. It's been around almost as long as the Staghorn and is a legitimate business. They try things to keep people coming and happy.

I didn't see Chris or his family at any more Graniteer games that summer. I saw him once or twice at the Blue Line playing pool, but we just said hello. Trey was there those nights, and I never liked that guy. I didn't get him, and just didn't want to be in a position to provoke him. I never actually saw him get in a bar fight, but you always felt like one could break out when he was around.

Then one night when I got there to meet Ty, Chris was at the bar with two other officers, Larry and Matt. It was early September, a crisp fall day, but Chris was wearing this black, long-sleeved Under Armour pullover. Chris always, always looked like a cop, even when he wasn't in uniform. The other guys were wearing ordinary clothes—you know, a flannel or a T-shirt with jeans. Chris looked like he had just finished a shift with the SWAT team.

That night Chris and I got into a conversation about being a police officer, and he was quite passionate about it. And, once again, I was charmed—that's the thing about Chris. I was flattered when he said he thought I'd make a good cop. He said I was levelheaded and smart, and I was just what the community needed. He really sold it. The camaraderie, he said, was like family, and every day on the job was different. "You aren't chained to a desk," he said, and I liked that. "You know what's going on in the area. You keep informed. It's good work. You help people."

I read the police blotter in the *Record*, so I had it in my head that it was mostly minor stuff. Checking out calls on suspicious cars, suspicious noises, drunken neighbors, teen parties. Cars broken into, garages broken into, alarms going off at buildings, the cops always arriving after the fact.

"What do you do all day?" I asked. He probably should have been offended at that, but he wasn't.

"You'd be surprised," Chris said. "There are quiet days, but there are busy days, too. And busy nights, definitely. It's not what you think. You have to stay on your guard. And we do a lot of investigations."

"Oh, yeah?" I said. "What do you investigate?"

"Bad checks, fraud. Thefts. Vandalism. We work closely with the banks and businesses in town."

"Do you ever solve any of those thefts I read about in the paper?" I asked.

"What, you mean on the blotter?" He shook his head. "No, not really. That stuff is mostly kids, low level. I'm not going to put in hours tracking down the kid who took someone's laptop or cellphone from a car. A woman called this fall to report that someone stole the hostas out of her yard. Shit happens. We go over, express our sympathy, write it down. Our reports just help with the insurance."

I asked him about a story I'd read regarding a pig that got loose behind the meat market, and how the cops captured it. He winced, but Larry Peterson got into telling that story. He told it with pig squeals and everything. Chris wasn't happy. I guess he could tell I wasn't being entirely serious about the work they did. So after we'd had our laugh with Larry, Chris told another story, one that had made the front page in the *Castor Standard,* about a group of child pornographers they'd broken up. They'd gotten a tip, and then help from the county task force for violent offenders, but Chris and Chief Kramer had been at one of the houses where they picked up the guys, taking their computers and shutting them down. "Pasty, pale, sick fucks," Chris said. "You feel good when you put an end to something like that."

I looked up the requirements online for becoming a peace officer and saw that the state preferred candidates with college degrees, and that my four-year business degree would qualify me for the transition program. All I had to do was apply, take a pretest, and then—if I was accepted—do a semester at the tech college in Brainerd, two hours away, followed by a ten-week skills course. I told my dad I was thinking about becoming an officer and he got real excited. He kept bringing it up, then he talked to some of his friends. Turns out he knew Harry Carver, the retired officer, and he called him up to get some pointers. I was embarrassed, but once I'd mentioned it, the whole thing kind of took on a life of its own.

I filled out the forms. Harry sent over some old books I could use to study for the test. Chief Kramer, who Chris introduced me to, recommended better ones that would actually help me to prepare. They needed good officers, he said. At first I would only be part time, but they were always requesting another full-time officer and it wouldn't be long, he thought, before they'd get the funding.

Once I passed the qualifying test, I was on my way. My parents were happy to give me the tuition money as a Christmas gift, and that winter I took the classes I needed and got my CPR and First Responder certification. The course work, some of which I could do online, covered search and seizure, methods of arrest, criminal statutes, narcotics detection, principles of policing, and police ethics. We learned a little law, our rights and the rights of others, how to Mirandize. We learned a lot of general stuff about the structure of law enforcement in the state and best practices for police officers. We went through a lot of information and some scenarios. Basically I learned where to go to find statutes and what I'd need to know to uphold and enforce the law. They were preparing us to take the written post-test and to find resources and be serious about paperwork and reports, but not much more. We'd have guest speakers sometimes who told stories, and they would tell us what really happened at a scene, as opposed to what was supposed to happen. I'd say that in the field, about forty percent of it is useful.

The real training began the following summer. I'd been commuting during the semester, but I moved up to Brainerd for the ten-week skills course. This was more like boot camp. It had a more military feel to it, lining up in ranks, morning inspections, and lots of running. Lots and lots of running and physical training, obstacle courses and the like. Mostly we were still on campus, but we'd go to shooting ranges and even out to Camp Franklin to use their obstacle courses. If you did something wrong or failed inspection, you paid in push-ups or extra laps.

These days were full of scenarios and real training on equipment. We learned how to use Tasers—and we all got tased in a controlled situation to understand what that means. We were pepper-sprayed, too, and let me tell you that is a bitch. If I'm pepper-sprayed, I'm out of commission. I can't see or do anything. It's not like the movies where people keep coming at you and are able to push through it. Pepper spray, for me, is incapacitating. I'm helpless. And we were made to understand that if we are helpless, it is an option to shoot to protect ourselves. I knew after that experience that if I got pepper-sprayed during a call, I'd be within my rights to shoot. I wouldn't want to, but I could in good conscience go there.

We practiced etiquette and defusing situations. The training focused on the kinds of calls we would most often receive. We spent two full days going over traffic stops of all kinds.

We went out on the road and practiced using radar units in squads and laser guns. We practiced with one another how to approach cars, how to address people in cars. We learned the telltale signs of drug use or intoxication. We learned how to spot things that are out of the usual and how to approach those things. We enacted all sorts of scenarios with one another. We acted crazy and we acted violently and we diffused and subdued one another. We practiced appropriate use of force and how to handcuff and use zip ties. We practiced speaking in our police officer voices, learning the various protocols. We learned how to be professional under duress and how to be strong and effective.

We learned how to deliver a baby. We practiced using defibrillators and made makeshift splints and breathed into the mouths of manikins. We spent a fair amount of time at the firing range, and cleaning and assembling our weapons. We had all sorts of drills to simulate shooting situations. Manikins on wires flew across the room like haunted-house ghosts, while we learned to hone in and shoot. We practiced in low light, indoors and outdoors, because we would need to qualify in each of these settings. We did drills in padded clothing with paintball guns that nonetheless let us know the consequences of our errors or inability. Every training involving a gun began and ended with safety and the hope we'd never need to use our weapon. In that way, it had much more the feel of a war game for a war we would never fight. We weren't soldiers, after all. Our training officers always made it clear we were preparing to serve the public and that our motto was to protect and serve.

In our spare time we watched old episodes of *COPS* and other reality television. We watched to get a sense of the environment, and for a laugh. We watched the stupid criminals, and we heard even more stories about them. We saw an officer dip his finger into a white bag of powder and say, "Oh, yes, cocaine." We laughed, knowing no cop would ever test a substance like that, never stick his finger into a bag of evidence.

We learned sight lines and approaches to buildings and homes where security alarms had sounded in the middle of the night. We were told to always expect danger, always expect the worst case. It informed how we approached cars on routine stops and how we approached doors with screaming couples behind them. We even participated in a school shooting drill, and we all prayed we'd never have to escort children out of a school with their hands over their heads. We took it seriously. We trained like our lives depended on it.

Then most of us went off to all the small towns in Minnesota and took up our posts. After a few months of pulling over women speeding on their way home from potluck dinners or teenagers terrified of getting their first ticket, after helping old people whose cars were stuck in the snow and filling out reports

for stolen bikes and Virgin Mary statues, after school lunches
with elementary school children and countless lectures on safety
and how to be a good neighbor, we forgot to be afraid.

Chapter Ten

There were types like Trey on the training course. Especially, it seemed, the guys from Deer Lick County, northwest of Brainerd. Some of them had small penis syndrome and thought just by putting on a badge they'd have authority. They wanted the power, and they didn't know a thing about how to get respect. Some of them were bullied as kids and now they were going to get their revenge on the tough guys. Some of them were lifelong bullies getting their professional accreditation. Some of them had just grown up in a world of violence and drugs. They could have become criminals just as easily as they became cops.

And then there were guys who got into it for the guns. They had all kinds of information about guns, and they'd talk about them endlessly. They also played lots of hard-core video games. The two guys we had like this were twin brothers, Jake and Jock Sisk. They brought in their video games and found others who wanted to play. Unfortunately, they were in my apartment, along with a good guy named Chad Flaten from a small town near

Hastings. They had contraband as well, namely automatic weapons.

We weren't allowed to bring our own guns to the police training. To tell you the truth, it hadn't occurred to me to bring one. I only had a shotgun for hunting, but most of the other guys had handguns. The Sisk twins—one instructor called them "The Cisco Kids," but we called them "The Sicko Brothers"— were the most vocal and detailed in their discussion of guns. It was something, because they couldn't string many sensible words together on ordinary topics, but they could talk about guns.

One night they brought in two duffel bags and laid one on the kitchenette counter, another on the couch in the small shared living space. They unzipped them to reveal several big guns.

"What the hell? Jock, what do you think you're doing?" asked Chad, who was sitting on the couch.

"Exercising my legal, constitutional, and I might add God-given right to bear arms," Jock said.

"Bear arms against who?" Chad asked.

"Against you if you try any funny stuff, homo," Jock said, wiggling his hand in Chad's face. Jake thought that was funny.

"There are rules about weapons here," said Chad.

"They're registered," said Jock.

"That's not the point," said Chad.

"Oh, shut up, you fucking pussy," said Jock. At which point Chad, wisely, left the apartment.

"You better not narc!" Jock yelled after him.

I stayed in the room, and soon enough four more guys crowded in to see the goods.

"Gentlemen, gentlemen," said Jock, holding up two large handguns with extended clips. "Let's go to the lounge, where we can all enjoy the beauty of this fine collection."

I trailed them to the lounge but hung back. Of course, that is where Chad had gone to escape, so now he retreated, with his book, back to our apartment. He gave me a significant look as he passed by, but I just ignored it.

The Sicko Brothers gave their own seminar that night. There were about a dozen guys in the lounge. All of them, even ones I would say were good guys, I mean getting into policing for the right reasons, knew a shitload about guns. Some of them had never seen these models, but they could talk about them all. They could date them and talk about the features, their relative merits and weaknesses. A few of the guns were modified, and they knew all about modifications, legal and illegal, too.

To tell you the truth, it freaked me out. The message that night, delivered in no uncertain terms by the Sicko Brothers, was this: "If you think people in your communities don't have these weapons, you are wrong. These are easily obtainable and easy to use. Our instructors aren't going to give us this information, but you all had better be prepared. Meth is everywhere, and with it comes weapons and people who will use them without thinking twice. Most of the time they are used to kill other meth heads and dealers, but they can also be used to kill cops. Don't ever forget it."

Seriously, it was the clearest, and most profanity-free speech I ever heard from either Jock or Jake. And I thanked God that I wasn't going to be a peace officer in Deer Lick County or, as it sounded from guys from bigger markets, in Castor or Duluth or any of the Twin Cities suburbs.

The video games came out the first night. The guns didn't come out until five days later. And the outings to shoot the guns didn't happen until midway through the third week of our ten-week training. There was a small group who did that; the rest of us didn't get involved. Still, no one said anything and I guess that was the beginning of our initiation into the Blue Wall.

"Those guys are freakin' idiots," Chad said. "Someone's going to get hurt." We were both naturally cautious, I guess. But no one did get hurt. No one got hurt at all. And that is something, too. That is something I thought about after Chris Miller's death. It just seemed for so long that despite everything, nothing would ever go terribly, terribly wrong. Everything was sort of fixable. Even the dangerous stuff didn't lead where our parents had made us think it would when we were kids. Consequences. People like the Sicko Brothers were emboldened because, really, there just didn't seem to be any consequences.

Still, I could see a good number of these guys were not going to be happy news to their communities.

"I heard they want to be in the sheriff's department, but the sheriff in Deer Lick won't hire them," Chad said.

"That's good," I said.

"Yeah, those guys are going to get themselves, or someone else, killed."

I just nodded.

"Sheriffs are elected. They have to actually care about their constituents and their reputation."

"Well, all cops have to think about their reputations," I said. "You can't get very far working in a town without the support of the public."

"It's not like sheriffs."

"I don't think there's drugs in Maurus like there are in Deer Lick," I said. "In Castor, I guess. I don't really know."

"They're there all right, but they're not the peace officers' responsibility. They mostly are out in the counties, and the sheriff's department responds. There are task forces, specially trained units, to deal with that. Any local police force that gets involved with drugs on its own is just asking for trouble."

This was the message in our classroom, too. Call for assistance. Never respond to a code alone. And if you see signs of bigger activity, drugs or gangs or something long term, back off. Bring it to your chief. Don't get yourself killed.

We didn't have the Sicko Brothers, but we had Trey. One day I asked the chief why he tolerated Trey's aggressive attitude. Trey had been particularly harsh at a traffic stop. He spotted someone speeding through town at three in the morning, but the guy he pulled over was a guy who worked a late shift at Champion Tools on his way home from work. He had the wrong guy, but he just wouldn't admit it or back down. He made the guy get out of the car. He was verbally abusive.

I was on duty the next day when the complaint came in. Thanks to Trey's boneheaded bullshit, there was another guy in town who hated the cops and would certainly be telling the story of his forty-five-minute traffic stop, complete with threats and profanity and a search of the vehicle, to all his buddies and for a long time.

"Chief," I said, behind his closed office door, "why do you put up with Trey's shit?"

"Paul," he said, "we need Trey. You don't know the valuable stuff that he does."

"No, I guess I don't. All I see is how hard he makes it for the rest of us."

"He also makes it safe for the rest of us, or safer."

"I know you send him out on some rough calls, but doesn't that just feed him?"

"I send him on those calls because he is effective," Chief Kramer said. "I could spend an hour with those guys and they wouldn't tell me anything. Trey knows how to talk to them; they respond to him, and they give up information."

"Yeah, but—"

"No buts. This job is mostly about helping people, but there's more than one way we have to help. You gotta figure out what is required, and the uniform and badge aren't going to do all the work for you. You have to apply the required force, be it with your voice, your language, or other tactics. I send Trey out, when possible, to manage the douche bags. And that means I don't have to send you. Sometimes I have to send him on other patrols, other calls. Things that aren't particularly his strengths. But he'll grow over time. He'll learn how to bring what is appropriate to the variety of duties."

"I hope so," I said.

"And you'll grow, too, Paul. You'll learn how to use the force available to you. You'll learn where force is needed, and step up to the plate. The goal is to have a group of officers who can handle all the calls properly. It's not easy. There will be slip-ups, times guys lose it a bit. That's natural. But in the end, Trey could wind up saving your life. Some of the work he's done that we don't talk about, he may already have saved your life."

When I thought about that later, the "things we don't talk about," I couldn't help but wonder if Trey had almost gotten me killed. If Trey and the chief knew about Lisa Hawkins, if they decided that was just another incident on the learning curve, and one best forgotten, well, they might as well have put the gun in Chris Miller's killer's hand.

Chapter Eleven

I was only a police officer for two years. I guess you could say I didn't have time to grow. I didn't have time to learn all the things there were to learn. Or I might not have been cut out for that part—I might just be weak. I might have just been unwilling to see Maurus for what it really was until it was too late.

I was focused on growing up in the ordinary way. I bought a house I could fix up, across from the ballpark. I loved the town, its history and its present reality. Every day on the job was interesting, and I was part of the community. I had purpose and life was good.

And there was still baseball. I joined a men's league, where I had the benefit of again being one of the younger players and one of the better ones. I batted cleanup, though I had been farther down on the batting order for the Graniteers. I played third base, because my arm was better than most of the guys on the team. It was a great group of guys, most of them in their thirties and forties, married with kids. Tim Lang was on the team. He recruited me.

It was low-key. I just wanted to make good plays and get on base, not embarrass anyone. The pitching was slow, much easier for me to hit, but I didn't show off. Our sponsor was Arnold's Bar and we wore T-shirts with their the name on the back. Of course, this meant we had to show up there after the games on Thursday nights. That's how I got to know some of the bartenders and regulars, Ashley and Carl Frisch, Sean Wellinger, Bill Truitt. At the beginning of the season I went with Tim. "Put in an appearance," he said. "It's good community relations." And he was right. We drank our beer and we got to know some of the people and their challenges.

As a cop, I did feel some kind of status in town. I also felt a responsibility to represent the force well. Tim was a good role model for how to be off duty in a public place. He'd been an officer in town for twelve years and knew everyone.

He conveyed a real sense of duty in all the things he did. And he was a great listener. He had his one beer and introduced me to some people. He remembered if they had a sick relative or had lost their job or whatever. He patiently listened to stories he'd heard many times before. I caught on pretty quick—this was our job. I probably would have stopped going to Arnold's and gone to the Blue Line to throw darts after those first few weeks. But Tim showed me how much it mattered to be at Arnold's. So later in the season, when he went home to bathe his kids and put them to bed instead of going to the bar, I carried on and took his place.

I met Julie that summer, too. She was Missy Lange's friend. I liked her right away—she was cute and easygoing. She was a dental hygienist, and she was very professional. She said she liked assisting the dentist in surgeries. When she cleaned a person's teeth and took the x-rays, she could tell what was going on as much as any dentist. She pointed out to him which teeth, if any, were in trouble, and she was always right. It could be a gross job, especially if people had gum disease, but she relieved pain and healed people, and that made her feel good. She said I had good teeth. "Hey, I never miss a floss," I said.

Julie sometimes came to the games still dressed in her pastel scrubs. I thought that was really sexy. Scrubs are underrated. She was slim and her pants, even though they were drawstring, were tidy and compact. She sat with my mom and they chatted away. After the games when we went to the bar, she was the perfect companion. She was respectable and wholesome, and I have to admit I liked the image I was getting. It was solid.

Julie and I were standing by the bar one Thursday night when Carl Frisch called us over to his table. Carl Frisch, Ashley's husband, was kind of a rough character. He was a meat cutter, but at Staley's, not the meat market. He worked behind the scenes, cutting up chickens and packaging the parts for resale, cutting up sides of beef and pork and wrapping them in Styrofoam trays. He'd been in a really bad car accident when he was sixteen. He was driving a Camaro with a T-top, and his best friend was in the passenger seat. They hit a patch of ice and Carl was ejected from the car and thrown into brush at the side of the road, but his friend, who was wearing a seatbelt, was decapitated by a piece of sharp metal when the car flipped into the barrier. There wasn't anyone in town he hadn't made feel the bump on his head where he has a steel plate. He described himself as a great guy with bad luck.

Of course, hanging out at Arnold's every night didn't suggest particularly good life choices. I'd say Carl found about half his trouble and the other half found him. He and his first wife had lost a son to SIDS, and the marriage ended shortly thereafter. He met Ashley on the day he got out of jail for illegally hooking his apartment complex up to free cable—twice. The first time he'd gotten a warning, but he just couldn't help himself. It was that kind of thing with Carl—he meant well. It's just that his good deeds involved significant risk and serious consequences. Illegal good deeds.

Still, it was easy to feel for him. He was a hard worker and he clearly loved Ashley. He swore the steel plate helped him predict the weather. He got headaches when it was going to snow or get icy, which may have been more the memory than the metal in his head, I'm thinking.

"Hey, Paul, you know, you guys should look into something," he said.

"What's that, Carl?" I asked.

"There's a house on Sixth, and there's something not right going on there."

"What have you seen?" I asked, getting serious, pulling out a chair and offering Julie the other.

"Carl," Ashley said. "What are you doing?"

"It's OK," I said. "Carl, which house is it?"

"It's the yellow house on the corner," Carl said. "It's a rental, and the people living there are up to something."

"People coming and going?" I asked.

"People coming and going," he said. "People who aren't from around here."

"Carl," Ashley said.

"What? I'm trying to be helpful," Carl said. "I'm doing a public service, here."

"Yes you are, Carl. We depend on people like you to keep your eyes open."

"I'm not saying it's terrorism. It's drugs. Believe me, I know what drugs looks like. Before I got clean the last time, I could have been one of those coming and going."

"I appreciate you telling me, Carl. Maybe those people will get some help."

"Yeah," Carl said. He looked at Ashley. "I wish someone would have helped me out—"

"By getting you arrested? By sending the cops to your house?" Ashley asked.

"Yeah, if it came to that," Carl said. "You don't know what your bottom will be, but everyone has to hit bottom before they can start climbing out. Some people never do. I'm just one of the lucky ones."

"Yes, Carl, yes you are," I said.

"I know, but for the grace of God," Carl said, "I could be right back down there." Then he took a few gulps of his beer. There was a half-empty pitcher on the table, and I wondered if it was their first one.

"We all hope that doesn't happen, Carl."

"I'm good now."

"Yes, Carl," Ashley said, putting her hand on his shoulder, "you're really good now."

"I don't even drink," he said, dragging his nearly empty beer glass through a puddle of condensation on the table.

I just looked and nodded. He could see I was looking at the beer.

"What, this? This isn't drinking," he said. "I used to drink a bottle of Jack Daniel's like it was nothing. I used to drink tequila from the bottle, don't bother with the lime and salt. This is no more harmful than pop, you ask me."

I nodded.

"It's like a crack addict, or a speed freak. When he gets clean, he still drinks coffee. He still drinks Red Bull. He needs caffeine just to stay sane, just to get to what other people call normal. For me, I still have beer and wine, the occasional cocktail, like a gin and tonic. That's just like my coffee, just to get me to normal levels with everyone else."

This was clearly not going to go anywhere. I slapped my hand on his other shoulder and stood up. "Carl," I said, "Thank you for the information. I'm going to look into it. See what we can do."

I took Julie's hand and we left the bar. On the way to the car, she said, "So what do you think's going on?"

"It's a meth house, we already know," I said. "Trey and Chris are working on it, figuring out who is there when, with the Castor task force. There's going to be a raid sometime next week.

"Wow, you didn't say anything," she said.

"I'm not really involved. Now Carl will think he's the hero—that he told us about it and look how fast we acted on his tip."

"He's a sad guy," Julie said.

"Deluded," I said. "All addicts are deluded."

Maybe I was deluded, too. Deluded into thinking I could be a good cop and settle down in Maurus and things would go smoothly. I had my house across from the ballpark, with new carpet in the two bedrooms, a 50-inch flat screen TV and an unfinished basement with possibilities. My mom saw this as another good sign. I'm not sure what she was saying to Julie in the stands, but they might very well have been making plans for turning the second bedroom into a nursery. I'm sure they both thought things would just run their course and we'd end up married.

I liked being a homeowner, mowing my lawn and getting the roof reshingled. The plaster walls weren't in very good shape, so Frank, my dad, and I took them down to the studs and put in new drywall. We opened up the kitchen wall and put in a breakfast bar, through to the dining and living room.

Julie had an apartment out by Kennedy High School, and we spent most of our time at her place. At first I just didn't want her to become too comfortable. But she was making inroads after a year. She had some clothes at my place, a bunch of products in my bathroom. We weren't living together; I said I didn't want to live with someone before I got married. Despite everybody clearly thinking that was where we were headed, part of me was holding back. I just didn't think Julie was the one.

Still, I probably would have married her if Chris Miller hadn't been shot. That next summer, when she fought for the bouquet at Chris's wedding, I knew time was no longer on my side. I put off thinking about it for the rest of the summer, but I knew Julie was expecting a ring, if not for Christmas then by New Year's Day.

Chapter Twelve

Somehow, we got through those holidays. My aunts were protective of me. As soon as we made it through the door, before I could even take my coat off, Aunt Theresa, my mother's oldest sister, asked for my help in the kitchen. First she wanted me to take some dishes off the high shelf, but then once she had me, she kept giving me things to do. Washing dishes, stirring the sauce, chopping onions. Never mind the men and the football game, the talk about hunting and sports and jobs and family.

I was happy to be in the kitchen with the women, my mother and Aunt Theresa, Aunt Jeanette, Aunt Bert, Aunt Marjorie, Aunt Lynn, Aunt Mary Ann, and my old Grandma Fran, who was near ninety. I almost cried when she reached up from her chair to hug me and give me one of her dry, smacking kisses. She was wearing a flowered dress as usual, with the smell of old perfume, and hose and black shoes. She didn't walk well anymore, so there was always a place for her at the kitchen table to sit and listen to the goings-on. Her daughters asked her for advice then immediately dismissed it. They reminded her of

Thanksgivings past, and she just laughed and slapped the table. If they teased her, she'd shake her head and cover her mouth. "Now, you stop it, Margie." But she clearly loved it.

My mother was the second youngest, so my aunts were mostly all grandmothers already. There was a lot to talk about the progress and accomplishments of the grandchildren. "Can you believe it?" Grandma Fran said to me, as I stood next to her, chopping onions. "I have twenty-six great-grandchildren. Not grandchildren. *Great*-grandchildren. God is good." She knew all their names and who they belonged to. I asked her who her favorite was and she laughed. "Oh, I love them all! They all have their talents, just like you, Paul. Dey're And, also like you, dey're every one angels. Paul, are you going to play baseball again dis year?"

"I don't know, Grandma," I said. "We'll see."

"You're such da good baseball player, Paul. I always love seeing you play." Grandma Fran had the old Will County German accent. Her parents emigrated from Bavaria and though both she and her husband, Alfonse, were born in this country, they grew up in German-speaking homes and went to German-speaking schools. The next generation mostly didn't have even a trace of the accent, although they'd all spoken German at home. A couple of my uncles had it, probably kept up from the workplace. Uncle Jerome and Aunt Jeanette, the dairy farmers; and Aunt Dolores, who also came off a farm; they still talked the old way. Even my cousin Ben, who would one day take over Uncle Jerome and Aunt Jeanette's farm, he talked like that. But mostly you don't hear it much anymore.

And although I'm used to my grandmother's Catholicism, sometimes my aunts and even my mom can surprise me. My mother still prays the rosary, and she'll say some old-fashioned things. But after Thanksgiving was over, Aunt Jeanette took me into the little side bedroom where all the coats were kept. She said, "I have something for you, Paul. Keep it in your car, or in your coat pocket. Use it when you need it." She pressed a plastic container into my hand. It was an old clear container that they used to use when cameras had film. It was filled with water.

"That's Holy Water," she said. "It's been blessed. You just keep it and stay safe."

"Thank you, Aunt Jeanette," I said. "You don't have to worry about me. I'm not in any danger."

"There are lots of kinds of danger," she said. "Some only God can protect us from. God loves you, Paul. And I love you. We're all prayin' for ya."

I thanked her again and we hugged. In the moment, I was confused by how I was meant to use the water exactly. I wondered if she meant for me to throw holy water at the killer if I encountered him again, like a vampire. But when I found it in my coat pocket the next day, I knew she didn't mean that at all. I opened it up and dipped my thumb in it, then pressed it to my forehead. It was just water, but I didn't feel right pouring it down the sink. I put it in my glove compartment and more or less forgot about it.

Christmas was more complicated. I went with Julie to her parents' house on Christmas Eve and was without protection. I could tell people were uncomfortable about me being there. It wasn't just our unclear status—here it was another year and we weren't engaged—it was the new layer of Chris Miller's murder. There was an elephant in the room, and too many topics to avoid. I had to admit I hadn't been hunting that season, hadn't done much of anything. I talked to Julie's brother Dave about a remodeling job he was working on, right down to the nails and screws he used and where he got them. It was a safe topic and neither of us wanted to let it go. The plight of the local hardware store.

Julie's mother tried to mother me, but mostly by speaking in an unnaturally high and cheerful voice, and it strained all of us. I've noticed through this whole thing that talking loudly at someone is a way to keep your distance and still seem nice. Everyone was talking loudly at me, in high, pleasant voices or about dull, meaningless topics. I felt like hiding, but there was nowhere to hide. I was glad when we could go to church for midnight Mass and get out of there.

On Christmas Day, I went to Frank's around noon. His wife, Joan, left cold cuts and salads out all day and my parents and family members made the rounds to see the kids' presents. Frank's girls, Clare and Patty, were in third and fifth grade. It was pretty clear they didn't believe in Santa Claus anymore, but they were still playing along for one more year, Clare more than Patty. Every time someone came to the door, they excitedly jumped up to show them what Santa brought. They were thankful for the gifts my parents had given them, even wearing the new striped sweaters from Old Navy with tape telling the size running down the front and their new winter stocking caps in purple and pink.

Between visitors, we played Sorry! I was struck by the girls' kindness, the civilized nature of the game. They were adamant that we should not send people backward. That was mean. Patty and I had a sort of secret agreement that we would help Clare win. Each time we switched pieces to advance her instead of sending her back, we'd act like we made a mistake and didn't know what we were doing. "You can't change it! You can't change back!" Clare shouted. Patty and I relished our roles as the world's stupidest Sorry! players.

It was a day free of Chris Miller, and I didn't want to leave. I ended up sitting on the couch watching television with Frank after the girls went up to read books with Joanie. When I kissed Patty good night, I smelled her hair, sweaty from wearing that stocking cap all day. She had that simple kid smell, and that simple love for me, her uncle. "Sleep tight," I said. "Don't let the bed bugs bite," she replied, then skipped off upstairs.

"They're really good girls," I said to Frank.

"I know it," he replied. "It's all their mother's doing."

I was called in twice more to repeat my testimony. Everyone was angry and on edge, frustrated by the lack of progress. Blame was being placed on the chief and the department. Things had not gone well. The murder investigation seemed to have given way to an investigation into the botched murder investigation. The questions I was asked the second and final time I was brought back to the station were more about procedure, not the crime scene. Who had interviewed me when. What had been said when I was in the ambulance, and in the sheriff officer's car. The support of the community didn't extend very far beyond support of Chris Miller's widow and children. Most of the contempt was reserved for me, but there was plenty to go around.

I resigned effective Tuesday, December 18. I made an appointment with Chief Kramer the day before and showed up at two p.m. Jean was on the phone but she buzzed me in right away and I went straight into the chief's office. I could see Kenny at the desk, doing something on the computer. He didn't look up to greet me.

The chief was relieved that I'd made this decision myself. I could have played out the leave, though it was clear without him saying it that eventually I would have been let go. This relieved us both of the burden of a report, the equivalent of a dishonorable discharge, a permanent record, so to speak. Chief Kramer let me know I was doing the department a favor, making it possible for them to hire someone else. He said he needed all officers on the street, and that I had to know how tight things were with an officer on leave.

The chief stayed on his side of the desk throughout the brief interview. I put my keys, attached to a ring with the Maurus Graniteers mascot, on his desk. He frowned and nodded.

I asked how the investigation was going and he said, "Oh, you know, pretty cold trail. Not many leads, but we're following them all."

"You have leads, then?" I asked.

"There's always people who will call in, think they saw something, think someone is suspicious. It doesn't add up to much in the end."

"Still no gun," I said, just to make conversation. He shook his head.

"If we could get the gun, that would be a big break." I thought he might ask me—*You sure you didn't see where the guy went?* But we'd been through it so many times. I wondered, too, if on some level he didn't quite believe me. Even though the story was part of the written record and no one had expressed doubt, I wondered. I thought about apologizing again, and the words, *I wish* came to my lips, but I didn't say them. I just nodded.

"Well, I guess I should be going," I said.

"Yeah," Chief Kramer said. He rose from his chair but didn't come from behind the desk. He kept his hands on his hips, no handshake. He just seemed tired. "You'll get a call from HR. They'll send you some paperwork—shouldn't be too complicated since you were part time." I nodded and left his office, closing the door.

Kenny had disappeared, so I walked over to the desk, Harry's desk. On the side was a small box with my coffee mug and photos in it. They'd already packed me up. Jean was still on the phone, but she gave me a perfunctory smile as I opened the door to leave. When I got home, I dumped the box, photos and everything, in the garbage can in the garage. I went inside and got my two uniforms from the back of the closet and stuffed them in the garbage can, too.

Chapter Thirteen

I had never thought of myself as busy, or my life as full, until it was suddenly completely quiet and empty. I threw myself into finishing the basement, a big job that could distract me those winter months. It got me out of the house for trips to Menard's and Home Depot for supplies. Julie got tired of hanging around watching me work.

When I wasn't working on the basement, I was watching TV. I upped my subscription to Netflix to three DVDs at a time and loaded up my queue. I hadn't been to a movie theater in a while, so there were new releases to watch. I also watched a lot of movies I'd already seen. I turned on the set as soon as there was any sign of darkness. That was a dangerous time, about 3:30 or 4 o'clock, when the day was over and a long night lay ahead. As the sun cast long shadows across the lawn, I could feel my mood slipping. When Julie called to check on me or see what I was doing, I was almost always watching a movie. I didn't ask her what she wanted to watch or wait for her to come over.

Movies were comforting. They'd been such a big part of my teens, especially in winter. That was the heyday for video stores, and we had one in Maurus, right next to the bakery: Video

Quest. It had been around for a long time, and the collection went way back. The owner, Patty Freeh, didn't use a computer and she didn't have a system. She built her own shelving, which filled the place like a maze. Each film had a numbered tag hanging under the empty case. If the tag was there, the movie was available. By the late 1990s, there were lots of missing films, and they just never had a tag hanging by them. Patty didn't bother to replace the movie, unless it was something really popular, but she didn't take the film box down either.

As Patty got new films, she didn't put them in sections, like action and comedy and drama. She just gave the film a number and put it on the shelf next to the last one. There were thousands of tapes in there in no order at all. It really was a quest, wandering those aisles for a title that caught your interest. I don't even know where the numbers started.

Since nothing was computerized, Patty couldn't tell you if she had a film or not. To keep track, she simply clipped the number of the film you rented to a card with your name on it and put it in a file box for return the next day. When you brought it back, she could see from the card if it was overdue and whether to charge you a fine.

It wasn't hard to keep up with the new releases, but there were always old things she was adding to the collection, too. I think this was why I really got to like movies. We just wandered around and picked up things based on the box. Over time, I got to know the contents of that store. I could find things for my parents or Frank or for my friends. Other people didn't appreciate the hunt. When VHS tapes went out and everything moved to DVD, Patty liquidated her stock and got out of the business. For a while, I couldn't find any of the older movies. Then Netflix came along. When Chris Miller died, I started watching all those movies, like *Stand by Me* and *Dead Poets Society*, kind of corny movies about kids and loss of innocence. Once you tell Netflix you like that kind of movie, they give you all sorts of others just like them.

It also made me miss Ty. I thought about calling him, telling him I'd just seen *A River Runs Through It*. Ty was the only one who was interested in things like River Phoenix's drug overdose or would know who Gene Hackman was. When we found the movie *Breaking Away,* deep in Patty's collection, it was like our own secret, like finding some really valuable artifact in an archeological dig. A movie with kids swimming in quarries in a small town. Wow, that was us. Ty even went to the library and got tapes to learn Italian, though no one knew but me.

But Ty was lost to me, and I knew it. He lived just over in St. Albans, and worked for an insurance firm in Castor. He and his wife, though, they'd sort of moved on from Maurus. The one time I went over they talked about wine and food and a play they'd seen in Minneapolis that sounded really weird. We hadn't had much in common then, but still, before the Chris Miller shooting I could have gone over and he would have tried. But now, I just knew, it was better I not try to get in touch. I could feel his disappointment in me even across that distance, especially in the evening, watching an old movie from the '80s or '90s, the dark and cold closing in.

I didn't put any movies about cops in my queue. Or any war movies. I'd had enough of heroes to last a lifetime. But I did think about Tim O'Brien when I thought about Ty. In Minnesota, you can't get through high school without reading the Vietnam stories of Tim O'Brien, who is from Minnesota. My high school English teacher, Mr. Sartap, was really into the 1960s, and teaching us about Vietnam and the protests and all that. He was mostly bald but had a long ponytail down his back and always wore jeans. He had been a hippie, I guess, though I think he was too young for Vietnam, so he was kind of a fake hippie. He brought in his guitar to play Bob Dylan songs, another great Minnesotan. He made us watch a show about Woodstock and write profiles on the bands and singers and stuff. We thought it was really lame. We made merciless fun of the guy.

He had us read a bunch of stories by Tim O'Brien, some of which were true and some of which were just stories, but they all seemed true. In that winter after Chris Miller's death, I kept thinking of two in particular. In the first one, soldier Tim is in a firefight and discovers that he is a coward. While other soldiers engage the enemy and even run out into danger to drag back wounded soldiers, Tim flops around on the ground, crying like a baby. When we read it in high school, I had wondered why he was so ashamed about it and felt the need to go on and on for a whole book about it. But after Chris Miller, it seemed like a perfectly good subject to obsess about.

There was another story, where the main character, who is really Tim if I'm remembering right, has gone off to a cabin on the Canadian border right before he has to report for basic training. He's been drafted and he is considering whether or not to escape to Canada. He has a plan that involves taking out a fishing boat and just crossing over. I had no idea it was that easy, but I guess a number of people did that, just rowed over to Canada or hiked in someplace. This guy agonizes about his decision for a week, and he can tell that the man who runs the fishing cabins knows what is going on. But the man doesn't say anything or try to stop him. In the end, though, Tim goes and does his tour of duty. And he says he does it because he couldn't bear the alternative. The alternative was that everyone in town, his parents included, but mostly the old guys who fought in World War II, would disown him.

In class, about a third of the students, including Ty, said they would have gone into the army if they were drafted. When Mr. Sartap polled us, the rest of us raised our hands and said we would have gone to Canada. Ty gave me a look of deep disappointment. That look almost made me put my hand down.

Instead, I said: "What? What do you want me to do? Go to the jungle and get zapped by gooks?" I expected him to laugh, but he didn't.

"Paul, you couldn't ever come back again. You'd lose your family forever," he said.

"No I wouldn't," I said. "I'd get amnesty in a few years when the war was over. Meanwhile I'd hang out in Canada and smoke weed."

He shook his head, and I was surprised how seriously he was taking all this. "You don't know that," he said. "What you would

164

think at the time is that you could never come back to the United States again."

"I don't care. I'd be alive, wouldn't I?"

"Paul, you'd be a *coward*," he said. He said it like it was the worst thing a person could be. Even then, it sounded like such an old-fashioned word to me. As kids, no one called anyone a coward, and who cared if they did? If you wanted to embarrass someone, or get him to fight, you'd call him a baby, a girl, a pussy—or worse, a homo or a retard or a faggot, but not a coward. If I had understood the meaning of that word, how it would feel to have a whole town, everyone you ever knew, disappointed in you like Ty was in me that day, I might have acted differently in that alley behind Arnold's Bar. If I'd really understood or anticipated the silence and shame that engulfs the guy who runs from the fight, I might have acted differently that night.

A lot of the kids who said they would have gone were from military families. They said they understood that it would be shameful for their families if they fled to Canada. Sarah Groh said that it would dishonor the sacrifice made by her grandfather and great-uncles who fought for their country. The whole thing didn't make sense to the rest of us, the idea of fighting for your country. Again, it sounded like an old-fashioned idea that belonged to our parents and grandparents but not to us. Kind of the way being a Catholic was more important and more real to our parents than it was to us. Those generations had lived in times of war, and in their day there were lots of nuns and priests everywhere. It surprised me that words like *duty* and *honor* and even *coward* meant something to Ty and Sarah. We had only ever really known peace and security. The bombs that fell on Iraq in the 1990s were like fireworks to us. Our ideas of heroes came from video games and movies, action heroes and superheroes.

I knew that Ty's silence now, after Chris Miller, was him letting me know what it means to go to Canada. I lost Ty and John and all of Maurus. And though my family was mostly supportive, I also knew my dad was ashamed of me. He didn't say it. We all pretended that everything was fine and the same as before, but I knew. I wished some days he would just come out and say it. But I was afraid. I was afraid it might break something in me, break it permanently. I didn't have anything that winter, and if I lost my family, if I lost my father . . . well, then I might not have kept on living.

Julie kept asking if I wanted to talk about Chris Miller, but when I shook my head, she didn't push it. She could have said I was shutting her out, because I was. And she just kept asking, which was her right, but wasn't going to get us anywhere. She thought everything was about Chris. If the cold was bothering me, or I was worried my truck wouldn't get through the winter, she asked me if I wanted to talk about Chris's murder. She went straight to that.

Finally one night things came to a head. It was a bitter cold day, and when Julie came over after work I was lying on the couch in the dark living room, watching something as usual. She had clothes at my place by then and so changed. There wasn't much food in the house.

"Why don't we go to House of Pizza," she said.

"We can have it delivered," I answered.

"It will be cold by the time it gets here," she said. "And I want to go out to eat."

I just shook my head. "Call and order what you want. I'm going to take a shower. I'll go pick it up, but I don't want to go to House of Pizza."

"What about somewhere in Castor? We could go to the White Horse, they have those seasoned fries you like."

I shook my head and walked back to the bedroom, pulling off my shirt. When I was shaved and dressed, Julie was in the living room. It was very quiet, no television, and I thought maybe she'd left. I stopped in the hallway and checked the thermostat. It was set to sixty-eight but the furnace was having trouble holding that temperature against the below-zero temperatures outside. It was only sixty-four degrees in the house. I put my foot up to the vent in the hallway. There was warm air blowing out, so it was working.

There was just a single lamp on in the living room, casting a yellow light. The room seemed dark and cold. Julie was wearing her coat and sitting on the couch. "I'm sorry, Julie, it's so cold in here. The furnace just can't keep up."

When she looked up I saw she was crying. Her nose was red and her eyes swollen.

"What's wrong?" I asked. I knew I shouldn't, but I felt angry. Was she really upset that we weren't going to House of Pizza?

She sniffled, and wiped her nose on her sleeve, which was wrapped around her hand. She just shook her head.

"I'm sorry I don't have food here," I said. "And that I don't want to go out." I wasn't sorry, though, and I didn't sound sorry either.

She shook her head again. "That's not it," she said. She just looked up at me, with that look like I knew the problem and was just pretending to be dense.

I knew I should go over and sit next to her, but the thought of it made me slightly sick. I sat down in the armchair instead, sort of collapsed into it, more like a challenge than an invitation to discussion.

"I don't know why you won't talk to me about it," she said.

"About what?"

She just kept shaking her head and looking at me. She was having trouble talking because of the crying. "Chris Miller."

"Jeez, I just don't want to go out on the coldest fucking night of the year. How is that about Chris Miller?"

"You—you don't want to . . . to run into anyone," she said.

I just looked at her, probably not with the most understanding look.

"And you won't . . . you won't . . . *talk* to me." Her voice cracked when she said it, and she started to cry harder.

"You gotta stop this," I said. "You're getting hysterical."

She shook her head, and didn't stop crying. We just sat there in silence until she got it together somewhat. The tears said everything. She looked exhausted, her eyes bloodshot, her hands trembling slightly. But I just let her. I didn't answer. I stayed in my chair. I was exhausted, too.

"This is the end," she said. "The end of us."

I just nodded. What could I do?

"I can't do this, I'm sorry," she said. She got up and went to the bathroom for some tissues, and still I didn't get out of the chair. I could hear her, blowing her nose, running the tap. She came back, using toilet paper to wipe her nose. And still I didn't get up.

"I don't want to leave you, Paul," she said. "I love you. I want to have a life with you. But this is impossible. And I don't see any way it is going to change. Do you?"

I didn't respond.

"*Do* you?" she insisted.

I just shook my head.

"If you won't talk to me, there's no way forward," she said. "If you won't let me help you, if we're not in this together, then what am I supposed to do?"

"Nothing," I said. "It's my fault."

"It's nobody's fault," she said. "You are who you are. I just want you to understand that this is not about what you did. This is not about Chris Miller. This is about us, how you've decided to be with me. And I want more."

I nodded. I didn't have anything to say.

"I deserve more," she said, and I nodded again.

"If you do want to talk, we can try," she said. "But right now it looks to me like it's over."

She went to the door, and I still didn't move. I felt rooted to that chair, and just braced myself for the blast of cold air that would come in when she left. "I'll come back Sunday afternoon, during the Viking's game, to get my stuff. I'll leave the key on the table."

I didn't even move. I just waited for the cold air, and listened to the door open, the storm door unlatch, then the front door firmly shut. The cold moved through like a wave, and I shivered. After a while I got up and went and got a beer. Then I turned on the television and stared at it, not thinking about anything at all. When the beer was finished I turned off the TV, brushed my teeth, and went to bed. In the morning when I woke up I felt relieved.

And of course, she was right. Everything was about Chris Miller's murder. If I was worried about my truck breaking down, it was because I knew I wouldn't have a job for long. If I was worried about the crowds at the mall in Castor for Christmas shopping, it was because I didn't want to run into anyone I knew. Ty didn't call about the annual deer-hunting trip the week before Thanksgiving. I knew they were still going, but I wasn't invited. And I knew the conversations going on out there, in the truck on the way up to the cabin, around the fire. That whole weekend I was a total bastard. Even that last night about getting pizza. There wasn't anything that wasn't about Chris Miller's murder. And I didn't want to talk about it.

On Sunday afternoons, I went to my parents' house and watched the Vikings with my dad. My mother kept pushing me to talk to Father Jonas. I wanted her to stop bugging me about it, so I finally agreed to go with them to church one Sunday in January, though I had no intention of visiting with Father Jonas. Kelsey was there with her mother and the boys. I was surprised, though I guess I shouldn't have been. I'd heard some rumors that a fight was brewing over the Chris Miller Memorial Fund, between Nicole and Kelsey. Nicole wanted half the money that wasn't designated specifically for the children or for her. Kelsey wanted it split four ways, a share for each of the boys and one quarter to Nicole. I wondered if church was a bit of public relations on Kelsey's part. I didn't see Nicole in the pews, though she may have worked the Saturday night service.

We always parked on the west side of the church and came in near the front of the sanctuary. That way we avoided most of the people in the foyer who came in and talked before Mass or hung out afterward. We kept our coats with us. My parents always sat on the far left side, opposite the musicians, near the stand for the reader. When you're sitting on either side, you can see everyone else, not just Father Jonas up at the altar. Frank and his family sat in the center section toward the back. Joanie liked to visit with people, so they came in and out the main doors. And Kelsey sat near the musicians, a place where a lot of families with small children sat, because the parents could exit easily to the crying room or bathroom or keep them occupied with a good view of the singers.

There was another set of pews, even higher up in the back. I guess this would have been the balcony in an old church. That section always emptied out after Communion, before the final blessing and hymn. Those were the people who came down the aisle in their coats and then just kept going out the door. My father said once that these were the Bohemians and Poles. He said Germans would never do that, but I saw plenty of Germans in the mix.

Sometimes my parents went to the parish hall for donuts after Mass, but we usually left right away. We didn't even go over and talk to Frank and his family. My dad was efficient about this, to avoid the traffic jam in the east lot. I was quite pleased with the seating arrangements, because I also had a great view straight ahead of Kelsey and her kids. They were well behaved and serious. The middle child, Kyle, loved to sing and manage the choir books. Shane was more stoic, but he held hands to say the Our Father and shook hands with those around him at the sign of the peace. He went up for Communion and jerked his head in a little bow before receiving the wafer from Father Jonas. Kelsey had to push little Zach along because he was always veering left and right down the aisle, but he kept his arms folded tightly across his chest to receive a blessing, smiling when the priest pressed his hand to his small head.

I didn't really want to give my mother the satisfaction, or any ideas, but it was nice to be in church. When it was clear after that first week that no one was likely to confront me, I agreed to go every Sunday. Father Jonas gave short, simple homilies, the choir was good, and I got to see Kelsey and other people in town, even if I didn't talk to them.

When we were kids, Ty and I had been altar servers. All the boys were encouraged to try it in fourth grade, and even some girls volunteered. Most were too fidgety or didn't like it or did something to get cut from the list. Bill Kleis yawned really loudly from his chair in the middle of Mass, and that was the end of him. Sadie Fuchs could not hold the book still for Father Jonas to read the prayers. He kept jerking it into place, and she kept half closing it or leaning out with it. It was funny to watch, but I guess not for Father Jonas. Ty liked serving and was a really good altar boy, and I kept it up because of Ty. We asked to be put together on the schedule.

Being back there, seeing Kelsey and thinking about Ty, reminded me of our first visit to the quarry. The swimming quarry was in a county park near St. Albans. We found out about it the summer after freshman year, when John Wendinger's older brother agreed to take us there as long as we stayed away from him and his friends. Greg Wendinger had just gotten his driver's license, and his parents made it clear he wouldn't have access to the family car unless he took his brother where he needed to go. Greg solved this problem by taking his brother where *he* wanted to go instead. On hot days, Ty, John, and I were always at the ready in our swim trunks and with our towels around our necks, hanging around the Wendinger house until Greg wanted to go for a swim. Usually we went to Kramer Lake, but one day he said we were going to Quarry Park instead.

The only problem at the quarry was finding a place to hang out. The swimming area was mostly enclosed by walls of granite, and there were only a few outcroppings of flat rocks where you could put your towels. In the summer, the place was mobbed with kids from Castor. The only thing in short supply at the quarry was supervision (no lifeguards and very few parents). Of course, that was just the way we liked it.

There was a line to the two high ridges where people could jump off into the water below. The granite ledges were a test of our early manhood. Surprisingly, Ty, our leader in most things, was the last of us to go off the high ridge.

You had plenty of time, snaking around with the kids in front of you, to see how high up you were and get scared. But the ledge you were standing on was so narrow that there was no turning back. Sure, kids got to the top and wanted to turn back. But the ones behind them were ruthless, yelling at them to jump, threatening to push them off the ledge, calling them all the usual names. Eventually, it was just better to jump than to suffer the abuse.

Ty took one look at the kids jumping off the ledges and shook his head. "That is really dangerous," he said.

"Seems like a lot of kids are doing it," John said.

"You could so easily hit your head on a rock, break your back, and be paralyzed for life," he said. As he did, another kid jumped off the ledge, doing a perfect flip. The kids waiting hugged themselves against the breeze and stomped around.

"You could slip off that ledge so easily," Ty said. "And that would be it. Game over."

"It must be safe, or they wouldn't allow it," I said.

"Yeah, don't you think they'd shut it down if that happened?" John said. "It must be OK."

"Jeez, I can't believe adults let this go on," Ty said. "It's so irresponsible."

We found a place to put our towels and Ty and I sat down against a rock. "Let's just swim," Ty said, but John, still standing, was having none of it.

"I'm going to jump," he said, dropping his towel at Ty's feet.

Ty just shook his head. Another kid, who had been standing on the ledge quite a long time and was now being subjected to a loud chorus urging him to jump, finally stepped off the rock. His feet clawed the air but he stayed mostly upright and entered, with a loud splash, grabbing his nose as he went into the water. When he surfaced the boys on the ledge clapped and shouted congratulations. It seems he was a virgin jumper.

"I'm definitely going in. How about you?" John said to me. I was sure it would be OK, but I wanted to watch a bit more first.

"I'll go later," I said, and John took off, picking his way in bare feet through the clusters of other kids to the line at the ledge.

That's when we saw the girls. They called out to John as he went past, and we saw him point over in our direction. It was Kelsey, her obnoxious cousin Ellen, and Grace Dietzman. "Hey, look," Ty said. "It's Kelsey."

This time he did lead the way, picking up his towel and John's and heading down the little trail to the girls. I followed, of course.

"What are you guys doing here?" Ellen asked.

"Same as you, I guess," said Ty.

"John's going to dive, huh," said Kelsey.

"How come you guys aren't jumping?" Ellen asked. "Scared?"

Ty shook his head. "That is really dangerous," he said. "I don't know why the park allows it." Ty could say things like that and not get made fun of.

"I don't know how they could stop it," Grace said. "I've never heard of anyone getting seriously hurt."

"Do you guys come here a lot?" I asked. Somehow it had been off our radar until John's brother Greg told us about it. Greg was with his friends getting high somewhere, and we had strict orders to be back at the car at four p.m.

"I've always come here," Grace said. "We ski in the park in winter, too." Grace's parents were from Minneapolis, and she was smart and seemed to know things. When she got accepted to college in Chicago, Ty said, "I wish we knew we could go to schools like that. I never even thought to apply out of state." It wasn't surprising she would know about the Quarry before the rest of us.

"This place is cool," I said. It was getting awkward. We needed to sit down or move on, but there wasn't much room.

"Can we join you?" Ty asked.

Kelsey stood up and moved her towel to make room for us. She sat down on Ellen's towel, swatting at Ellen's legs. Ellen pouted but moved over. The area was shaded so there wasn't any sunbathing. Ty put his towel down and we both sat on it. I felt self-conscious about my hairy legs. It felt like Kelsey and Ellen were staring at them.

I took more time to look at Kelsey, too. She was wearing a bikini, though she didn't have much of a figure. The bikini had tiny neon flowers all over it and was plain, like a bra and underwear, pretty modest. Ellen's bikini was more revealing, and she had more to reveal. The top tied like a halter and showed cleavage, and the bottom was under her belly. It wasn't attractive, and she looked like an older woman, not a fourteen-year-old girl. That was Ellen, though. She seemed like a divorced woman even in junior high. Grace had on a one-piece navy blue Speedo like someone on a swim team would have.

"What have you been up to this summer, Paul?" Ellen asked.

"Not much," I said. "You?"

Ellen shook her head. "That's sad," she said.

I didn't know what she was talking about, but I hardly ever did. I felt like she was baiting me. "How about you, Kelsey?" I said.

Kelsey shrugged and giggled. "Just hanging out," she said. "Babysitting." She giggled again.

"Grace just got back from Europe," Ellen said.

"Oh, yeah?" asked Ty. "How was that?"

"It was good," Grace said. Ty asked what countries she went to and if she saw relatives, and she gave us the facts, but the conversation wasn't going anywhere.

"Want to swim?" I asked. Kelsey did, but Grace wanted to stay back with her book and Ellen had a magazine. They would do some non-sunbathing.

We made our way down to a granite slab at the water's edge. We could see here that there were larger chunks of granite several feet below the surface. "See?" said Ty. "That's why people shouldn't be diving off that ledge."

"I think they'd have figured out by now if it was dangerous, Ty," I said.

We both made shallow dives out away from the edge. Kelsey was more tentative, letting herself in slowly and squealing at the cold.

The water felt great. The quarry was deep, and there was no slimy lake bottom, no weeds growing up and tickling your legs. It seemed clean. We waited for Kelsey and then swam to the other side, about fifty yards, and grabbed hold of a large rock.

This side of the quarry was even more steep, with a giant pile of granite and sheer walls. Two guys in baseball caps and running shoes were making their way down over the rocks. They weren't dressed for swimming. They had tattoos, and in any other setting I would have been nervous about them. They were clearly from Castor.

"Hey, look," Kelsey said, pointing up at some vines growing along the edge. They had raspberries on them, though not many were ripe. "Can you reach them, Paul?"

178

I pulled myself up onto the rock and picked some raspberries, which I passed down to Kelsey and Ty. Kelsey dipped hers in the water then into her mouth.

"What are you doing, washing them?" Ty asked.

Kelsey laughed. "I guess so."

"'Cause that water, I mean," said Ty, "lots of kids swimming in it, and I don't see a bathroom anywhere around here."

"Oh, eww!" Kelsey said. She scrambled over to the rock and pulled herself up next to where I was sitting with another handful of berries. "That is so gross!"

She sprinkled me with cold water, and shook her head, spraying me with more water from her curls.

"What are you, a dog?" I said. "Stop that."

She looked at me, her mouth open in shock. "A dog!" She reached down and started to splash me with the water in earnest. Ty grabbed her leg and there was a slight struggle before he pulled her back in the water.

"Kelsey drank pee water, Kelsey drank pee water," he said when she bobbed back to the surface.

"You guys are gross," she said, but she was smiling. She put her hand on Ty's shoulder while she wiped the water from her hair and face.

And I had this pang, seeing her hand on his shoulder, their smiles. This was before she started dating Chris, a brief moment when someone else could have had her. She moved around and held on to Ty, her arms around his neck. "Give me a ride," she said in a pouty voice.

"What?" I could see him blushing.

"Give me a ride back," she said, like it was obvious.

Ty looked over at the other shore. I let myself into the water and moved toward them.

"Come on, Ty. Giddy-up," she said.

"Yeah, Ty," I said. "I want a ride, too." I swam up behind Kelsey, put my hands on her bare shoulders, and pushed down lightly. But she just went under, let go of Ty and slid out between us. She emerged a short distance away.

"No fair, Paul Thielen, that was my ride," she said. I was treading water, as was Ty.

"Race ya!" she yelled, and started swimming for the other side. Ty took off then, intent on beating her. I watched her even stroke, her kick, weak on the left side but sending up a high wake on the right when she wasn't breathing. I could make out the girls' towels and see that John had joined them. I started to make my way back, slowly and steadily, preparing to go to the ledge and jump, to lose my quarry virginity.

Chapter Fourteen

I ran into Kelsey in Staley's in early February. She was by herself, sort of hunched over the shopping cart as she pushed it down the aisle. When she saw me, she smiled weakly. Usually when I ran into people those days, they talked in that false tone, sort of light and standoffish at the same time, if they acknowledged me at all. It was like they were doing me a favor, and I shouldn't get too comfortable. Not Kelsey, though. Her smile was tentative but real.

So I thought, she knows we are bound in this thing, although we had not talked once since it happened. I walked over to her, clutching my shopping basket in front of me for protection.

"Hi, Kelsey," I said.

"Hey," she said. "I see you've become a churchgoer."

"Yeah," I said. I was surprised she had noticed. "It makes my mom happy."

"That's important," she said. There was a pause, and she added, "Moms are important."

We were in danger of the conversation ending there, so I just asked the first question that came into my head. "How are you doing?"

She shrugged, then her eyes widened. "How are *you* doing?" she asked, as if suddenly realizing I might not be doing all that well.

"Oh, you know. Hanging in."

She smiled.

"Eating right, I see," she said, gesturing to my basket, which contained a bag of frozen tater tots and a couple frozen pizzas.

"Yeah, you know, single guy food."

"Doesn't Julie cook for you?" she asked, tilting her head to the side.

I shook my head. "Julie and I broke up."

"Oh," she said. "Sorry." She winced like it was physically painful to hear. "I'm sorry."

"It's not—it's not because of . . . what happened," I said. I was afraid she thought Julie had abandoned me along with everyone else after the incident. I didn't want her feeling sorry for me.

"Oh, I know," she said. "I mean it's too bad you broke up. You seemed good together."

"Yeah," I said. "She's really great. It just wasn't working." I was tempted to say more, but I just stood there.

"I could fix you dinner sometime," she said.

I felt the full weight of that. No one but my family had called or invited me anywhere. And though they'd offered their best attempt at normalcy—I now felt how much I'd missed the simple invitation of someone wanting to spend time with me. I hoped she wasn't just making conversation. But it also cut right through me.

I tried to play it cool by reaching into her cart and considering the items: "Hmmm. Chicken, ground beef, Hamburger Helper." I picked up a box of Cap'n Crunch and shook it. "Breakfast of champions."

"How about Friday," she said. She was looking at me steadily, not smiling. It was scary, this idea hanging between us.

"Friday is good."

"Six o'clock?"

"Six it is."

"You know where I live, right?"

"I do."

"Don't be late," she said. I went straight to the checkout, although I had planned on buying a few more things. I didn't want us running into each other in a different aisle, and I was sort of afraid she might change her mind.

I hadn't heard from her by Friday, so I figured dinner was still on. When I drove to Frogtown, I thought about parking my car on Third Street and walking the last two blocks. I circled around the cul-de-sac at the park and back up to Third, but then returned and drove into a space at the park, facing the river. I didn't like the idea of someone seeing my car in Kelsey's driveway, but I knew from experience that a car parked on a side street could look suspicious. I really didn't want anyone calling the Maurus cops to check on a suspicious car and the license plate turning up my name.

I'd brought a six-pack of Heineken in bottles, as fancy as I get. I walked up the drive to the kitchen door and rang the bell.

Shane pulled open the door, with Kelsey right behind. "Hi, Paul, come on in," she said. I felt relieved that the kids were there. I also wished I'd dressed a little more casually. I was wearing jeans and a plaid, button-down shirt. I wished I'd gone with the polo shirt I had considered first or a plain T-shirt.

Kelsey had on leggings and a sweatshirt, with thick wool socks pulled up over the leggings. Her hair was pulled back with a barrette in a sort of bun, with a lot of hair falling around the sides of her face. It was very relaxed, but also looked good on her. It made me think of her curly hair when we were younger, the way it made her face look brighter and sort of nestled into her hair. I came into the small entry, which had a few steps going up to a second door, into the kitchen, and another set of stairs going down to the basement. The whole vestibule was a jumble of children's shoes and hats and mittens. I started taking off my shoes.

"Oh, you don't have to do that," Kelsey said. "Don't bother." But I did anyway, putting them carefully on the rug by the door. Then we went up into the bright kitchen.

"It's just sloppy joes," she said.

"Oh, good," I said. "I brought beer." I handed her the six-pack.

"Thanks!" She went to the fridge to put it away. Shane was keeping an eye on us both. I could hear a commotion in the other room, where the two other boys were playing.

"Just a second," Kelsey said, and went to check on them, shouting their names. I was alone with Shane, who was clearly suspicious of me.

"So," I said to Shane, "still want to be a pitcher?"

"I'm a pitcher now," he said. He looked surprisingly like his father. He had the same open face and high forehead, the same putty nose.

I nodded. "That's good," I said. He was studying me. I needed a beer. "What grade are you in?"

"Fourth," he said.

"At Kennedy?"

"I go to St. Willibald's," he said. "We're Catholic."

"Yeah, I'm Catholic, too," I said. "I went to St. Willibald's."

"With my dad?" His eyes widened, despite his clear attempts to stay guarded. Poor kid.

"Yes, exactly. Your dad and I were in the same class." He wanted to know more, had a sort of pleading look. I just smiled.

"Tell me a story about when my dad was little," he said. It was a command, not a question.

Of course, my mind went blank. I was sure I had stories, but nothing came to me. Then I saw little Chris Miller up on the altar with Father Jonas. "Do they still have the school Mass on Thursdays?" I asked him.

He nodded.

"Your dad was an altar boy—"

"A server," he interrupted.

"Yeah, a server for the school Masses—and Sundays sometimes, too. One time, when the priest put the incense in the censor— You know what that is?"

He nodded.

"You know how they spoon it in and smoke comes out?"

More nodding.

"Well, your dad was supposed to be holding the censor still, but he looked down in it and got smoke in his face and that made him sneeze and—"

Kelsey had walked back in, dragging along her middle child. She had him by the wrist, but he was trying to wriggle out of her grasp. She looked at me kind of worriedly, while I finished. "And he sneezed and dropped the censor."

"Did the church catch on fire?" Shane asked, quite seriously.

"What are you two talking about?" Kelsey broke in.

I shook my head at Shane. "No, nothing like that."

"Did everybody laugh?" he asked.

"Yeah," I said, smiling. "We all thought it was pretty funny." I stood up.

"Was the priest mad?"

"No, no," I said. "He knew it was an accident." I didn't have anywhere to go with this. Maybe it wasn't as good a story as I thought. "Your dad was a funny guy. Everybody liked him."

When he heard his dad mentioned, Kyle, who was still twisting at the end of Kelsey's arm and protesting his fate, fell silent. Kelsey looked at me with some distress. I hadn't meant to talk about Chris tonight. But there it was.

"My dad died," Kyle said. Kelsey dropped his arm and put her hand on his head, moving smoothly from coercing to comforting.

I nodded at him. "I know it," I said. "I'm sorry." Kelsey looked up at me with a sad smile. As if to say, *This is my life.*

"Mind if I get a beer?" I asked her, already moving to the fridge.

"Oh, yeah, sorry!" she said. "Go right ahead. Opener's on the door." Kyle joined his brother at the kitchen table, which was set for five.

I took two beers from the fridge. "You want one?" I asked her.

"Yes, I'll have one with dinner," she said. "Shane, pour the milk, will you? We're almost ready."

I helped Shane with the gallon of milk while Kelsey dished up the sloppy joes, chips, and corn. I went with the two boys to wash our hands in the main floor bathroom while Kelsey persuaded young Zach to leave his LEGOs and join us at the table. After the standard grace and genuflections all around, we dug in.

It was wonderful, really, comfortable and easy after the first awkward moments. Kelsey asked about my folks and Frank, and we didn't talk about Chris anymore. I asked about her mom, who I knew was divorced from her stepfather and living on the other side of Main Street. She said what a big help her mom had been with the kids. Kyle told us some stories about his grandmother and what board games she had over at her house. Little Zach was particularly funny on the subject of Grandma's inability to build a fort. Kyle was interested in sharing their experience of eating blue cheese, which was only sort of blue in places, and which he had decided he did not want to try again. He was a fan of the cheese that is a powder on macaroni or of string cheese wrapped in plastic.

I wasn't really sure how long I should stay. After dinner, I offered to help clean up and began clearing dishes over Kelsey's protests. Zach wanted to show me what he was building, and Kelsey encouraged me to go to the living room with the younger boys while Shane helped her clean up. Kyle was immediately drawn back into the things he had wanted to do with the LEGOs, and was quick to spot where some pieces of his spaceship had been stolen to beef up his younger brother's ship.

As far as kids go, I did have some experience from Clare and Patty, though they were not really into LEGOs. Most of my experience with children consisted of running around outside with a big band of cousins' kids, letting myself be a human jungle gym with kids clambering over me.

Now I sat down on the floor and crossed my legs. Kyle knelt down beside me, his hand resting on my leg. Zach took his place on the other side of me, and both boys held up their ships for me to see. It was sweet, but I also felt on edge, a responsibility to handle this correctly. These boys didn't know who I was. I was just a friend of their mother's, someone who knew their dad. I focused on the LEGOs, admiring their work and offering up an idea for each of them. Zach wasn't interested and told me his ship was done.

Kyle, however, took the ship from me and got busy making modifications. He sat down close to me, sort of nestled into the back of my crossed legs, facing away. Zach stretched out on the other side, propping himself on my other crossed leg, studying his brother. I took the carton of tiny pieces and went to work on selling Kyle on some interesting ones. LEGOs had gotten much more complicated since I'd had them, and the boys were less flexible about assigning parts meant for, say, a Star Wars land vehicle, to the outside of a spaceship. There was a lot more searching for parts than actual building.

Kelsey came in and announced it was bath time, and I was grateful for this clear sign that I should go. This, too, seemed right. I said goodbye, and Zach gave me a perfunctory hug. As Kelsey led Kyle and Zach upstairs, Shane walked me back to the entry and turned on the light for me, as his mother had instructed. I put my hand on his neck, sort of a fatherly, guy gesture. It was moving, the way he was the man of the house. I wondered if he'd taken on the role immediately, when his dad left to be with Nicole, or if it had happened after his father's death.

He stood at the door while I put on my shoes, but he didn't say anything. "OK, goodbye," I said. As soon as I got outside he turned off the light. I chuckled as I made my way down the dark porch steps and then was startled by the motion-activated floodlight that went on when I reached the corner of the house. It lit my way down the gravel drive, my shadow stretching out in front of me. The night was icy, completely still and glittering. The snow was heaped on both sides of the street and around the cul-de-sac at the park.

I began to feel unsteady, emotional. I crossed over into the arc of the streetlight and focused on my parked car. As soon as I closed the door, safely in the driver's seat, I was overcome. It took me completely by surprise, and I'm still not sure about the mix of emotions. I started to cry, and I put my hands on the steering wheel and let my head fall forward. I was shaking, crying in bursts, as if the stress of the previous weeks was taking me over. It was cold, really cold, a layer of ice crystals had formed across the windshield. Even so, I was sweating. It was like a long, low-grade fever was breaking.

I didn't think it could be about Kelsey. I'd barely interacted with her all evening—the focus had been on the kids. We'd felt like old friends. There hadn't been the romantic spark I'd felt in Staley's. It had been simple and even the kids had acted like this was normal.

Maybe it was the normalcy that I'd been missing. Maybe that was what I was desperate for. I wiped my face and turned on the car, blasting the defroster, which blew out cold air and filled the car with a white noise roar. I got out and scraped the windshield, but I continued to cry, just quietly now and not with my whole body. I wiped the tears before they could freeze on my face, and back in the car I wiped my nose along my sleeve. I felt the boys' simple weight against me, the simple reality of human contact. For a few minutes, I even forgot whose sons they were.

Chapter Fifteen

But the next day, and the day after that, it wasn't the kids I was thinking about. It was Kelsey. When I got up that Saturday I sent her a text, thanking her for dinner. She texted back: "good 2 see u 2" and a smiley face. In the following days, I looked at that text a lot. The whole evening gave me renewed energy.

I went to the gym, out on Highway 41, for the first time since the incident, and it started off well. The place was full, but mostly with middle-aged women. I didn't see anyone from the department. I recognized some people, my mother's friends and some others, but no one who would give me trouble. My mother would be happy to hear from her friends that I was getting out.

It was the usual New Year's resolution crowd. Ryan greeted me at the desk. While he scanned my ID and got me a towel, we made small talk about the seasonal rise in memberships. It would all be over in a few weeks, he said, and things would be back to normal. He was using that fake friendly tone with me, letting me know he knew what I'd done and not to confuse his professionalism with real friendliness. I put my earbuds in, ran on the treadmill, did a few free-weight circuits. Nothing that would require a spotting partner. Nothing that would require me to remove my headphones.

It felt good to work my body and get out of the house. Everyone there was wrapped up in what they were doing, all determination, distracting themselves with the television screens or their own music. Gyms have become very quiet places now, everyone in their own little world. Physical activity as escape. A lot of places that used to be social centers are like that. Everyone's just getting down to business.

But then, after thirty minutes running on the treadmill, when I was doing a circuit on the machines, I saw Trey come in. I saw him in the mirror and felt the adrenaline rush. He leaned in when he talked to Ryan at the desk, and Ryan nodded in my direction. Trey was basically lying across the desk, the way some guys do, and turned his head to look over at me. I just kept up my reps and didn't make eye contact. No reason we had to get in each other's way.

Trey took his stuff into the locker room, and in came Kenny Streator. Kenny looked bigger, and I figured he and Trey were buddies now, lifting together. In the mirror, I saw Kenny also look over at me, talking to Ryan, then head off into the locker room.

That was my moment to leave, but I didn't go anywhere. I moved to the next machine, adjusted the weight, tucked my legs under the cushions, and started my reps.

Trey and Kenny walked, purposefully, right past me. Trey leaned down over my head and smiled into the mirror. It was menacing—I was hoping to be shunned instead. Kenny didn't do anything, just walked by, gripping the towel wrapped around his neck, and they moved to the free weights for their warm-up. I kept looking straight ahead, counting my reps, but I did turn off my iPod. I left my earbuds in, but I wanted to hear what was going on. I was on alert, trying to calm the pounding in my chest.

I had three more machines to do, about twelve minutes with breaks. Trey and Kenny had turned their attention to their regimen, and Kenny was lifting, Trey adding weight and grunting out short bursts of encouragement. I wiped down the machine, walked to the far side of the room and the drinking fountain, then returned to the next station. I only had three minutes left when the energy in the room shifted.

"FUCK!" The barbell fell with a loud clang. All the women on their treadmills and stationary bikes looked over to see what had happened.

Nothing serious, just Trey trying and failing to lift a weight that was too heavy for him. Kenny had been in place and helped as far as one is able to settle the weight into its cradle.

"*WRAAAGH!*" Trey roared, slamming his fists on the bench. He stood up and shook out his tattooed arms, rippling with muscles. He turned in my direction, looking more like an ape than a man. Then he started walking my way.

"What's wrong with you?" he asked.

I just shook my head. I did pull out my earbuds, to pay full attention. He kept coming my way.

"What's wrong with you, pussy," he said. Now the women were looking at me, still churning away on their ellipticals, trying not to be alarmed.

"Trey, leave it alone," I said. But he was right in front of me now. I released the weight on my calves and prepared to get up, but he blocked my exit.

"What kind of pussy machine is this?" Trey said. I just held his gaze, thinking about how to diffuse the situation.

Trey leaned over and pulled the pin holding the weight. "Oh, come on, tough guy. You can do better than that," he said. He pushed the pin back in a couple notches down.

"Trey, that's enough," I said.

"Come on, let's see you lift it. It's only 130, surely you can do that," he taunted.

Kenny had come over and stood a few feet away. "Trey," he said. "Let's go."

Trey just ignored Kenny and kept looking at me. "Can't do it?" he asked.

I didn't engage. Not engaging was the number one rule. He knew that as much as I did.

"Come on, Trey," Kenny said. I resolved to stay quiet, let Kenny draw his attention away.

"I want to see if this pussy can lift some weight," Trey said. "Can you, pussy? Or are you afraid?"

I didn't move my gaze, but didn't answer.

"Are you afraid of getting hurt? Afraid someone's going to hurt you?" He leaned in, grabbing both armrests, and the muscles in his left bicep twitched. I could smell his sweat and see the anger in his eyes.

"Trey, leave it," Kenny said.

Then one of the women, on a nearby treadmill, yelled out. "Hey, leave him alone, you bully." We both swung our heads to look at her, and even Kenny was speechless.

Trey didn't move. He just smiled, then looked back at me and laughed silently, shaking his head. "Need that nice lady to fight your battles?" he asked.

"No," I said, though I knew I shouldn't. I just couldn't stay silent on that one.

"Hey, lady," Trey said, looking up at her, rising to face her but not moving from the station. "Do you know who this is? Do you know who this fine citizen is?"

"It doesn't matter," she said. "He wasn't bothering you."

"This," he said, extending his arm to point at my face, "is Chris Miller's partner. The guy who left the scene when Officer Chris Miller was shot."

"I don't care about that," she said. "Just leave him alone." This lady, she was probably a few years younger than my mother, was tough. She talked to Trey like he was an unruly teenager bullying a younger kid in the park. How do you get authority like that? Fearlessness?

I didn't care if it was Kenny, or this lady, I just wanted someone to draw Trey off of me so I could escape. I could see Ryan in the mirror, his back turned, folding towels. Kenny called Trey again. The lady kept up her steady pace on the treadmill.

Trey reached over me and pulled the pin from the machine, this time tossing it behind him. The pin made a pinging sound as it hit the floor. "Go fetch," he said, and moved away. "Go fetch," he said, louder, "you bitch." Then he turned to the lady, "You can take the little bitch with you when you leave, you bitch," he said. She didn't respond, and he and Kenny went back to their bench. He pounded his fist into his hand: "Let's *do* this thing, motherfuckah!"

I got up and walked to the drinking fountain. I didn't retrieve the pin, and I didn't acknowledge the lady on the treadmill. I went to the locker room to get my coat, keeping my eyes forward, not looking at Ryan. I threw the towel in the bin and left. It was near zero out, and my nose hairs froze and my throat hurt when I breathed in. I didn't wait for the car to warm up. I just threw the defroster on high and backed out of the parking lot. At home I didn't bother to shower, just threw some water on my face and changed my shirt. I hadn't even worked up much of a sweat, truth be told. I called Frank to make plans to work on my basement the next day. Then I opened a beer and sat down on the couch and watched college football for the rest of the afternoon and into the evening. The phone didn't ring. No one came to the door. Outside, it was dark and cold and quiet as hell.

After Julie and I broke up, I drove around a lot, through the cold, empty streets of Maurus. It was like being back on patrol. When I'd get anxious, unable to stay inside but unsure where to go, I traced the old police routes, in and out of neighborhoods, all the way out to the Agamis and back. First I'd trace the even blocks of downtown, then I'd drive the coved neighborhoods of Quarry Trails. Finally, I'd cut through the high school parking lot and back onto Route 2, across Highway 41 and the river, and out to Fraser Lake and the smaller Agamis. I didn't spend much time there, where few people came in winter and the lake roads could be icy and unplowed.

I drove during daylight, and sometimes at dinnertime, never at night when I might have been viewed as suspicious. As I drove, I just looked at the houses. I kept the radio off, so the only sound was of the heat blowing from the vents and the snow under my tires. It's very quiet in the winter, and people keep their homes closed up tight. In the evening, I could see the light in dining rooms and kitchens, upstairs where kids were doing homework. Occasionally there was the glow of a big screen television, or the curtains were tied open and I could see the giant heads of newscasters against blue backgrounds and the news ticker along the bottom of the screen.

That winter there wasn't a thaw, so people didn't take down their Christmas lights until March, although no one turned them on after mid-January. Looking at the packed rows of ramblers like the one I grew up in, I remembered the names of people who had lived there. I remembered their stories: the lost child, the teenager killed in the auto accident, the house fire. I thought about the kindnesses of people helping neighbors shovel walks or clean gutters. I remembered the meanness of people who wouldn't answer the door when I went out selling candy for football, and the surprising generosity of a man who gave me a twenty dollar bill, but only wanted one candy bar for it.

When I came home, dispirited, my mother would get angry. "All these people are sitting on money," she said. "These damn Germans, they're tighter than tight. Sure, they leave money to the church and charity when they die, but would it hurt them to give a little now?" I thought the twenty would make her happy, but she had the same reaction. "Oh, yeah, see? He's sitting on a pile of money, too. What did you do to get it out of him?" Then she went down another path. "Maybe he's going senile and doesn't realize he gave you so much." She actually wanted me to return it, to ask him if he really meant to give me a twenty or if it was a mistake. She wanted me to bring change to him, said I was taking advantage of him. My father calmed her down. "Jeez, Marilyn, just see it for what it is. He wants to support the football team. He was feeling generous. Maybe he won a pull tab at the parish festival. Leave the kid alone."

On my self-imposed patrols, I drove over the Horst twice, once where it passed by the old granite company site, and then again farther down, by the Lutheran church, on the way out of town. I drove along Main Street and past Arnold's Bar and the Staghorn. I even drove down the alley behind Arnold's Bar, more than a few times. I counted to myself as I covered the distance from the scene of Chris Miller's murder to the post office parking lot. Thousand and one, thousand and two, thousand and three into the parking space. Three seconds. Pause. Then three more seconds back to the scene. Maybe thirty seconds total, away from the scene, that defined me forever.

On my drives through town, I saw people shoveling or using their snowblowers. I saw kids with sleds. Snowmen appeared and turned into shapeless ghosts under more snow. Snow forts appeared and disappeared. The parking lots in town stayed half full with shoppers at the meat market, the bakery, Staley's, the dollar store where Video Quest used to be, Lynn's, the Blue

Line, the pharmacy. Snowmobiles ran in and out of the ditches, their tracks across lawns and down along the banks of the Horst. Tracks in graceful arcs past the Lutheran church and out of town. Frank and the other landscapers in town who removed snow in winter dumped truckloads on the edge of the golf course and near one of the baseball diamonds behind Kennedy. The kids turned these piles into sledding hills. A few cross-country skiers moved like bugs, all poles and legs, across the athletic fields.

I drove slowly but I didn't stop, and I tried not to think. I just observed and somehow felt a sense of peace and purpose, even if it was a false one. This was what it had meant to serve and protect, just to be present. This was more or less what I had signed on for, and what I missed.

I'd move out beyond my patrol route and across the river, to the Agamis. The lake neighborhoods were quiet in the winter, no one around during the week and even most weekends. The smaller cabins on the smaller lakes even had closed shutters over the windows, untouched snow all the way up to the door and covering the driveways. On sunny days, the snow was blinding. Here and there someone had an ice-fishing shack set up, and a path in to the lake.

Fraser Lake was the largest and had no public access. That never stopped people from going there. It was stocked, which made it worthwhile for some fishermen to make deals with residents or just make their own access and set up their fish houses for the winter. I know some people think it's trashy, but I love the sight of a lake dotted with fish houses.

Out there I remembered trespassing onto a private beach when a resort home sat empty one summer, for gorgeous late-night swims. This was in high school, once Ty had a car. We passed a bottle of tequila as we lay after a swim on the manicured lawn. Kelsey was already off with Chris, and it was mostly just a group of guys at the beach that summer. We were good kids, despite the drinking and trespassing. We always took the empty bottle and any other trash with us when we left. When we borrowed a canoe, we brought it back. Ty's family had a cabin up in the Boundary Waters area, and he was used to canoeing and camping and wilderness stuff. "Leave no trace, people!" he would say when it was time to go.

The Agamis were not part of regular police patrols, especially in winter. As a matter of policy, we only went in when residents called us. We didn't see them as part of the town, these wealthy out-of-towners. Usually the calls were for house alarm malfunctions. The city people were particularly nervous about noises and security. They weren't used to the country and they both feared and idealized it.

As kids, we hadn't just used their beaches. We'd also taken canoes and rowboats, and even hotwired a pontoon boat one hot day in September when we cut school. It was such a ridiculous thing to hotwire a pontoon boat, which chugged along on the lake at a slow speed. Of course, we were neither the first nor the last. Problems only occurred when the property didn't get back where it belonged. As safety officers, we'd calm the owners reporting stolen canoes and kayaks and tell them we expected the merchandise might turn up. Sometimes a neighbor called to report an "extra" boat at their dock or in their yard, or canoes were found in the woods by the main road.

After two weeks, my desire to see Kelsey again had gotten even more intense. I looked for her car at the gym parking lot, though I was working out at home now, too. I wished I'd asked her more about what she was doing when I was at her house for dinner.

After Chris Miller's death, I'd taken down my Facebook page. There were some pretty ugly posts at the time. But now I went back, looking for Kelsey. She didn't have a page either, and when I Googled her I got a bunch of articles about Chris's death. I downloaded the single published photo of her with the kids taken at the funeral.

I also found a link to a website called "Behind The Blue Wall," about police officers and domestic violence. The site was a chronicle of suspicious suicides by women in relationships with police officers. The gist of the site was that a lot of law enforcement personnel were getting away with murdering their spouses, fiancées, and girlfriends.

The site bummed me out. I found myself reading through the various cases—a shocking number of them—and then some other articles about police officers and cover-ups of domestic violence. I wasn't all that surprised that police officers were perpetrators of domestic violence. I knew that anyone could be an abuser, and most of the violence we lived in, the simple, daily violence that I'd come to recognize as a police officer, was domestic. I'm not trying to be alarming, here. But if you're paying attention, you realize that life is full of violence. Frank's wife, Joanie, talked about seeing a woman hit her kid in a grocery store in Castor, which you hardly see anymore because it's so frowned upon. Joanie was outraged, but she didn't say anything. No one did. She said she was scared of the woman.

My mom yelled at some teenagers who were picking on a younger boy at the park, and they swore at her and laughed. Even the boy getting bullied laughed at her. It had shaken her up in terms of what she saw as a total breakdown in society. But I didn't agree. Society was made of this stuff. Alcohol and poverty brought a lot of violence into view, but I knew most of the men—and women—we arrested on domestic charges were mostly not drunk, just angry.

What went on behind closed doors, especially during the recession, was bad. People were losing their jobs and in my two years on the force I'd seen some real desperation and plenty of meanness. There had even been a suicide, a man with four kids who had been unemployed for a year and whose house had just gone into foreclosure. Everyone said he had a long history of depression. People say all sorts of things—everyone has a theory, an opinion. The point is, there is violence everywhere and you don't have to go far to find it. We live with it.

I thought about Trey, and who would be stupid enough to marry him? But the truth is, he was sweet to his wife, as far as I could see. I'd heard him say that men who beat up women are scum. And we all knew this executive at the bank who beat up his wife. We had gone to that house a number of times. We didn't disclose, but he kind of shaped our picture of what a true abuser was like. We'd called an ambulance to that house, twice.

But she always went back. A lot of those women married to abusers, they could take care of themselves. It wasn't clear, sometimes, who you needed to protect. Trey hated women getting hurt. He didn't bully women. I'm sure he ignored them, played them, maybe even cheated on them, but he didn't physically hurt them.

Still, if he had, would one of us have intervened? If we'd been called to an officer's house on a domestic, what would we do? We'd probably just try to separate them and get them to cool off.

Responding to domestics, we used our judgment. We didn't always make an arrest. If we went straight to an arrest on couples fighting, we'd have to lock up too many people. Although we had training about zero tolerance and talked as though we were tough on domestic violence, the reality was much more complicated.

The way we handled domestic calls was this: We'd go inside and do a lethality assessment. Was anyone hurt or likely to get hurt? We separated the parties and got their stories, individually. If there were kids there, and there often were, we talked to them, too. Sometimes they cowered and were scared and wouldn't say anything. Sometimes, especially if they knew us from the school visits, they would tell us a lot. The kids were a great source of information. They know what's going on and they'll give it up, mother or father or both. It wasn't just men who were perpetrators. You'd be surprised what some of these women can dish out.

Then we'd meet back together and share stories. We'd decide whether or not we were going to make an arrest. Sometimes, if the problem was mostly verbal, if the kids said it was just an argument, if the couple got it together once we arrived, we would suggest a cool down. We wouldn't make an arrest. But more often, we did take the man into custody. Most often, we got the woman to a relative's house or the shelter, and same for the kids, or called in family services. We'd cuff the guy, get him in the back of the squad car, and take him to Castor, the only jail, and get him booked. It could be a really long ride to Castor, the guy yelling or pleading from the backseat, telling you his troubles and his side of things. You hope for a stoic perpetrator, someone who gets the part about remaining silent. I don't know why they didn't see that it helped them, made us more sympathetic, if they just shut up.

I tried to imagine putting Trey in the back of the squad, taking him to Castor. Or Kenny, or Tim Lang, which was impossible to imagine. That just wouldn't happen. All I have to do is remember how I was treated at the scene of Chris Miller's murder. We sat in the back of the ambulance and the back of the squad and talked like colleagues. It was only later my status changed, and before that it was impossible for them to think of me as involved, as anything but another potential victim, as their brother.

Chapter Sixteen

Finally, I just went ahead and called Kelsey. I was nervous, but she acted like she was expecting the call. "Do you want to do something sometime?" I asked.

She paused, and I almost said, "Forget it, bad idea," but she answered: "I've been wanting to go to the antiques mall in Alex." I realized she was recommending a place we wouldn't be recognized, somewhere far from town but not too far. I also realized she had been thinking about this in the weeks since we'd had dinner, too.

Alex was Alexandria, about ninety miles farther up the interstate. It is a resort town, a lake town, but there wouldn't be people from Maurus there in the winter. And it was close enough to go there and back in an afternoon. She said the kids would be at her former inlaws' house for a whole weekend in two weeks. There was a long weekend for school. What about going on that Friday? More insurance against running into people if we went on a Friday. I agreed. I'd pick her up at eleven.

For two more weeks I had to distract myself, but I didn't have much luck. I worked out, helped Frank on a remodel job, and finished the ductwork in my basement. I went driving. I watched television, but I couldn't tell you what I watched. I had all sorts of visions of how that day in Alex would go.

In the end, we didn't go to the antiques mall. We were both giddy and giggly from the moment I picked her up, quite the opposite of the ease of that first dinner with her kids. I went to the door, determined to play it cool, but she looked so beautiful. Her hair was straight and shining, spilling over the hood of her parka. The coat was light blue and fit close to her body, skimming the top of her jeans. I led the way, trying to swallow my smile, and opened the car door for her. She thanked me and slid into the passenger seat. You would have thought my Chevy Cavalier was a sports car. Even the way she pulled down and fastened her seatbelt was sexy.

The atmosphere in the car was electric. It was painful, really, to feel so out of control emotionally. I asked about the kids, but she threw off that topic. She didn't want to be a mom that day. This day was a vacation from all that. About halfway to Alex, she said, "You know, I don't really care about the antiques mall."

I looked at her and raised an eyebrow. "Did you have something else in mind?"

"Well, I've always liked this resort on Gull Lake." She smiled, truly a glorious smile, wide open and her eyes bright.

"Are they open this time of year?" I asked.

"Yes," she said. Still smiling, she added, "And they have a vacancy. Or at least they did when I called Wednesday."

"Well, call them up," I said. She had her cellphone in her hand and made the call. We just looked at each other and laughed. She used her phone to guide us in to Windhover Resort.

It was cabins, which was even better than a lodge. The woman who took my information and my credit card clearly suspected us. She could tell we weren't married. I only gave my name and address when checking in. She probably thought we were having an affair.

"Being spontaneous, are you?" she asked.

"I can't tell you how much I needed to get away," Kelsey said. "I'm so happy to be here."

"Well, it will be pretty quiet this weekend," the woman said. "There will be snowmobilers—the lake is still safe for that. If you want to rent them, it's all in the brochure. Just ring the bell at the house if no one is in the office, after seven a.m. and before six." She handed me the brochure and the key, and we went off to cabin eight.

Kelsey shed her parka and dropped her big purse at the door. I realized now the bag probably had extra clothes and at least a toothbrush in it. She threw herself on the bed, her arms stretched to either side. "Oh Lord, I haven't felt this free in a long, long time."

And it's true. We both felt free. We'd been locked inside the Chris Miller murder for three four months, through all the holidays and the long winter. It almost felt like we were here under false identities, like we weren't ourselves. No one knew us and the murder was very far away. I was focused in that moment on how bad it must have been for her, with the kids. With

Chris's family, the confusion of yet another change after the divorce and remarriage, this one even more difficult for the boys. I'd also heard something about problems over the money that had been raised to support the family, what the split should be between Nicole and the kids. But we didn't have to talk about any of that. We were Paul and Kelsey. Residents for one weekend only of cabin eight, Windhover Resort, Gull Lake, Alexandria, Minnesota.

I wanted to rip her clothes off and climb under the covers right away, but I was pretty sure that wasn't how she expected things to go. She lay on the bed with one arm flung out to the side, the other folded over her forehead. She was in a private space, or just enjoying being away. I went back to her bag and picked it up.

"I think you might have me at a disadvantage," I said. "I really didn't think this was going to happen." I reached in and pulled out a makeup case. "Did you bring two toothbrushes?" I asked.

She propped herself up on her elbows. "I brought something even better than that," she said.

I raised my eyebrows again. I reached for the zipper, half teasing and half asking permission to look inside.

"Go ahead," she said. "Open it." I delicately peeled back the zipper, cradling the contents in my hand. I shuffled through the bag, tossing the eye shadow and other stuff onto the nightstand. Then I found it, the beautiful blue-wrappered square of a condom, two of them folded together. I pulled my hand back and covered my mouth.

"Kelsey O'Neal Miller!" I said. "What is this?" and I tapped on them to reveal the corner without lifting them from the bag. I walked toward the bed. "And why are there only two?"

She shrugged. I pushed back on the edge until they were safely in the bag and took out a lipstick instead. I dropped the makeup case and sat down next to her on the bed. I turned to face her. I put my hand on her stomach, lifting her sweater. She flinched just a bit, still propped on her elbows, looking up at me without fully turning her head. I twisted off the top of the lipstick with my other hand, popping the lid off onto the bed.

I straddled her then, and she shifted higher on the bed. I tugged the sweater higher, and she reached down and pulled it with both hands over her head. Her stomach was flat and her skin was smooth and even. She was wearing a lacy pink bra that clasped in the front. I hovered with the lipstick over her. She reached up and took it from my hand, then sat up so we were facing each other like kids on a swing. She tugged at my belt and freed my T-shirt from my jeans. I helped by pulling off my shirt and unhooking my belt, leaving it hanging open.

She applied the lipstick to her mouth heavily, sensually, then leaned in and kissed me square in the center of my chest. She made small, perfect kisses across my collarbone, and I lifted her face and kissed her on the mouth.

I'm afraid we made a mess of the bed in cabin eight with that lipstick. And I, too, couldn't remember a time I'd felt that free.

Afterward, though, I made a discovery. She had a burn scar. It was on the inside of her arm, pretty significant. "Kelsey, how did you get this scar?" She pulled her arm away and hid it.

"That's nothing," she said, crinkling up her nose.

"No it isn't," I said, grabbing her wrist. She just looked at me.

"I'm a klutz," she said. She kept her arm against her body, not giving it back to me. I let go of her wrist.

"No, you're not," I said. Kelsey had been on the volleyball team briefly in high school. She quit that, too, when she started dating Chris.

She was quiet, but she looked a little stressed. I knew she wanted to tell me something but couldn't. "Did someone hurt you?" I asked.

She shook her head, no. After a pause, I asked, "So what happened?"

"I knocked a pot off the stove. Boiling water. It splashed my arm."

I didn't believe her. Not the way she hid her arm. "Was someone else involved?"

She was quiet, then she nodded. "I don't want to talk about it," she said.

"Is that person still around?"

"No," she said.

I didn't want to ask if it was Chris. I didn't want to bring him into the room yet.

Eventually we talked about Chris's death when we talked about the kids. Zach didn't understand what had happened at all, and Kyle was sketchy on the situation, thinking his dad would come back someday, thinking he was off on police work or at Nicole's.

At the funeral he knew all the fanciness was because his dad was a hero, but he kept thinking Chris was there somewhere in the crowd of policemen and he just couldn't find him. He'd kept asking, "Where's Daddy?" And when Kelsey pointed at the casket, which was closed but topped with his photo, Kyle just got frustrated. "Not his picture. I want Daddy!"

They had all seen a therapist a few times, she told me, paid for by the police department. Or not exactly paid for, because only the children and Chris's actual wife, Nicole, qualified. She had to pay out of pocket to go with the children, and once she figured that out, she stopped the treatment. The therapy wasn't helpful anyway, she said. But the point had been made to the boys that Daddy wasn't coming back and it was serious business. Still, Kyle had the most trouble, good days and bad days.

I told her I'd been offered counseling, too, but hadn't taken them up on it. We were still in bed on Saturday, late morning. We'd ordered pizza to the cabin the night before, but hadn't moved much from the bed. We were going to have to go out, however. I, for one, wanted to go to the drugstore for more supplies, and it had been a long time since we finished the pizza.

"It could be helpful for you, Paul," she said.

I was skeptical, staring at the ceiling.

"It's been pretty rough, huh?" she said.

I pulled her closer. "I can handle it."

"Anybody would've done what you did," she said. "Any of those other cops would have done that. All you did was keep it from being a double homicide."

I kind of wished she hadn't thought it through like that. I wondered, like always, exactly how much conversation had taken place about me. She rolled over so we were facing each other. She looked good in the morning, natural, relaxed. Her face was small against the pillow. The Windhover had quality ones. I moved my face closer to hers, and found it reassuring, lying there looking her in the eye. It felt OK to talk about the murder.

"It just caught me totally off guard," I said. "It was reflex, really. I heard the shot—I didn't even see Chris go down. I guess I knew what was happening, but I didn't even think."

She nodded. She was very sweet. "I'm so glad nothing happened to you," she said. And I felt grateful to her. I believed her.

I don't know why I couldn't get this comfort from Julie, but I couldn't. Maybe it was Kelsey's part in the whole thing, or our history. We had both been changed by this event, both kicked out of our lives and into different ones. There was no place for either of us, the ex-wife and the cowardly partner, in the heroic martyr's story.

"And it's not true that others would have done the same thing," I said. "They wouldn't have. I would've thought, with my training, that I would have acted differently. I could have just ducked down. The car door would've protected me. I could've gotten a better look at the guy—"

"And gotten yourself killed," she said.

I was quiet a minute. I pushed her hair back behind her ear. "No, I wouldn't have gotten killed."

"You don't know that," she said.

"Yes," I said. "Yes, I do."

She didn't push me, or ask me how I knew, so I didn't have to tell her. I didn't have to give her the scenarios I'd run through all those weeks, the many ways in which I could have done the right thing and seen the guy, and stopped the guy.

"Life didn't go the way we thought, huh?" Kelsey said. "Chris kind of screwed things up for both of us."

I sighed and rolled away from her. "I screwed things up for myself," I said. "Chris didn't do anything."

"Well, he sure wasn't the hero everyone is making him out to be," she said. I was quiet. I hadn't expected her to say that— no one had said that, as far as I knew. I had never said it aloud. You couldn't say something like that. But here she had, she just came out with it.

"He was in the wrong place at the wrong time," I said.

Now she was quiet. "Yeah, maybe."

I turned, propping myself on my elbow and raising my eyebrows. "What?"

She pursed her lips and shook her head.

"Do you know something, Kelse?"

She rolled onto her stomach, put a hand to each side of her head, propped on her elbows, looking down into the pillow.

"Kelsey, do you know something? Something you didn't tell the police?"

"It isn't anything," she said. "It can't be anything."

I tugged on her elbow and sat up. "Tell me."

She shook her head, and I tugged her again, more insistently. "It's silly," she said.

"Nothing is silly. Anything could be a lead." I got out of bed and picked up my jeans and boxers from the chair. I pulled them on, getting serious. "Come on, Kelsey. Tell me."

She sat up and pushed some of the bedding away, but then she put her hands over her face. "You're going to think I'm an idiot for even suggesting there's something to it," she said.

"Well then, just tell me," I said. I picked up my socks and sat back on the bed to put them on. "What does it matter?"

She dropped her hands into her lap. "It's just that, now we've made a big deal about it. But it isn't anything."

"Kelsey," I said, looking back at her. "Tell me."

"It's just pot," she said.

"Pot?" I stopped putting on my socks. I turned and folded a leg beneath me, directing my full attention to her.

"Yeah," she said. "I know. It's stupid. I mean, pot is no big deal. People don't even get arrested for it anymore."

"What about pot and Chris?" I asked. Chris was a pretty straight-and-narrow guy. He was strict about drugs and DUIs. After the bust on the meth house, he was always suspecting people of being on meth or of there being meth labs everywhere. He kind of drove me crazy.

"He thought there was a guy growing pot, outside of town."

That was possible. "Who?"

"Jim Kastenbauer," she said.

I remembered Jim from that summer with Frank's friends. I hadn't thought about him in years. I smiled. "That's very possible," I said.

"See, it's stupid," she said.

214

"It's not stupid. But I don't see Jim Kastenbauer shooting anyone, ambushing a cop behind Arnold's Bar over pot."

"I know. It's totally ridiculous. See why I didn't tell the cops about it?"

I refocused. I needed to find out what this was about. Kelsey was clearly spooked, and probably not for nothing.

"When was this? This suspicion of Jim?"

She made a face. "Yeah, see, it wasn't even this past summer. It was the summer before last. Before we split up."

"Did Chris have trouble with Jim? Did Jim threaten him or something?"

"I don't know what there was between them. Chris didn't like Jim. He said Jim thought he was smarter than him, treated Chris like he was an idiot. Not about pot. But when Chris stopped him for a traffic stop or speeding or something."

That was easy to picture. Jim was smarter than Chris, but he didn't need to provoke the guy. Jim wouldn't care much for cops either. Maybe he'd slipped further into his hippie farmer identity. Who knew what he was up to.

"How do you even know Jim Kastenbauer?" she asked. I told her about Frank and following the Graniteers. I asked what she knew about him, which wasn't much, just that he was farming on his dad's land, living in a trailer.

"Damn, that sounds like when I knew him," I said. The Kastenbauer dairy farm wasn't even technically in Maurus. It was in the township, so still within our jurisdiction, but it wasn't a place I had concerned myself with very much. And in the two years I was on the force, Jim Kastenbauer's name had not come up once.

"At first Chris thought he was into meth," Kelsey continued. "All *Breaking Bad* with that trailer and stuff. A mild-mannered guy with a trailer and not really socializing in town."

I had to laugh at that, too. "Chris was kind of big on uncovering local meth rings," I said.

"Yeah, but it wasn't that. Something was going on with Chris. Chris was involved in something. That summer he was gone a lot, out all weekend sometimes, coming home tanned. He said it was a case he was working on, but he couldn't talk about it."

"What?" That didn't sound right at all. There was no undercover stuff going on.

"I figured he was having an affair. Then it turned out I was right, he *was* having an affair, with Nicole. But he insisted the affair didn't start until around Christmas. Not that summer."

That sounded right to me, but I didn't let her know I knew about the affair the whole time. I thought it might even have started at the Christmas party.

"I confronted him when I found out about Nicole. I asked him what had been going on all summer. And he got quiet. He said that wasn't an affair. He said it was an investigation, but that it had fallen through. He said it had ended and I wasn't to say anything to anyone about it."

That didn't make any sense at all. We didn't have secret investigations. I tried to remember back to the summer of 2011 and what was going on. Everything had been pretty routine.

"I figured he was lying. That either it was a different affair, or he didn't want me to know how long he had been fooling around with Nicole. I said he was a coward—"

I probably cringed when I heard the word. She looked at me, kind of scared. "I'm sorry," she said.

"No, no, it's OK," I said. I reached out and touched her leg.

"But what is a coward if not someone who knowingly hurts someone and won't do anything to stop?" she continued, softer now. "That's the real definition. A cheater who doesn't have the courage to make a choice, make a decision, stop hurting his wife and kids."

She was really angry. I moved closer and squeezed her knee beneath the bedspread. I wanted to change the subject. "I'm sorry," I said.

She shrugged. "No, I'm sorry. I haven't thought about the affair for a while. I can't really talk about that anymore. No one wants to hear about it."

"You can talk to me," I said.

"I know," she said. "You can talk to me, too."

"Hey," I said. "Should we get up? I'm really hungry." That's how we left it, but I knew I'd have more questions, and I might have to pay Jim Kastenbauer a visit.

Chapter Seventeen

It was going to be tricky, but Kelsey and I weren't about to stop seeing each other after that weekend. We had the talk, too. "My boys like you," she said. I wasn't going to start hanging out at her house with her boys, not for a good long time anyway. "That would be a disaster," I said. "Not for me, or us, but, you know, people will flip out. Your former inlaws for sure."

Zach was in pre-school Tuesday and Thursday mornings, so Kelsey came to my house after she dropped him off. We had a couple of hours and were mostly just eager to, you know, jump each other's bones. We were in that silly, happy phase. I guess the danger of getting caught, the secrecy about our relationship, made it more exciting and kept our interest high. But I also think I was energized by the sudden release from isolation. It was a thrill to get texts on my phone again, to hear the phone vibrating, to have someone who wanted to talk to me who wasn't related to me. Sometimes I tried to think about a future for us in Maurus. But I didn't ever get very far with that.

My mom, of course, knew right away something was up. For one thing, I was eager about going to church. It was a way I could see Kelsey, even from across the sanctuary. And I was happier in general. One day in her kitchen she asked me, "Who's the girl?" She caught me off guard, being so direct. "And why's it a big secret?"

"Oh Mom, there's no girl," I said.

"Yes there is," she said. "You can't fool me."

"*Oh Kay*," I said, as if she were crazy but there was no use arguing with her. This was how Frank and I usually tried to get her off our backs. I don't know why, because the tactic wasn't effective. As usual, she just continued with her advice.

"Don't get me wrong," she said. "I'm all for it. You need something positive in your life. I just hope you're not seeing somebody's wife—not going to get yourself in trouble."

"Whatever you want to think, Mom. But there's no girl."

"Whenever you're ready to tell me about it," she said, still serious and concerned, "I'll be here."

I also couldn't stop thinking about Jim Kastenbauer. What had happened between him and Chris? I knew it wasn't about pot. When I was at the academy in Brainerd, we spent a few days on drug laws in the state and arrest policies. It was brought home to us that we shouldn't hassle people about a little pot. At the same time, growing pot for sale and distribution was serious. If someone had a pipe on his person, or a joint, we were encouraged not to take that too seriously. But in a car, if we found a bag of pot, or if a person was carrying a large quantity (this amount was never specified—we'd know it when we saw it), then an arrest was warranted. If we suspected someone was a dealer, that was different. The person changed categories, from an alternative kid or aging hippie into a criminal, a deviant, someone with more going on than just a bad habit.

The concept applied in more ways than one, of course. An addict of any sort was seen as a victim; the criminal was the dealer. The addict could be our friend, lead us to the dealer. Addicts were somewhat to be pitied—although of course they could be toxic to a community. They could be stealing or mugging to get money for a fix. They could be violent and unable to control their violence. But in actuality . . . well, yes, there was stealing and breaking into houses, but not for pot. Drunks were dangerous. Meth heads and heroin addicts were very dangerous. But potheads, well, they seemed fundamentally not a risk. Like the worst that could happen is they would fall asleep. Which was a problem if they were driving, but otherwise not so much. They were not robbing or stealing to pay for pot, and they were not violent.

The previous summer, two city workers discovered all these pot plants growing near the Quarry Trails subdivision in a place where excavators and others could dump clean fill. The lot was overgrown with weeds, and on one side some kids had carved out moguls for riding BMX bikes. The guys from the city were bringing over a load of fill and one of them noticed (probably from experience) the leaf. It wasn't a stray maple seedling. On closer inspection, they discovered there were about a hundred plants out there, somewhat scattered in with the weeds to reduce the chance of detection.

The city guys called us, and we went over with Brent from the Castor drug task force. Brent was quite sober about the situation, unlike me and Kenny and the city workers, who had all but exhausted our *Bill & Ted's Excellent Adventure* routine. He was also not at all concerned. Looking around, it was going to be impossible to tell who in these neat, new houses had planted the plants. Brent had done a quick online search, and there were no known dealers or folks with drug offenses in that neighborhood. He told the city workers to just destroy the plants and forget about it. Back at the station, the jokes about Minnesota weed and ditch weed went on for about a week, and then we stopped. But for me, we were in new territory. If we didn't really care—if the task force didn't really care—about growers, then we'd moved pretty far in decriminalizing pot. I mean, Tim Lang and Larry Peterson talked about a time in the '90s when you could get jail time for being caught with a single joint.

No one, not even Chris, would have a top-secret pot investigation going on. It just wouldn't be worth it. This idea that he told Kelsey he was on the job was bothering me. I didn't remember anything about that summer, certainly not Lisa Hawkins and her dropped missing person case. I didn't ask Kelsey about it again, because it seemed more likely he was covering another affair before Nicole. I also started thinking about what he said to Gary, to take care of Nicole if anything happened to him. Maybe he had been into something. Maybe it hadn't been entirely grandiose.

Finally, I went over and paid Jim Kastenbauer a visit. He had been busy since the Graniteers days. The trailer was more like a little pre-fab house. He'd built it out. This was early April and a late snowfall had melted under a day's rain. It's probably the only truly ugly time of year in this area. The patches of snow were sickly-looking, and the fields were still frozen but mostly exposed. The lawn was muddy—Jim had a dog. His car was parked under a metal awning on a concrete pad, and the dog was chained up to one of the posts. There were buckets and dog toys around, and a grill that had been left out all winter.

He had a bunch of garden beds made out of cement blocks in neat rows in front, and one of those plastic buildings where people start plants off to the side. It looked like a handmade job, and I thought briefly he could grow pot in there. But there didn't seem to be heaters or fans, just plastic sheeting over wood. This time of year it would be too cold for pot plants to grow outside, even under plastic. Next to it was a very large fenced garden plot. Everything seemed very out in the open. And kind of pathetic, small and poor.

The dog announced my arrival, and Jim came to the door. I saw him looking out at me, but then he disappeared back inside. When I came to the door, he opened it and greeted me.

"Hiya, Wonderboy."

The door was open just enough for me to use it as an invitation to come inside. I pulled it wider and stepped inside, and Jim stepped back just enough to make room for me to enter. It took me a minute to get my bearings. The place was a bit like a science lab and lit up like a UFO. On the counter in front of me were jars of beans, a couple jars with mesh metal lids filled to various levels with sprouts, and a bunch of plastic yogurt containers marked with scientific names. The place was damp and smelled like dirt.

The light came from the odd glow of fluorescent lamps set over flats of seedlings. He had installed lights under the kitchen cabinets and had rows of little seed pots under them on both sides of the sink. There were more flats with lights covering the table and benches of the built-in banquette, and larger seedlings in trays along the floor leading back to the bedroom. The only thing on the counter not related to plants was a large bottle of Jack Daniel's.

Jim didn't move from his place near the door, and I stood at the edge of the counter, just staring.

"You've been busy," I said. Jim looked more or less the same after ten years. The lines in his face had deepened, and his skull was more pronounced under his thinning hair. Without a cap, he looked much older. His sadness had changed to a sort of edgy resignation, not bitterness or anger but right on the brink of both. There was no warmth in him. He could have used a grow lamp himself, or maybe it was too much artificial sunlight and not enough real warmth that had shrunk him. He was still lanky, wearing a long-sleeved gray T-shirt over a white undershirt, tucked into jeans that were as faded as the pair I'd last seen him wearing at the ballpark all those years ago. And just like then he wore work boots, which had been tracking mud through the trailer.

"Someone mentioned your name not long ago, and I just thought I'd come over and see how you're doing," I said.

"How I'm doing? I'm doing great," he said. "As you can see, I've made incredible progress."

I chuckled, making a joke of it. But I also looked around more closely. The seedlings were carefully marked with colored tabs, a variety of things I wouldn't be able to recognize, not at that stage. But they weren't pot plants, and there was nothing to suggest a hydroponic operation. Later, I decided, I'd ask to use the bathroom and check that out. But this looked like regular spring planting to me. Excessive, but not necessarily suspicious.

"And you?" Jim said, the hint of a smile on his lips. "You have distinguished yourself recently, too."

I just looked at him, not sure what to say. It was a little weird that he wasn't asking me in, that we weren't moving to the living room. I just nodded. I pointed to the couch, "Mind if I sit down?"

"No, no, make yourself at home," he said. He stayed by the door until I was seated—maybe he was thinking about whether to offer me a drink or not. He didn't, just came and settled into the recliner. I was sitting in an overstuffed chair facing him. "So, is this a business call?" he asked.

This was going to be harder than I thought. He didn't trust me. For the first time since Chris's death, someone was treating me like a cop. But I didn't want to be a cop in this situation. I wasn't a cop. "I don't have any business, not anymore—unless you're looking for some landscaping work," I said.

"You criticizing my lawn?" he asked. I couldn't tell if he was serious or not.

"No, it's just that . . . I've been doing some landscaping with Frank."

He nodded. "I heard something like that." Now it was my turn to be suspicious. Why would he hear that about me? We both sat with our suspicions, in awkward silence. I wasn't sure what else I had planned on talking to him about. I didn't want to bring up Chris right away. I didn't want to mention Kelsey at all. Clearly the farm wasn't a good subject to introduce, but I didn't have anywhere to go. The room was very small and there was a very large elephant filling it.

"Frank is doing well," I said, though he hadn't asked.

He nodded.

"It turns out Frank is the smart one," I said.

"Frank was just lucky," he said. "Frank knew his capabilities and no one expected more of him."

This is the way I remembered Jim. He didn't say much, but when he did, it was surprising. Distracting. Is that what the problem was, high expectations? Was it too much to expect someone to attend to his partner at the scene when shots were fired? Every conversation, again, was really about Chris. I needed to get the focus off of me.

I noticed the stacks of books around—including a full bookshelf behind him. Whiskey, plants, and fine literature. That was Jim Kastenbauer.

"What are you reading?" I asked, gesturing toward a stack of books on the end table.

He smiled and picked up the top book, a dog-eared paperback. "Nietzsche," he said. "Heard of him?"

I'd heard of him of course, but I had no idea what he was about. "Heavy stuff, no?"

I wished he would offer me a glass of water. I would feel much better somehow with something to drink. As it was, I felt like he was on the verge of throwing me out. He just looked at the book cover and returned it to the stack, not answering my question.

"What's it about?" I asked.

"Superman," he said. "It's about superman."

I didn't know what he meant by that, if he was joking or not. "You have quite a garden out there," I said.

"Yup," he said. "I'm quite the gardener."

"Are you still into the organic farming? That seems to be getting bigger and bigger."

"We're still strictly Roundup ready out here. Monsanto central. You wouldn't believe our yields. Of course, it's not fit for human consumption. Not really fit for animals either."

"So you aren't making any headway with your father?" I asked.

"Next year he's giving me an acre behind my house," he said. "If I don't get in any trouble." He said this last part with a sneer, and it stuck with me. What trouble was Jim's father worried about?

"What are you going to do with it?" At least he was talking to me.

"I'm going to pasture it and get some sheep. It will take years to get the soil back in any kind of shape. I've got a quarter acre out there in crops now." He was talking, but he wasn't getting any friendlier. I remembered his comment all those years ago about not wanting to be a poor truck farmer. "I haven't seen you at the farmer's market."

I shook my head. "Why don't you get your own land and some of those free range cows?" I asked. He snorted.

"No one's going to give me a loan," he said.

"Not even with this land—I mean, you're going to inherit it someday, or your father cosigning?"

"I'm afraid I'm stuck here," he said. "Believe it or not, this place still has a large mortgage on it, and the old man's let me know he's not going to be party to any of my nonsense. Starting a farm without support or machinery would be a fool's errand."

"Sounds kinda mean," I said.

"My dad? He's a hard motherfucker. His way or the highway. Or no, not even the highway. Just his way."

"So you're making a go of it with the farmer's markets?"

He shook his head again. "Child support—the younger boy's in college now, the girl will follow."

"So what else are you doing?"

He looked at me sharply. "I'm resourceful," he said.

That was the only opening, the only suggestion that he was involved in anything that wasn't on the up-and-up. Mostly, he struck me as a frustrated guy, a bit of an eccentric. I couldn't really understand the idea of not being able to get out of the situation. If he was resourceful, why not move away? Why not go to the Cities, or partner up with someone in this new natural food world? Why let yourself stay chained to this place, like the dog out there, just getting increasingly bitter about it?

"So you never remarried," I said.

I knew I made a false step. He was wondering what my game was. And he made his move. "Not me. But you? I thought you'd be married and have a couple kids by now."

I must have blushed, because he said, "Delicate subject, Paul?"

I shook my head. "No, not at all."

"Maybe you are playing house with someone else's wife?" he said. I'm sure I blushed deeper, although of course it wasn't true.

"I wouldn't do that," I said.

"No, no, of course you wouldn't," he said. He was staring at me, and I felt accused, though I couldn't have said what I was being accused of. The whole thing was uncomfortable. I broke my gaze and looked at my hands in my lap.

Jim stood up and went over to the counter. He took down a glass, only one, and poured himself a half inch of whiskey. Then he came back. It just made things worse. I didn't know what I was supposed to do. I couldn't leave—he'd just poured a drink. One thing was clear—Jim was now in charge of this interview.

He leaned toward me, resting his elbows on his knees, and swirled the whiskey in the glass.

"So tell me the truth, Paul," he said. "What do you remember about that night?"

"What night?" I asked, though I knew what he meant. He sat up and took a sip of whiskey, then resumed his position, leaning toward me but without giving the impression he was trying to get closer to me. He didn't answer.

"The night Chris Miller was shot?" I asked. That phrase was like a single entity, a title, a solid thing. I'd heard it said so many times, said it myself so often, but it still sounded strange here, in this room.

I tried to make a joke of it, or get control back. "I thought we were talking about wives."

Jim put the glass down on the end table, pushing the pile of books back to make room. Then he opened a small drawer in the table and took out a pack of cigarettes. He did offer me one of those, but I don't smoke.

"What happened?" he asked.

"The guy pointed the gun at me," I said. "And I panicked."

He didn't look at me as he lit the cigarette and took the first drag. "Who?" he asked, the cigarette in his mouth.

"The shooter," I said. I felt stupid. What was he getting at?

Jim leaned back, then nodded as he blew out a long stream of smoke. "Yeah, but who was it?"

Now it was my turn not to answer. What the hell was he up to?

Jim sat up straight again and cocked one eyebrow. Did he really think I knew and just wasn't saying? Did he think I was an accomplice? I know some people thought that, but not anyone rational, not anyone who knew me.

"I didn't see him," I said. "Not really. He was wearing a dark hoodie. He was tall, about six foot."

"That's what they said in the paper," he said. "That was the description."

"Yeah. Because that's what I told them. What I saw."

"A guy in a hoodie, about six feet tall," he said.

"He pointed the gun at me. He shot Chris in cold blood," I said. I didn't know why I felt this need, still, to defend myself. Now I really wanted to leave, but I couldn't without looking guilty of something. Of hiding something.

He took another drag on the cigarette. "Not the murder weapon, though," he said.

"What do you mean?"

"The murder weapon was a shotgun," he said.

"Yeah," I said.

"He pointed a shotgun at you?"

I couldn't figure out his game. Of course it was a shotgun. That was the murder weapon. I tried to turn things back to him. Ask a question instead of answering a question. "What other kind of gun would it be?"

He didn't take the bait. He would have been a great interrogator. "Just so you're clear," he said. "I mean, you know what you saw. I don't. I wasn't there." He took another long drag on the cigarette and leaned back, exhaling a column of smoke. We were silent a moment.

"Were you?" I asked. My voice was steady and clear, although I didn't feel even close to steady. Jim didn't flinch, didn't react, didn't change his expression at all.

"I don't go to bars much," he said. "In fact, I don't go out much at all."

"What about that night?"

He shrugged. I didn't like it at all, but I couldn't bring myself to ask him again. I didn't have the confidence. I couldn't play the cop here, not with Jim.

"Look," I said, "if you know something about that night, you should tell the police."

He nodded, and tapped the ash from his cigarette onto a saucer on the end table.

"There's an anonymous tip line," I said. I didn't like how much I sounded like a cop.

"Anonymous, huh?" he said. He picked up the glass of whiskey. "And they follow up on all these tips?"

"Are you saying you already reported something? That it wasn't followed up?"

"I'm not saying anything," he said. "It's all very interesting."

"No it isn't," I said. "What's going on, Jim? If you know something, why don't you just tell me? Why don't you tell me what was between you and Chris?"

He squinted and cocked his head. "What do you mean, what was between us?"

"I know there was something, an altercation of some kind." He took another drag on his cigarette while I was speaking.

He shook his head, blowing out the smoke. "There was no altercation," he said, his face expressionless.

"Then what's your interest? How are you involved in this case?"

"I'm not involved," he said, as if the very idea was ridiculous. "I'm not involved at all."

"But there's something," I said.

"No, Wonderboy, there's not anything." He leaned back again. "I'm just screwing with you. Relax."

"Don't call me that," I said. He raised his eyebrows again, but didn't say anything. We sat in silence while he smoked.

"It seems to me like you're suggesting the Maurus police aren't doing their job," I said. "But I know they're doing all they can. It's a cold trail. If you know something, anything at all, you should call the tip line. It's not just Maurus working the case. There are state agencies involved, too."

He upended the glass and poured the rest of the whiskey down his throat. "If you say so," he said, putting the glass on the end table with a loud rap. "You're the guy who was there."

"Yeah, well, like you already know. I didn't get a clear look at him."

"I got it. Dark hoodie and six feet tall. Approximately. That's all you saw before you left the scene," he said. I felt my cheeks burn.

"Yes, I left the scene. I backed out of the alley. A coward."

He stood up, taking his glass. "I didn't say anything about you being a coward," he said. "I'm sure most people would have done the same thing—don't let them tell you otherwise. A guy points a gun at you—a shotgun—and what are you going to do?" I couldn't tell, but it still felt like he was mocking me. He had moved back behind the counter to the bottle and was refilling his glass. He still didn't offer me anything.

"If you're not going to offer me a drink, I'll get going," I said, standing up.

"Well, I'm not offering you a drink," he said. He took a sip, not moving from the kitchen. When I got to the door, I stopped and faced him.

"Don't judge the whole police department because of what I did," I said.

He shook his head, still slightly amused. "As far as I can tell, you're the only one who acted honestly. If you're telling the truth, that is."

"Why would I lie?" I asked. "I resigned, you know."

He nodded, but he didn't say anything.

I took the door handle, but I felt more confused than ever. "I don't know what this was," I said.

"Hey, you came here," Jim said. "I figured you had business with me, but I still don't know what it was."

"It was just a visit," I said. "I just wanted to see how you are."

"Yeah, OK."

I opened the door, but before I walked out, something caught my eye. It was behind him, on the counter, under the cupboard. I saw the LED display, the knob and the set of buttons, the antenna, and as I walked onto the narrow top step, I knew what it was I was looking at. The dog barked at me all the way to my car, and I got in, facing the trailer. Jim wasn't at the window. I sat there a moment, thinking he would appear, but he didn't. I sat looking at the dog, who seemed mad, lurching against his chain and barking wildly. It was a police scanner. Jim Kastenbauer had a police scanner. What would he be doing with one of those?

Chapter Eighteen

The next time Kelsey and I got together, we did not jump into bed. I was thinking about Jim and that police scanner. Kelsey was the one who had put me onto Jim, but was it just a random instinct on her part, or did she know he was involved in Chris's death? Nothing about my conversation with Jim led me to believe that he was involved in drugs. Had I invented a connection between him and Chris? Had he suggested it himself? Did he know, for example, that the shooter was not six foot tall and wearing a hoodie? This was when I started to doubt my own account in earnest. This was when I started to think maybe I had invented that vision of the shooter. Had I even looked out the window toward the shots? Had he pointed the shotgun at me? Jim Kastenbauer was only about five foot nine. Did he know the exact height of the killer?

What I wanted to do was go to the cops, ask someone if they'd looked into Jim Kastenbauer, what they knew about him. But lots of people had police scanners, just for entertainment. I wasn't actually sure what I saw on his counter was a police scanner. It could have been a portable weather radio or something. It wasn't even turned on. That box, whatever it was, might have been on that counter for years.

I met Kelsey at the door and gave her a quick kiss.

"What's wrong?" she asked. She turned and I helped her take off her hooded sweater—these gestures were routine now. She could tell instantly when I was having a bad day. As we walked into the living room, I just draped the sweater over the couch.

"Jim Kastenbauer," I said.

She shook her head, as if clearing it of cobwebs. "What about him?"

"I went to visit him," I said. "I had the weirdest time over there."

"Why did you go there?" she asked.

"You know," I said. "The thing you said about pot." I had kept moving, and spoke to her from the kitchen as she slid onto one of the stools at the pass-through.

"You said that was nothing," she said. "You went over to see if he was growing pot?"

I got us a couple of beers and brought them around to the small dining room table. I wanted her to know this was going to be a real discussion. She swiveled on the stool to face me, but didn't come over. "I wanted to see what was up," I said. "I wanted to see if he knew anything."

"About Chris?" She looked lost, perched there on the stool.

"Yeah," I said.

"Why would he know anything about Chris?"

I made a face. Was she going to pretend she wasn't the one who suggested Jim Kastenbauer was involved in the first place? "But you're the one who suspected him."

"I didn't *suspect* him," she said. "I don't suspect him." She got off the stool and came to the table, but neither one of us sat down. "I mean, Chris thought Jim was a wiseass. He thought that about a lot of people."

"But he had trouble specifically with Jim Kastenbauer," I said.

"I don't know," she said, waving her arms, impatient for some reason. "I don't know anything about Chris's life or what Chris was doing."

"Hey, hey," I said, trying to calm her down. "I just want to figure this out."

"Why?" she said, loudly. The thing with women is, it's so hard to just talk to them without things immediately getting emotional. We had barely started talking, and her pitch was rising already. "Isn't that the Maurus Police Department's job? What is there for you to figure out?"

"Come on, Kelsey. Hey, sit down. Have a beer." I sat down, but she remained standing behind her chair.

I passed her a beer and she put her hand over the top of the can, claiming it. "We all want to figure it out," I said, cracking open my can. "Everybody in this town, in this *state,* wants to know who shot Chris Miller. Maybe me most of all. I should have seen who did this. I should know already. I should have pursued him and taken him into custody. I should have shot him."

"It's probably not even someone from around here," she said. "It's probably someone from the Twin Cities, some drug thing or robbery gone bad. Some random thing."

I hadn't expected her to react this way. We both knew it wasn't some drug dealer in the Twin Cities. I guess I'd thought she would be interested in what I discovered and might help me determine what was going on. "It could help me if I put things right. If I was the one to figure it out."

"Well, I didn't mean to say it was Jim Kastenbauer. That was random. I don't think it was about him at all."

"I'm not sure," I said. "We had a really intense visit. And I trust your instincts. You picked that up from Chris, that there was something going on between them."

"You shouldn't have gone over to his trailer," she said, dropping her hand to the table.

"Why not? Why shouldn't I? I know him from before, you know."

"It just—you and I shouldn't be involved in anything about Chris. You more than anyone should not get involved. Let the police figure it out."

My face fell at that, and she saw it. "I'm sorry," she said, softening. "I didn't mean that the way it sounded. I meant I just wish I could get away from it."

"I know," I said. "I don't want to talk about it any more than you do. But it's important. He has a police scanner."

"What?"

"He has a police scanner. In his kitchen. On the counter. For hearing police calls."

"So?"

"He could have heard the call about the welfare check. He could have known we were going over there, that we were going to be behind Arnold's Bar."

"And he could have gotten there and staked it out in the time it took you to get there, from his house in the country?"

"I don't know. We didn't hurry over there. It took some time." I was thinking about Chris and Nicole and their long goodbye kiss. Chris had to collect his stuff, and I was the one in a hurry to leave. I had been thinking about Julie, about going over to her place. Nicole and Chris had started me on that track.

"Lots of people have police scanners," she said. "My stepfather had one. He had it on all the time."

"He was a volunteer fireman," I said. "Jim isn't."

"Oh Jesus, I can't take this shit right now!" she said. She put her hands over her ears like a child.

"Kelsey, what's going on?"

She dropped her arms and looked at me. She pulled out the chair only enough to slide into it. She was trying to keep from crying. She didn't look at me, just started tapping her beer can. "It's all this bullshit about Nicole and the money, I guess."

"Why? What's happening?"

"Nicole and Gary have lawyers, and we had a meeting this morning. It was pretty awful."

I pulled my chair over closer to her so I could take her hand. "Why didn't you tell me?" I asked.

"I was trying not to think about it. It was supposed to be just to sign papers. But they're not agreeing to the split."

"What? Can she do that?"

"It's just . . . that skank thinks I'm trying to get the money. I don't care about the money. I don't want the money. I want my kids to get what's rightfully theirs, what people raised to go to them. She's the one who gets the death benefits. The life insurance. Chris had her as beneficiary for everything. Not even his kids. But she wants it all. She's the one."

"I'm sorry," I said. We hadn't really discussed her financial situation. She talked sometimes about getting a job but hadn't made any serious moves in that direction.

"It's not just that. She's seeing the kids."

"What? When?"

"When they go to Chris's parents' house. She goes over and sees them. They all do things together, like a *family*." She spit out that last word more than spoke it. "She wants to have some kind of formal visitation agreement."

"You don't have to do that, do you?" I asked. It seemed more than unreasonable.

"I can't keep her from seeing them when they're at their grandparents' house," she said. "I don't have a basis for a restraining order or anything."

"You don't have to take them to their grandparents', though, do you?"

She looked down. "I wouldn't do that. They're Chris's parents. They lost their son. I wouldn't take away their grandchildren."

"Are you worried about Nicole doing something?"

She looked at me, anger taking over her features. "Chris wanted them to call her *Mom*," she said. "Can you believe that? As soon as they were married, my kids started calling her *Mom*."

I shook my head. "But they don't think of her as their mom, Kelse."

"That's not the point," she said. "She's not having regular visitation."

"Of course not," I said. She held her beer in both hands. I was afraid she might throw it, or squeeze the can until it exploded all over the room. I just wanted to diffuse the situation a bit.

"Skank," I said. She looked up at me, surprised. When she saw I was imitating her, she smiled.

"Greedy bitch," I said. It felt kind of good, to say something bad, something I'd never actually say to anyone. The fight over the money was pretty low. The idea the kids would call Nicole *Mom* was just embarrassing. Kelsey let out a little giggle.

"Whore," she said.

"Selfish asshole," I said.

"Skanky, no-good, husband-stealing, blond-ass bitch." She was beaming now.

"Ooh," I said, proud of her. Kelsey never talked like this either. "That's good." She let go of her beer and sat up straight, looking at me, her back pressed against the chair. We sat in silence a moment.

Then she pushed her beer away, crossed her arms on the table and put her head down between them. I moved even closer so I could tousle her hair. "Hey," I said.

"When is this going to be over?" she asked, looking up at me, her eyes shining with tears.

"I don't know," I said. "I wish I knew."

Later, when we'd moved to the living room and turned on the television, she said: "I don't hate Nicole."

"Yeah, I know. You never say anything bad about her."

"She did me a favor," she said.

I muted the television, it was a commercial break, and looked at her. But she kept her eyes on the screen. So I faced the screen, too, though I left the TV on mute, and let her speak.

"Chris was not a great husband," she said. When she didn't elaborate, I weighed in. "He could be a handful. Kind of cocky."

She was quiet, and I almost turned up the sound when the show returned, thinking that was all she was going to say. But then she continued, almost at a whisper. "I'm not talking about that."

I took her hand, which was cold, but I didn't look at her. I turned her arm face up, and moved my hand along her forearm to grasp her bicep, my thumb tracing her burn scar. She didn't pull away. When I looked over at her, tears were streaming down her face.

"He could be mean," she said, her voice catching on the words.

I turned to her, held her. "I'm sorry Kelsey," I said. "I'm sorry that happened to you."

She explained to me that the controlling behavior had started in high school. Chris didn't want her to play volleyball or be on teams. He didn't want her to sit with anyone else at the diner or talk on the phone with friends. She said it would have been worse if there had been cellphones then, but even so he'd call her house just to see if she was on the line with someone else. She had to answer the call waiting and just lie. After high school, she almost got away from him. They broke up twice, but he kept pulling her back. He did love her, and she loved him. Then she got pregnant and felt stuck.

"What did your family say?" I asked.

"They liked him—everyone liked him."

"Still, they must have seen it—the controlling stuff."

"He could be subtle about it. When I told my mom, she said he was just attentive, that it was nice. My mom felt like my stepdad never talked to her, like he ignored her. She said she'd like someone to dote on her the way Chris doted on me."

"But why didn't you tell her he hurt you?"

She shook her head. "That didn't happen until later. And it was only a couple of times. He was usually really good. He *was* sweet; that wasn't a lie. He brought me flowers—he was romantic. And he didn't mean to hurt me."

I cocked my head to the side. "Oh, so you made him burn you?"

"That was just once," she said. "And it really was my fault."

I just looked at her, incredulous.

"No, I know," she said. "It was wrong. But we were having a fight. It was in the kitchen and I was cooking. I turned away from him to take the pot of spaghetti and he grabbed it away from me, sloshing it onto my arm. It was an accident. But not, not really. I mean, he wanted to hurt me, just not that bad. I was in shock and he finally took me to the hospital."

"He wasn't going to take you to the hospital?"

"He didn't expect it to be so bad. When he realized, he was sorry."

"Did you ever call 911?" I asked.

"What? Are you crazy? Plus, it wasn't that bad. He just needed to work on his anger issues. Usually he kept it together. He was so sorry afterward about the burn. He took me on a trip up to the North Shore to make it up to me. He felt terrible. That was before Zach was born."

"Kelsey, why didn't you leave him?"

"I couldn't," she said. "I just couldn't."

"Were you scared of him?"

She shook her head. "I thought I could predict it and, you know, handle it. But I needed him. Or I thought I did. I know it sounds stupid."

"It doesn't sound stupid. And he did have a gun."

That shocked her. "No, Paul, no. Nothing like that. He never threatened me. He wasn't dangerous."

"OK," I said, still stroking her arm. She gently pulled it away. "I'm sorry that happened," I said.

"It's OK," she said. "It's over. And really, it wasn't that bad."

I tried to forget about it, but of course what she'd said about Chris bothered me. I thought about the two of them in high school. She had just seemed really into him. She hadn't seemed controlled. But I should have wondered when she quit volleyball. She had been really good. She had friends on that team, Gina and Stephanie.

I laughed, remembering how I thought she went out with Chris to get away from her cousin Ellen, who was always telling her what to do. Out of the frying pan and into the fire.

I thought about that afternoon on Gull Lake in cabin eight, how she lay back and said she felt free, staring at the ceiling, going into herself. Free from a whole lot more than the craziness of Chris's murder. Free, in fact, maybe because of Chris's murder. That was the first time I seriously believed Chris could have done something to get himself killed. That Chris could have hurt someone. That night I even considered whether Kelsey could have hired Jim Kastenbauer to kill Chris for her, but that was, of course, ridiculous. In the middle of the night, my head went in all sorts of directions. It was hard to hold on to the simple truth that Chris Miller was ordinary. Not a hero but not a monster either.

I thought about how Chris had been when we worked together. He was obnoxious, but like Kelsey said, he wasn't dangerous. He was always showing photos of his kids and sharing cute things they said. Kelsey did seem more reserved, quiet, the few times I'd seen them together. I remembered when they'd come to the Graniteers game. She'd lost her spark. I thought it was just having kids, but that was only part of it. She'd learned how to make herself small and uninteresting, so that Chris could shine. Maybe it was self-protection. Kelsey hadn't ever come with him to the bar, and I figured she was just home with the kids. And of course, she was.

And what about Nicole? I'd seen them together at the bar, once their relationship was out in the open. She was so in love with Chris, but they'd only been married six months, still in the newlywed phase. Maybe all she'd seen was the prom king side of him. Dairy Queen and chocolates and flowers. And maybe Chris had been trying to change. Maybe it was a fresh start of sorts for him.

In the end, I wondered why Kelsey told me about the violent streak. What did she want me to do? Or was she telling me because I couldn't do anything? Did she just want to tell someone, before the real version of Chris disappeared, before all that was left was the hero.

Chapter Nineteen

Knowing about Chris made my relationship with Kelsey even more serious. She'd been hurt in a big way. Not how I thought, from the affair, but more deeply and over a longer period of time. As we got deeper into April, she began to have trouble getting away to see me, finding time without the boys. And I ached without her, wanted her with me all the time. I had to restrain myself. I didn't want to be needy—or worse, controlling.

In addition to the predictable fantasies, I was having very complex daydreams about domestic life. I could see myself playing ball with Shane, carrying a sleeping Zach up to bed like those movie dads. I like little kids. And there were daydreams about being on the water—I've always loved the water. Kelsey and me on a boat together, fishing. On a pier, kissing, her foot dangling in the water. Kelsey in a bikini. Me untying it. Swimming at Lower Cormorant Lake. Me and the boys in a canoe on the Horst River, wearing our bright orange life vests.

"Do you like boats?" I asked her one warm Saturday at my house. The boys were with her mom, visiting her aunt and uncle in the Cities for the weekend, and she'd been able to spend the night. The fishing opener was the following weekend, Mother's Day.

"Oh, no," she said. "That's right. You fish."

"You say that like it's a bad thing," I said. She laughed.

"I like boats," she said. "I have a very limited attention span for fishing."

I smiled. "You just haven't been fishing with me yet."

"Oh, OK then. No one gets bored on your boat, huh?"

"No," I said. "And hey, aren't you the girl who picked up frogs with her toes?" I don't know why I said it, or why I hadn't mentioned it anytime before. I was making eggs and she was getting juice. She closed the refrigerator door and placed the juice firmly on the counter. Then she came over and turned me around, away from the stove, to face her.

"What?" I asked, spatula in the air, sausage links sizzling in a pan behind me.

She put her hands on my cheeks and kissed me, a long, slow, passionate kiss. "I knew right then you were the one for me," she said.

I'm not sure how I looked. I was taken off guard. I didn't think she'd forgotten that day at Frogtown, but had always thought it didn't really mean anything to her. In a way, her oversized response to my comment seemed like a joke at my expense.

"I'm surprised you even remember it," I said softly, turning back to the stove.

"What? Are you kidding me?" She stood behind me and put her hands around my waist, pressing her head into my back.

"I mean, nothing happened. Afterward."

She straightened up and moved her arms around my chest. "It was the most romantic thing that ever happened to me," she said.

I just turned and looked at her, putting down my spatula. She held me tighter, pressing her hips into mine. "What are you talking about?" I asked.

"It was the first time a boy ever looked at me like I was beautiful," she said.

I put my arms on her shoulders, looking past her face into her hair. The curls were gone, but her hair was still flecked with gold where it caught the sunlight from the kitchen window. I hadn't realized I was so transparent, at fourteen, but of course I was. "It was the first time I thought a girl was beautiful," I said. I ran my fingers through her hair, brushing it back over her shoulder. "Even just seeing you out of the corner of my eye, from my bike, from a block away, I knew you were beautiful."

She leaned into me and rested her forehead against my shoulder. I put my hand on her neck, under a golden wave of hair. "You are beautiful," I said.

She shifted slightly, even deeper into my arms, and tilted her head up to kiss me. "I love you," she said.

"I love you, too."

I turned so I could switch off the burner under the sausage and eggs and walked her backwards. We moved together, kissing, down the hall to the bedroom. I was glad not to be fourteen, with that youthful awkwardness. I was glad she was not fourteen, too. Her body was strong and responsive. And yet, all those years meant nothing, and we made love with the innocence and freshness of teenagers, something that was not part of our usual courtship. The passion and hunger, yes. But the innocence, the discovery, the newness—that came from our first encounter on Third Street all those years before.

Afterward, we started again with new eggs. Then we went downstairs to work on the paint job in the basement. Kelsey put her hair in a high ponytail while I set up, pouring some paint into an empty ice cream tub for her to use on the doorframe into the laundry room, setting up the stepladder. After painting, the basement project would be complete. For me, it was another sign of moving on. Frank and I had been working on machinery and lining up seeding jobs. The long winter that started November ninth was coming to an end. Soon I'd be back out there. Kelsey stood on the stepladder and took the plastic container of paint and a brush from me. She looked adorable with her oversized yellow gloves and one of my old, paint-splattered Graniteers T-shirts on.

I wanted to talk more about fishing. I wanted to make a plan, if not for the following weekend, then soon. I wanted to get the fishing licenses at Fleet Farm for me and the boys.

"Did Chris ever take the boys fishing?" I asked.

"No," she said. "He didn't really fish. That wouldn't be his kind of outing."

"What a shame! Especially living where you do, right across from the Horst. I fished there all the time as a kid."

"That wasn't really Chris's speed. He was more into Jet Skis and waterskiing. He did take Shane and Kyle canoeing from our house twice. You can go down the Horst all the way to Castor. I'd bring his truck to pick them up at the end."

"Well, I want to take them fishing. I think Kyle will especially like it."

"He would," she said. "He's a patient guy."

"Aw," I said. "Why do you act like it's some kind of torture? Have they really never been fishing?"

"Zach hasn't," she said. "Chris's dad took Shane and Kyle once, to a cabin on Mille Lacs. They liked it OK, I guess."

"It doesn't have to be anything big," I said. "We could just take some poles over to Frogtown to start. Or there's a public pier at Lower Cormorant Lake."

"Uh, yeah," she said. "Let's see."

"What?"

"Just make a plan with me first," she said.

I couldn't think what her reluctance could be. "We will wear safety vests if you're worried about that," I said.

"No, it's not that. I just . . . I just want us to have our privacy a bit longer."

I don't know if I was more surprised that she said it or that I hadn't expected it. I paused and dipped my brush, then returned to the trim I was working on.

"You don't want people to see me with the boys?" I asked.

She didn't answer, so I said, "Or with you?"

"Not yet," she said. The depth of our secret hit me again then. I realized I'd sort of let it go in my head, wasn't thinking of us as secret anymore, even though I hadn't told anyone about us. It hadn't been hard to keep so far, because no one was interested in my life. But it seemed to me we'd already started to let our guard down. Kelsey parked in the alley behind my house, near my garage, in her car with the old Police Officer Wives Association sticker in the back window and the car seats. I'd wondered what might happen if my mother or Frank showed up at the house unannounced while she was over, but it had never happened.

"I haven't told anyone," I said. "I haven't told Frank, or my parents. No one."

"Me either," she said. She said it like she was proud of her restraint. But I felt sad.

"Not even your mom?"

She shook her head.

"Where does she think you are, all this time you're off with me?"

She smiled. "She thinks I'm having an affair."

"And she doesn't mind?" I asked.

"She minds," Kelsey said, more lightly than I liked. "She's being all quietly judgmental about it. But she sees I'm happy."

"And you don't mind," I asked, "that she thinks that about you?"

Kelsey turned and sat down on the stepladder. She put her brush on the top step, hanging over the bedsheet below. She wiped a strand of hair from her face with her yellow-gloved finger, as if to see me more clearly. She didn't say anything.

"We're not doing anything wrong," I said.

"I know," she said, poking down the long fingers of her gloves. "But people aren't ready."

My brush was dry, but I just kept whisking it back and forth over the chair-rail trim, careful not to get any on the wall above the wainscoting. "People aren't ever going to be ready," I said. She didn't answer.

I turned and dipped my brush in the paint, carefully wiping off the excess on the bucket rim. I took this moment to look at her. She was still playing with her gloves. "Kelsey?" I said. She stopped and looked up at me, clearly and directly.

"No," she said. "They're never going to like it. It's going to be a scandal, if it comes out."

I nodded, and just stood there with my brush hovering over the paint can. "It's Maurus," she said. "There's no point. Everyone is who people say they are. It's set in stone. Chris is the hero. Nicole is the widow. I'm the ex-wife. And you're the guy who left the scene. The coward and the ex-wife."

I felt stung. It was a feeling I'd had a lot, that slap-in-the-face sensation, but not with Kelsey. "No, I don't suppose people will think I should get the girl," I said. It was hard to say.

She looked exasperated, not sad. I wanted her to come down off the ladder and assure me that she didn't feel that way. I wanted her to say she didn't care what everyone else thought, that we'd be OK. But she didn't move from her perch.

"I don't mean it that way, Paul. It's only—it's very complicated. You know how people are. They're going to talk. And I'm not ready for this, for another round of people gossiping about me. People are just beginning to act normal, just starting to talk to me like I'm a regular person."

"Yeah," I said. I couldn't hide my hurt. I knew I shouldn't say anything else, but I couldn't stop myself. "It must be hard for you."

"Paul, just please try to understand. I have to think about the boys. They don't get what's happening, and if people start talking, it's another thing they have to work through. And I have to be respectful of Chris's death. It's only been six months. We need to make it seem like we didn't get together right away."

I turned to the wall, returned to painting, but my hand was shaking slightly. I wasn't going to be able to continue. I went at an unpainted stretch of wainscoting with the brush, to transfer the paint without messing up the wall. "I don't really feel like painting anymore," I said.

She didn't argue with me. "I know it's hard, Paul. I'm sorry." She hopped off the ladder and took her brush to wash it in the laundry room. When my brush was dry, I went over and got her ice cream tub and poured the remaining paint back into the can. Then I knelt to seal the lid, pounding it with the screwdriver I had used to open it. It was satisfying to pound on something and make dents in the lid. When I went into the laundry room, she was pinning up the wet rubber gloves on the line with clothespins.

"I love you, Paul, I do. But you have to respect this," she said. She sounded like she was reasoning with one of her boys.

I nodded, and moved to wash my brush at the sink. She came over and put her hand on my back, but I didn't acknowledge her. When I turned around with the clean brush, she backed up a step.

"Paul," she said. I could barely look at her. "Don't be like this."

"I guess it's just hard for me to see a way forward," I said. "For us."

"Nothing has to change. For now. We'll figure it out. It's simply going to take time," she said.

She leaned toward me and gave me a kiss, placing her hands lightly on my shoulders. I still held the paintbrush, though I let my arms fall to my side. I kissed her back, but we didn't embrace. I couldn't tell if she was reaching out to me or holding me at arm's length. She settled back on her heels and smiled sadly. It was the worst possible look, that pity.

"I'm going," she said. "You don't have to walk me to the door." I nodded.

"Call me, OK?" she said from the top of the basement stairs.

"I will," I said, but I wasn't sure when.

When the kids were in bed that night, she called me instead, and I answered. We kept it simple. She recounted the plot of a DVD she'd watched with the boys that she thought was funny. I guess she thought it was a way to make me feel included, but that's not how I felt. We didn't talk about the future. We didn't talk about anything real. We didn't make any plans.

Then, a few days later, I told my mother. It was another warm day, and she was hanging laundry outside. My mother is a champion laundry hanger. They own an old dryer, but she only uses it after the snow falls. She says they never had a dryer when she was a kid, and her mother hung laundry outside even in winter. "It would freeze on the lines," she told us, "and grandma would bring in the frozen pieces of laundry and lay them on the radiators. As they thawed and dried out, the house would keep moist and smell like clean clothes." That, combined with the ironing that her sisters did from an early age, was one of her favorite memories.

These days, in the new subdivisions like Quarry Trails, they've outlawed laundry lines. The new homeowners don't want to look out and see their neighbors' laundry. They think it is tacky, low class, country. I was surprised when I heard about that. Not allowed to put up a laundry line in your own yard?

Here in my mother's backyard her laundry was on full display to the neighbors, whose houses are close by. She hung her laundry with an eye toward modesty. Underwear and bras she hung in the basement, but socks and washcloths she hung on the inner line with larger items like shirts and pants surrounding them, then sheets and towels on the outermost line to shield the clothing from direct view. She began with the socks, which she had somehow separated to the top of the basket before bringing it outside. She could grab four in her hand and clip them with incredible efficiency, two to a pin, in a single motion fastening them to the line and tugging them straight.

"Mom," I said. "I've been seeing Kelsey Miller."

She froze for a second, shock registering on her face, her hands on the socks and pin. After a pause she went back to work, reaching into the basket at her feet for another bunch of socks.

"What do you mean, *seeing her*?" She tacked four more socks to the line.

"I mean what it always means," I said. "That we're romantically involved."

"How long?" she asked. I didn't know why she was doing this, since she knew I'd been seeing someone in February.

"A couple months."

"Let's go inside," she said. She took the rest of the damp clothes still in their basket with her. I trailed after her like a puppy. I hated this. I wanted no more secrets. That is why I was telling her, even if it got me in trouble with Kelsey.

She put the basket on the kitchen table and faced me. "So, after Chris's death," she said.

"Yes, of course," I said. "After. It was February—March before we got together."

She looked at me for a minute, thinking about it. Then she shook her head. "People aren't going to understand," she said.

"I know."

"Oh Paul, I actually wish it was just someone's wife."

"What?" I couldn't believe this would be so bad. My Catholic mother preferred adultery to a relationship with Kelsey Miller? What was I missing?

"Mom, we're not doing anything wrong," I said.

"Why do you have to make things more difficult for yourself?" she said, her voice pitched high. She was going to cry.

"Why can't you just, you know, do something to help yourself? Do something to move on? Instead of keeping this story alive, reminding everyone, giving them something new to talk about."

"I know," I said. "But I can't help it."

She wiped a few tears from her face. "What do you want me to say?" she asked.

"Nothing. I don't know. I just wanted you to know. Remember you said how happy I seemed? Well, this is why."

She just stood there with the laundry on the table between us. I hadn't ever known my mother to be at a loss for words. It was hard on her, having sons. Neither Frank nor I were all that communicative. "Sorry for the drama," I said.

She held her hand out for mine. I took it. Her hand was cold from being outdoors and the wet laundry. The back of it was soft, but the pads of her fingers were rough and chapped. I'd know those hands anywhere.

"Paul, you're a good person," she said. "You don't deserve any of what has been happening. I want you to be happy. That's all I've ever wanted for my boys. You deserve it." She should have stopped there, yet if she had, she wouldn't be my mother. "But I don't know why you—why you undercut yourself all the time."

"Kelsey's a good person, too," I said. "She deserves to be happy."

She nodded, but she didn't say anything. Then, "I like Kelsey. She just—she has a complicated life."

"Will you tell dad for me?" I asked.

She nodded. "That's probably best."

"Can we go outside and hang up the rest of the laundry now?"

She nodded, and we went back outside. I couldn't help but notice the worry line between her eyebrows. That was me. I put that there.

Chapter Twenty

In May they dedicated a stretch of Highway 41 to Chris. The Chris Miller Memorial Highway, between Maurus and Dasso. I saw the picture on the front page of the local paper. Nicole was front and center, still wearing that oversized police jacket, even on a hot day. Unsmiling, she looked puzzled about the whole thing. Chris's parents and his brother, Gary, stood on either side of her, beaming at the honor. A stretch of highway bearing the Miller name.

There still had been no arrest. There were, as far as I knew, no suspects. And as time passed, people seemed to relax a bit and accept that whoever shot Chris Miller was not going to strike again. It was over, maybe destined to remain a mystery. All that was left now was the commemorative stretch of highway and the broken family, which had been fairly broken even before the shooting.

Kelsey and I talked about moving, but we never got very far. Frank had a reputation now as a landscaper, and we had as much work as we could handle, even occasionally hiring a Mexican guy, Carlo, from Bel Clare recommended by Sister Dominica with the parish outreach ministry, Casa Romero. I worked hard, and I was saving money. I had my house. Kelsey didn't want to be far from her family. Her mother helped her out a lot with the kids. She was worried if she moved the kids that Chris's mother, too, would put up a fuss.

However, we opened up a bit more. Kelsey told her mother about us, and she took the news about the same as my mother had. Disappointed, but what are you going to do? It was summer, so when I went over to Kelsey's house, we did things outside with the boys, mostly at Frogtown Park or in their backyard. Her neighbors, a nice guy who worked with Maurus Quarry and his wife, and a couple with young kids who relocated from Iowa, found out. They were nice to us. The guy from the quarry said it was good she had someone to help her out with the place. The Iowa couple could see I was good with the boys, who played with their kids.

We went to my parents' house and Frank's house and had family to my house. My mom loved having the boys around. She treated them like they were her own grandchildren. She said there really couldn't be too much love for children who lost a parent; they needed all they could get. It was interesting to see her with the boys. In some ways she was more comfortable with them than with Clare and Patty. As a mother of sons, she knew what to do.

I also hadn't expected that I would learn more about myself from seeing my mom with Kelsey's boys. She was full of stories about how Frank and I were as children, as brothers. I hadn't heard some of the stories before. Shane especially loved to hear them. He loved being at her house, and every time he wanted to know where Frank and I had built the fort, and hear about when we kept rabbits until a hawk got them, and about the day Frank climbed up on the roof. She told him that I used to build bicycles, and in fact I had built one out of two wrecked bikes. Shane wanted me to teach him how to do that. When Shane got too enthusiastic about me, or wanted to do a project like building a bike, I could see that Kelsey was worried. She'd back off and I wouldn't see them for a few days.

This was easy to do, because I was working long days. Frank and I worked until seven or eight most nights, and at least a half day on Saturday. Kelsey could back off during the week and just check in with a text. Most nights I was too tired to drop by after work. I just wanted to shower and eat and go to sleep.

Kelsey and I didn't flaunt our relationship. I didn't go to Shane's baseball games, although he wanted me to. I played catch with him at Frogtown Park across the street, and he and Kyle and I fished like I had as a kid. That was on Sundays. I never stayed overnight at Kelsey's house. Some nights she would get her mother to watch the kids and come to my house. A few times, when she asked me to, I picked up the boys at her mother's house. Mrs. O'Neal didn't warm to the idea like my mother did, and I wasn't invited to their family gatherings. I suppose her daughter had more to lose. She definitely had more choices.

One of the nice things about a small town, at least in Minnesota, is that people are polite. They aren't going to say anything mean to your face. We tried to make it easy for everyone, let them get used to the idea. At church, I still sat with my parents. Kyle waved to me and smiled, and I nodded back to him. No one turned around to see who he was waving at. When it came time to offer the sign of peace, Kelsey and I made a peace sign to each other from across the rows. After Mass, we still left by different doors.

Time did not, however, make people forget I'd left the scene, and sometimes they let me know in the worst way. I was feeling comfortable enough about things by Memorial Day that I had signed up for the men's baseball league. Tim was no longer on the team—he was coaching his son's team, so there weren't any officers. There were twelve guys signed up, and I knew all of them in one way or another. I'd been playing ball with these guys for most of my life. There was even a guy who had been on the Graniteers with me.

I expected to play shortstop or third base. But when I looked at the roster that first game, I wasn't on it. Chuck, who put together the lineup, didn't say anything. I sat down, thinking I'd be subbed in later in the game. In the third inning of six, Chuck put in the other two guys on the bench, but not me. I went and asked him why he didn't put me in.

He looked me in the eye, and I could tell right away this wasn't going to be good. He looked back at the roster when he gave me the news. "Well, I was going to put you at right field, but *I can't really trust you to back anyone up,* can I?" He looked at me when he said that last part, for emphasis, or to make sure I understood him. As I say, I'd had that slap-in-the-face sensation a few times, but this was the worst. In fact, it sort of knocked the wind out of me.

I couldn't believe Chuck would say that to me—think so little of me that he would say that to my face. No sugarcoating, no excuse, no putting me off until I figured out what was going on. He was direct. They couldn't kick me off the team, but they could keep me from playing.

I sat on the bench and realized that I was a pariah. I'd heard that word—overheard it, really—one awkward visit to the bakery. I ran into a guy there who I knew only vaguely. We recognized each other and said "Hey," but that was it. The bakery was crowded and we had to wait. The woman behind the counter finally called my number, and when she saw it was me, her face sort of fell. Like she didn't want to even get me my box of donuts or touch my money. This guy, who was being helped farther down the counter, said to his wife: "So that's what it's like to be a pariah."

To tell you the truth, I thought he was calling me a piranha, though I couldn't figure out why he'd call me a man-eating fish. I didn't know what a pariah was. I had to Google it. "A person despised and rejected by everyone. Outcast, leper, untouchable." It was awful, to read that. It was so harsh. But when Chuck said what he did, I understood that guy in the bakery was right. I was untouchable, a leper.

The shunning was very effective. They didn't actually ignore me. Everyone talked to me on the bench, like this was the way it had always been. I sat there in my team shirt and cheered for everyone. Afterward, when the team went to the Blue Line, the hardware store being our sponsor that year, I went home. I've never been back inside any of the bars in Maurus.

No one, and I mean *no one,* questioned why I wasn't playing. Not *Are you hurt?* or *Why aren't you playing?* Not even my parents, who were at that first game. They knew right away what was going on, and they stopped coming.

I thought if I bided my time, they would relent and things would go back to normal. I went to practice and demonstrated my skills. The guys practiced with me like I was a full member of the team. But I was not on the roster. I thought if I showed loyalty, patience, perseverance, things would change. I wouldn't make a fuss about it. I'd suck it up. I sat on the bench for six games. But then Frank, who knew about the situation from my parents, said we really needed to finish a job on Tuesday night. It wasn't true, but it gave me an honorable way out. I called Chuck to let him know why I wouldn't be there and he said, "Thanks for letting me know."

Now and then I ran into someone who didn't know. Didn't know I was "the partner" or only vaguely knew about "the cop shooting in Maurus." Steve Briggs, who had moved to the Twin Cities, ran into me and Kelsey at a summer music event in Castor. "Hey, Kelsey and Paul! Cool!" he said. Then, "Paul, how is the cop life treating you?"

"What?"

"Aren't you a cop? I heard you were a cop."

"Oh, no, that was just part time. It wasn't going to turn into anything. I'm doing landscaping with Frank."

"Oh, cool. What kind of landscaping? Mowing lawns and stuff?"

"No, that's yard maintenance. We seed lawns, lay sod, build retaining walls, rock and edging, that kind of thing."

And we easily moved on to talk about his job and family. He said before he left how good it was to see us, and how good we looked together. He was happy for us. He seemed to have missed the whole Chris Miller story—the marriage, the kids, the divorce, the murder. I don't know if he was just out of it or what.

"That is what it would be like if we lived somewhere else," I said, once he'd left and we were settled on our blanket listening to the music. "We could have small talk. People could just get to know us for who we are now."

"I can't," Kelsey said. "I can't leave. Not yet."

I was working so hard at making things normal, I tried not to think about Jim Kastenbauer and his police scanner. I did ask Frank if he'd heard anything about Jim Kastenbauer over the years.

"I heard he had some hippie operation going, turning himself into a truck farmer."

"Organic. He's an organic farmer," I said.

"Yeah, OK."

"But anything else? Anything related to Chris Miller?"

Frank looked at me. "Paul, you should try to move on from that. I mean, as much as you can."

"But what do you hear?"

"Nothing about Jim Kastenbauer," he said.

"But other things? You hear other things about the investigation?"

"I hear all sorts of crazy things, Paul. Nothing worth telling you."

I looked at him steadily. "I want to know," I said.

"It's all rumor. Conspiracy theories."

"Like what?"

"Like there's a cocaine ring and the police and granite company are involved in it, hiding shipments in the granite warehouse under slabs or in boxes of tile."

I had to laugh. "Yeah, well, that is crazy."

Frank didn't laugh, though. "Paul, no one knows what happened to Chris Miller or why, and no one is going to ever figure it out."

"What else do they say?" He knew I was asking about myself.

"Bullshit. Piles and piles of bullshit."

"Yeah, like what?"

"You and Kelsey. That you had a motive."

I took a minute to let that sink in. "But I hadn't even seen her before—"

"You think that matters? People talk, Paul. Like I say. You don't want to know. And it's all bullshit."

"I'm going to have to move," I said.

"Yes, I think you are," he said. "I love you, brother, and you are a great partner. I don't want to lose you in the business or in my life. But in Maurus, this will never go away. You're never going to get free of it unless you leave."

Chapter Twenty-one

It was August when I finally learned about Lisa Hawkins. A guy we'd been doing a lot of work for invited Frank and me out to his house on Fraser Lake to do some fishing. There were five of us, in a very nice boat, but we only knew the guy who invited us, Stan. I didn't even know him very well. It was unusual to get an invitation like this, or be out at the Agamis at all. Other than the property calls when I was an officer, I never went out there. Most of our trips were caused by a security alarm set off by a squirrel or a cat. Sometimes a suspected gas leak or water main break, a boat not tied down properly that drifted off. It was almost entirely property calls.

Fraser Lake is the nicest of the Agamis, where we used to sneak in as kids. There are a few developers who have pushed the prices way up. As the Twin Cities have grown, and more money has poured in there, a new group of people have been interested in vacation homes. Unlike Alexandria, these aren't family resorts or cabins. The Agamis are sort of a world apart, people with money from the Twin Cities. Lots of these places, mansions really, were built where there were already big houses, teardowns.

The cove where Stan lived was the most recent part of the lake to be developed. Stan and another guy, Mason Parker, both had places in the cove. I'd say they were both in their fifties or early sixties, executives. Stan worked in finance some way, and I don't know what Mason did. The third guy, Spencer, was just up for an overnight. He was some kind of junior executive, a fund manager, he called himself, at Stan's firm. He was clearly there to impress his boss, but the guy was really obnoxious. I don't know if he thought Frank and I were trying to get his job or something. In any event, he seemed to resent us being there, honing in on his time with his boss. Or maybe he was afraid his boss saw him in the same way he saw Frank and me, just the hired help. Then again, he might have been just a plain old asshole.

These guys had some serious money. They were generous, too, wanting us to use their gear. Spencer had brought fancy, bottled beer, all different kinds, from a brewery in the Twin Cities. It was funny because Mason seemed to want to slum it, and he made a point of drinking the six-pack of Maurus beer he had brought. He also brought a bag of Cheetos, and Stan gave him crap for that. The snacks that day, bought and packed by Stan's wife, were salads of different kinds in plastic containers from an upscale grocery in the Cities. Not coleslaw and potato salad. Stuff like curry chicken and rice salad with grapes. There was also smoked salmon and crackers and fancy cheese. They could tell stories about that cheese, and really seemed to care what kind it was. Stan had a couple of large, iced coolers for the stuff.

Frank and I were the local color, part of the slumming adventure. Mason and Stan wanted to know where we fished, what we caught, and took our advice about bait seriously. Whatever. We'd been fishing our whole lives, but there wasn't any trick to it. A pole and some leeches, or if no leeches then worms, or whatever they had at the gas station was fine. But we talked it up like we were giving them the inside info.

Their fishing stories were exotic. They talked about fly-fishing in Montana and deep sea fishing in the Caribbean. Mason had been to Alaska to catch salmon, but we knew guys who did that, even who worked on Alaska fishing boats after school to save money. Spencer didn't have any stories like this to share. He seemed very comfortable with a leech, too. I suspect he grew up in a town like Maurus, and though it would have probably won him points with his boss, he seemed intent on not letting his humble beginnings show.

The Agamis are well stocked, so you always catch something. Most of what we caught we released because they were too small, but we did manage to catch several good-sized sunnies apiece. Actually, Frank caught the most, which gave us more status as locals-in-the-know.

The guys got looser with their talk as the day went on and the beers were consumed. They knew, of course, about Chris Miller, but they had no idea about my part in the whole thing. They didn't know I'd ever been anything but a landscaper.

Mason first brought it up. "Hey, did they ever catch the guy who killed that police officer?"

Frank looked at me, and we shook our heads no.

269

"That was such a mystery—bizarre, no?"

"In such a quiet place," Stan said. "You'd never expect something like that to happen in Maurus."

"It does seem like the police really botched things up, though," Mason said.

"What do you mean?" I asked. Frank looked at me, concerned, but I looked straight back to let him know I wouldn't say anything stupid.

"Oh, you can't expect a department like this, I mean a small town department, to be able to handle a major crime like that," Stan said. Although I pretty much agreed, it still gave me a twinge to hear Stan say it.

"It did seem like they were *particularly* out of their league on this one," Mason said. It was hard to hold my tongue. Clearly he was saying the Maurus Police Department was always incompetent, but even worse this time around.

"I don't know much about it," Spencer said, "but I heard the police chief interviewed on public radio and he—no offense, but he didn't seem so smart."

Spencer was a twat. But now Mason and Stan, relaxing to find they were all on the same page, joined in.

"How could there have been no witnesses?" Mason said. "If you ask me, the guy just slipped into the bar and blended in."

"With a shotgun?" I asked.

"Yeah," he conceded. "That doesn't make a lot of sense."

"So they never found the gun?" Stan asked.

Frank and I shook our heads.

"So, what's the word around here?" Stan asked me. "What are people saying in town?"

I shrugged. Frank was still looking at me intently. "Seems like there's no leads," I said. "No one knows."

We were quiet for a while, concentrating on the fishing. Then Stan said, "I haven't had a good feeling about the Maurus cops since Lisa Hawkins."

"Yeah," Mason agreed. "That was awful."

The name Lisa Hawkins registered with me, but just barely. It was a missing person case, the summer before. She was from Welker, out of our jurisdiction. Welker asked for help, thought she might have been in Maurus, when a friend or family member reported her missing. The investigation didn't go anywhere. As I remembered it, there was no evidence she'd been in this area.

"Who is Lisa Hawkins?" Spencer asked.

"I only know what I heard. The story didn't even make the paper," Stan said. Mason nodded in agreement.

"I know Bill Friedrichs, whose house is next door, and he said it was tragic, but what are you going to do? If the police didn't help, who was going to?"

Frank and I just stared out at our lines.

"So what happened?" Spencer asked.

"Lisa Hawkins is from some godforsaken little place down near Welker. I don't even think the town has a name, and it's a ways from here. She did some dealing on the lakes, small stuff, cocaine and prescription drugs."

I wondered when cocaine had become "small stuff," but I just listened. These guys were from a different world.

"Well, she got involved with this football player. Bill's neighbor. Bill says he's got some anger issues. Could be really nice, but also had some issues with people in his hot tub or playing basketball, things like that. He was very full of himself. He was a pro, played with the Rams for a few seasons."

"Fullback," Stan said. "He wasn't here long."

I had heard about this guy, too. In fact, I had heard about him from Chris Miller. Chris had been really impressed that this pro football player was moving to town, but moving to the Agamis wasn't exactly moving to town. We never interacted with these folks, except to see them at the hardware store or gas station, or pass them in their giant SUVs hauling boats down Highway 41. They didn't even shop at Staley's unless they had to. I'd heard a woman once complaining about the ice cream selection—no Häagen-Dazs or Ben & Jerry's. How could they be expected to eat Kemps or Bluebird? The Staley's clerk just shrugged. Why stock things just for them—they weren't going to buy enough to make it worthwhile. The gas station had some Ben & Jerry's, but not the flavor the woman's children liked, apparently.

Just like they thought our town was secretive, we had no idea what went on out there on the lakes. Oxycontin and other "small stuff" apparently.

"Well, this guy wasn't a big partier, but people did come up from the Cities. Lots of bling, you know what I mean? White guy, but he had a posse."

"He had a 22-foot Scarab, didn't he?" Stan asked.

"Yes, yes he did," Mason said. "He had a couple of fast boats. Bill was not happy about the noise."

"Did he call the police?" Spencer asked.

"Aw, no," Stan said. "You can't do that around here, not to your neighbors." Spencer lost a point with his boss there. "And you can't do anything about people having boats and Jet Skis on a lake."

"Plus," Mason said, "there was a cop who hung out there."

This is when I perked up. I actually looked over at Mason. He was standing with a can of beer in one hand and a cracker topped with salmon in the other, holding forth. "Who?" I asked.

"I don't know. But it was a local cop. He came out several times. Rode the Jet Skis. Drank the guy's booze. Hung out in the hot tub."

"When was this?"

"Uh, this was a couple years ago. The football player moved out over a year ago. After Lisa Hawkins. I think the cop probably encouraged him to go."

It was surreal. I believed right away that Chris was hanging out with this football player. I could see it clearly. But he would have talked about it. Man, would he ever have talked about it. He would have talked about nothing but that.

"So what happened to Lisa Hawkins?" Spencer asked.

"Lisa had some business with them. And then, before you know it, Lisa was romantically involved with the guy, this football player."

"What was his name?" Stan asked.

"It was something common, like Tim Smith or something. He hardly played, didn't get much notice. I looked him up online, and there was nothing there, just stats. He was brought in to back up Franco Van Buren, and that guy never got hurt. He was big, more of a blocker than a runner."

"I think it was Mike something," Stan said. "Mike Lee, maybe." I could see Spencer was wishing he knew more about football. I knew it was Mike Peters, but I didn't say anything. I wanted to hear the story.

"That could be it," Mason said. "I do think it was Mike. So anyway, then Lisa and Mike were an item."

"Local girl makes good," Spencer said, wryly. I wanted to punch that guy.

"And I only know what Bill told me about the rest," Mason said. "The story is that one day they were on the boat—not the Scarab, he had a Cobalt with a cabin—and things got out of hand. It was Mike and Lisa and this cop and two other guys from Mike's crew, or his posse, whatever they call it. Maybe other girls, I'm not sure. At least that many people.

"They were presumably high on something, drinking, who knows. Things went south. Things went bad, especially for the girl. I heard she was beat up pretty badly."

"With a cop on board?" Spencer asked.

"Oh, yes, that part was definite. There was a local cop there."

"Nice," Spencer said. "Classy."

"Who?" This time it was Frank.

"I don't know. Do you, Stan?"

Stan shook his head. "I never heard any names. Just that there was a cop there and he did nothing."

"I don't believe it," Frank said. "I don't believe there was a cop there."

Mason and Stan looked at each other. "Hey, for all I know, none of it happened," Mason said. "This is just what Bill said."

"How does Bill know what happened? Was he on the boat?" Frank asked, maybe a little too sharply.

"No," Mason said, not sounding the least bit defensive. Rich guys are like that. They just talk, like it's nothing to them. Sharing some information. No harm, no foul. "He wasn't there, but he did see them getting off at the dock. He saw them carry the girl off the boat. He saw the guy who he knew was a cop."

"Maybe he was mistaken," Frank said.

"Well, he wasn't mistaken about the girl. She was unconscious. And no ambulance came. Nothing. No cops. No ambulance. She was carried into that house and that was it. The next day her car was gone and Bill said he never saw her again." With that, Mason crushed his empty beer can in his hand and dropped it in the wastebasket by the cooler.

"Hmm," Spencer said. "Not good." We were quiet again, and then Stan caught another fish. With that, he decided it was time to head back and get out of the sun. We pulled in our lines and packed up while Stan drove the boat to the house. Frank and I sat quietly in our seats. Spencer looked a little seasick. He was wearing a baseball cap with radio call letters on it, some station I didn't know, probably classical or jazz, and he held it to keep it from blowing off his little pinhead. Frank and I were used to

275

being outside in the heat, not even wearing hats, and the breeze in my hair felt good.

Back on the dock, Stan proposed going inside for gin and tonics, but I wanted to get out of there. Frank didn't argue with me. We said we had a family thing to get to, and left. Stan did insist we take some fish, and he went inside for a plastic bag and ice.

"I hope you weren't offended by that story," Mason said.

"No, no, not at all," Frank said. I shook my head.

"It just doesn't quite add up," Frank said.

"No, it doesn't add up. That's true." Mason sort of chuckled, as though what it added up to was perfectly clear. I wanted Frank to stop, but I also needed more information.

"Did these guys, out at the football player's house, did any of them drive a black sedan by any chance?" I asked.

Mason thought a moment. "I only saw the cars coming and going along the lake road. I didn't see all of them, I'm sure, but these were strictly SUV guys. Lisa Hawkins's car was red. A little hatchback."

Stan arrived with the bag of ice, little discs of ice you get from a fancy refrigerator door, and he packed several barely breathing fish into it and handed the bag to Frank. "Doesn't get any fresher than that," he said. We said our goodbyes, shook hands, even with Spencer, and walked around the back of the house to the car, while the other three retreated inside.

In the truck, Frank paused before turning the key in the ignition. "Those guys are full of shit. I bet there is no such person as Lisa Hawkins."

"There is," I said.

He looked at me. "You know who she is?"

"Missing person," I said. "I don't know who did the investigation, but we turned it back over to Welker."

Frank just sat there with his hand on the key, looking at me. "You think it was Chris Miller, don't you? On the boat."

"Might have been. But I can't imagine him keeping something like a friendship with a pro football player to himself."

"You're right there," Frank said, smiling. "Chris always was a braggart."

"But if there were drugs involved—" I said.

"That doesn't seem like him."

I had no idea anymore. I had already lost confidence in what I thought I knew about Chris Miller. "Maybe he was on his own personal, undercover mission. Maybe he thought he was setting up some kind of sting operation."

"Sounds pretty rogue," Frank said. Then, after a pause, he added: "Sounds like Chris, too."

We were quiet again, and then Frank said, "But what about the girl? He would have reported that, right?"

I looked at Frank. "I don't know. I really don't know what he would have done."

Frank turned the key and the truck started with a roar. As we drove away I glanced back to see Stan watching us through the big picture window.

Chapter Twenty-two

I actually thought about calling the anonymous tip line. But what would I say? That I believed the hero Chris Miller might have been involved in the disappearance and possible murder of Lisa Hawkins? That his participation in the cover-up might be what got him killed?

What I really wanted to know was how Jim Kastenbauer was involved.

A few days later, I went out and asked Jim himself.

I found Jim chopping weeds in the big garden behind his house. I stayed at the edge of the plot. He had a hoe, I didn't think people still used those, and he was stabbing away at the ground and dragging the weeds from a row of cabbages. The place looked like a total mess to me.

"Hi, Wonderboy," he said.

"I wish you'd stop calling me that," I said.

He shrugged. "What's up?"

"I need to ask you something," I said.

"Yeah, sure, go ahead," he said. He hacked at the weeds some more.

"Could we—could you take a break, maybe?"

He stood up and took off his cap. The sun was bright and he wiped sweat off his brow. "I guess so," he said. "But I have a lot of work to do."

We walked to the side of his trailer, where there was a pipe sticking out of the ground with a hose attached to it. He turned on the spigot, found the end of the hose, and washed his hands. He poured water on his face and over his head, then put his cap back on. He stood up, wiped his face in one motion, and faced me, seemingly refreshed.

"Can we go inside?" I asked.

"Naw, I don't want to get the place all dirty," he said. "Afraid someone will see you talking to me?"

I just looked at him. He didn't understand things had changed since our last meeting. I was going to have the upper hand this time. "Why should I be afraid?"

He pursed his lips together, with only the slightest smirk. Then he said, "I don't know." He gestured to the picnic table, and I nodded. But I didn't really want to sit down either. We walked in that direction and stood there. Finally, he sat on top of the table and put his feet on the bench. "Well?"

"How do you know Lisa Hawkins?" I asked. He seemed to know this was coming. Still, he reached up and adjusted his cap.

"How do you know her?" I kept my eyes on him, my body squarely facing his.

"She's my—she *was* my cousin," he said.

My mouth went dry. I felt a slight pounding in my head. I nodded.

"She was a beautiful girl," Jim said. He seemed completely at ease. "Sweet. Younger than me. A little lost, but a really sweet girl."

"What happened to her?"

He looked up at me, and I saw a brief look of surprise, then a hardening in his face. "I think you know."

"No," I said. "I don't."

"But you were an officer then—you were his fuckin' partner." He'd gone from easy to anger so fast, it scared me a little.

"Jim, I honestly don't know what you're talking about," I said. "Please, please tell me what happened." Now I did want to sit down, but I couldn't. We were just going to have to be uncomfortable.

"So how do you know to ask me?"

"If I knew anything about her, I would have asked last time. Why didn't you just tell me then?"

Jim put up his hand, as if pushing me away. "I've done all my talking."

"To who? Who did you talk to? Chief Kramer?"

"Chief Kramer, yeah. Him. The sheriff got my letters and messages, too."

"Jim, you gotta believe me. I didn't know about this. I want to know." I guess I convinced him, because his face kind of dropped then into its customary sadness. He looked down as he talked and rubbed a blister on his palm with his thumb, like picking at a scab.

"Lisa was involved with the football player, Mike Peters, out on Fraser Lake," he said. "They went out on a boat—with Chris Miller—and she was never seen again."

"And you think she's dead?"

"I *know* she's dead," he said. "She's completely gone. Her car, her body. No phone calls, no texts, no hospital or morgue. Her brother talked to her two days before. She was fine. She was happy."

"What do the Welker police say?"

He sneered at me. "The Welker police? What do the *Welker* police say?"

"I understand they were doing the investigation," I said.

He leaned back. "Am I really supposed to believe you don't know anything?"

I held his gaze. "I don't, Jim. I heard her name, by chance, just the other day. I remembered it was a missing person case but was turned over to Welker. But I believe there was more to it. That's why I'm here. I want to know the truth."

He leaned forward, his elbows on his knees. "There's no truth," he said. "And there's no justice, either, except what you make yourself." He stood up and pushed past me, brushing my shoulder. He started to walk to the trailer, stopped, took a few steps toward the garden, but stopped again. I faced him.

"Hey, listen, sit down. Let's sit down here," I said, pulling out one of the weathered cedar benches for him. I sat down on the other side of the table. He came over but just stood there, his jaw working, challenging me.

"Tell me what happened," I said. "Tell me what you know. Sit down and tell me the truth about Chris Miller."

Jim kicked at the bench, roughly, then sat down. His eyes were red, and he stared at me. He was going to tell me, but he wasn't going to give me any credit for asking. It was too late for that.

"Her brother, Sam, he knew about Lisa dating Mike Peters. And he was worried, but she said for him not to worry, because Mike was a good guy, and because, well, because Chris, she tells him, this *cop* named *Chris,* was hanging with them." He spit out the words.

"And then she disappeared," he continued. "And we reported it in Welker, but told them she had been up here, on Fraser Lake." He paused to let it sink in. Then, "So the Welker police, they go to Maurus, and guess what happens?"

I shook my head. I wanted him to tell me.

"Nothing. Nothing happens. As far as I can tell, they don't even go out to Peters's house. They don't canvas the neighborhood or anything else that would seem like an investigation. Somehow Chris Miller's name never seems to come up in connection with her disappearance either. It's like they didn't even hear Sam say the name "Chris" or anything Lisa told Sam, because in no time at all the Welker police are telling Sam that Lisa was never in Maurus, and they suspect her disappearance is drug-related. You know what that means."

"No," I said, softly. "Tell me."

"It means *We don't care what happened to her.* It means *We're not going to look for her anymore, but we'll let you know*

283

if we hear anything. If anything turns up. It means *She got what she deserved.* "

I shook my head and looked at the table. His pain was palpable, behind all the anger.

"I go up there," he said. "I go up there to the station, too, and I want to know if they have checked out Mike Peters, and if they're protecting Chris Miller. I talk to the chief. I tell him I want to make a statement. I want to know what they're doing to find my cousin."

I nodded, and held his gaze. And the tears that were forming disappeared, his face shifted again to anger. "And so they send some guys from the drug task force in Castor around. They come out here to see if I'm growing weed. Which I'm not. But they think they can scare me. They think they can discredit me. And they can't, but they walk all over my father's land and go into his barns and search. They get my father all worked up, and he threatens to kick me off the property."

I could see the blood vessels bursting in his eyes as he talked, more rage than tears. I couldn't say anything. I just kept paying attention. I just listened.

"So I'm out, and it's only Sam. And nobody cares about Sam, down in Welker, what can he do? He can't force them to interview anyone, and before you know it Peters and his people have gone back to Minnetonka and the house is sold at a loss and there are new people in it. Nobody wants to hear Sam's speculations, or Sam's pleas. Sam goes a little crazy. I go a little crazy with him."

"I'm sorry," I said.

He just looked at me, saying nothing. Then, almost a growl, he said: "You don't have to be sorry. It's all over now."

I looked back at him. I don't know that it's over. I know what he's saying—someone got justice for Lisa Hawkins. This is why Chris Miller is dead. But I'm not sure yet if I'm talking to a murderer. A cop killer.

"Where is Sam?" I asked.

Then he started to cry. His face screwed itself up involuntarily and angry tears squeezed from his eyes. "Sam's dead," he said, in a growl that was more hoarse this time. Then again, like a punch to the face, clearly, he repeated: "Sam is dead."

I sat there. I wanted to know how. I wanted to know if Sam killed Chris, or if Jim did. I just waited, while Jim fought with himself, coughed out his angry tears, wiped his face, and pulled himself back together. I didn't know if he was going to make me ask the question. I didn't know if he was going to tell me, or if he was going to make me say it. He sat there, composed, just looking at me. I knew what I wanted to be the story. So I phrased my question.

"Did Sam get justice for Lisa?" I asked. And Jim nodded. He looked me in the eye and nodded his head, yes. I didn't ask any more. I could have asked if he was the one who called in the welfare check. If I had still been a cop, that is what I would have asked. But I already knew. I didn't have to make him say it. And then he'd listened to the scene play out on the police scanner. He'd heard me make the call, "Officer down." He knew I hadn't seen a six-foot man in a hoodie. He knew Sam wasn't going to shoot me. Sam expected to get shot by me. Sam was on a suicide mission. Jim waited to hear me shoot Sam. He knew before anyone else that I didn't do my job.

I got up, gripped his shoulder briefly, and left.

I found the rest of what I needed to know on the Internet. There was a brief news item about the death of Sam Hawkins of Welker. He died of an apparent self-inflicted gunshot wound in December, a few weeks after Chris Miller was killed. He had been concerned about his sister, Lisa Hawkins, who disappeared more than a year earlier. Lisa, the article said, was known to be active in the narcotics trade. Police described her case as open but inactive. Her brother had expressed frustration over the case, but there had been no leads. Hawkins's whereabouts at the time of her disappearance were unclear, but it was suspected she was not in Welker. The gun used in the suicide was a handgun, but Sam was the owner of several guns, including an automatic rifle and a shotgun. The two siblings had been more or less on their own. Their mother died in a car accident five years earlier, and the father was disabled and in a nursing home.

I found an obituary, too, on the funeral home website. It said Sam had graduated from Mankato State and worked since then at the technical college in Welker, maintaining and operating the science labs. He was an avid cyclist and had participated in several long-distance events. It did not have that line about who he was survived by. It just said, "He will be missed by family and friends," then the funeral information.

"Why are you so quiet tonight?" Kelsey asked. We were sitting outside around the fire pit, watching Zach doze in his chair.

I was thinking about Lisa Hawkins and Chris Miller, of course. I had spent some time after my visit with Jim reading, not just the stuff about Sam and Lisa Hawkins, but also visiting the old Chris Miller pages. The Facebook page had been overtaken by tributes and stories about another cop, this one from Badenberg, a small town near Alex. He had died of cancer a couple weeks before, and remembrances of him, full of the same clichés as had surrounded Chris, had pushed down the stories about Chris's murder. I scrolled and found the coverage of the highway dedication. Further back were a few posts by Chris's brother, Gary, from May, about missing Chris, with fewer than a dozen comments of support. I searched for news items but it was the same old stuff.

When I arrived at Kelsey's, I still hadn't decided if I would tell her what I knew. Right away Kyle wanted me to go out back to see the new tetherball set he got from Kelsey's parents. He wanted me to set it up so we could play. Kelsey seemed relieved to see me and sent the other two boys outside, too. Shane helped me find some tools in the garage, Chris's tools, and we pounded the pole in a spot with enough room for the ball to spin out on its farthest orbit.

After dinner and more tetherball, Kelsey and the two younger boys went into the brush at the back of the property and gathered kindling. Shane helped me bring chairs from the garage and build a fire in the fire pit.

The yards in Frogtown are narrow but deep. Thick brush separates the back of the property from the city golf course. It was fun to walk back there and look for golf balls. One night Shane had the idea of putting on his swimsuit, mask, and snorkel and going into one of the shallow ponds to retrieve lost balls. I went with him, wading in a bit but mainly standing guard and making sure he didn't drown. He didn't need the mask, as he didn't go underwater and mostly just mucked around with his hands near the edge until he found the golf balls.

We got half a bucket full, and he meticulously cleaned them and separated them by value. Then on a nice Saturday he set up a table on his property at the edge of the course, right by the 7th hole, and sold the balls back to the golfers who had lost them. The kid was a genius.

Kelsey brought wine in juice jars for the two of us, and we sat, the five of us, around the fire. The boys poked it occasionally with sticks, and a small duel broke out between Shane and Kyle. By the time it was full dark, nearly ten p.m., Zach sat with glazed eyes staring at the fire, his mouth hanging open, and Shane and Kyle were off running around with flashlights, playing some game of their own invention.

"You're awfully quiet tonight," Kelsey said.

"No I'm not," I said.

"Yes you are. All night. What's going on?"

I pointed to Zach. "Want me to take him up?"

"I'll do it," she said. "And then we're going to talk."

I nodded. "I'll be here."

She lifted Zach out of the chair and he clung to her like a monkey, wrapping his arms and legs around her. She called the other two boys. They protested, but not loudly or very long. Whining, they followed Kelsey inside. I sat with my thoughts, wondering how to tell her what I knew, or *what* to tell her. She was back in a surprisingly short time. Once the boys gave up, they must have completely given up.

"I'm such a bad mother," she said. "I didn't even brush Zach's teeth. He was basically asleep."

"You're a great mother," I said.

She snorted, and took her seat. Then she got up and put another log on the fire. Sparks flew and it rolled, but I used my poking stick to steady it. The rest of the fire collapsed and the new log fell, jutting out on one side.

"So," she said, settling into her chair. "What is going on?"

I poked at the fire a little more, and then I said, "I know who killed Chris."

She looked at me, then back at the fire. "Jesus," she said. "Who?"

I told her about Sam and Lisa Hawkins, Jim Kastenbauer's cousins, both dead. And she listened, sometimes looking at me but mostly looking into the fire. I told her about Mike Peters and Fraser Lake, and how I'd found this out.

She wiped her eyes when she heard about Chris hanging out on the lake and about Lisa. I wasn't sure if she was sad about Chris or about Lisa. I wished I could see her more clearly, make out the subtleties of her expression. Her face at the edge of the firelight was a play of light and shadow. Her hair was pulled back, leaving the blankness of her forehead. I could see her eyes, large and dark, but her small mouth all but disappeared.

"Are you OK?" I asked. She nodded, then wiped her eyes again.

She didn't say anything, so I just continued my story. I could tell she was taking it in, working through the details. She didn't ask any questions or say anything until I was finished.

After a long pause, she said: "That all makes sense." She wiped her eyes and sniffled.

"I'm sorry, Kelsey," I said.

She shook her head. "You don't have to be sorry."

"Yeah, but I am." We sat in silence some more. She poked at the fire with a stick she'd taken from one of the boys.

"Are you going to tell the police?" she asked. "There's a new chief now." By then Chief Kramer had retired. They'd replaced him with someone outside of the department, which was unusual. But the article in the *Standard* described the new guy as just another small-town cop. This was a promotion for him; he was from a much smaller town in southwestern Minnesota. There he had been one of two officers. In Maurus, he would manage a staff of eight.

I shook my head. "I don't think so. Do you want me to?"

She paused. Then she looked at the fire and said, "The killer's dead, right?"

"Yes," I answered.

"Do you think it would help them find Lisa Hawkins's body? To know?"

"Honestly, I don't know."

"It will get Jim Kastenbauer in trouble. He knew what his cousin did."

"It might. I think he probably called in the welfare check himself. He could be an accomplice."

She looked back at the fire. "Do you think he's dangerous?"

I shook my head. "No. Not at all."

"It will upset a lot of people."

"Chris is a hero. It will be a scandal."

She was quiet, and then said, "No. Let's not. Let's not tell anyone."

I nodded, and she added, "I want my boys to think their dad was a hero."

I picked up the bottle of wine and refilled both our glasses. We didn't toast, but it still felt like we were sealing a pact of some sort. Looking at each other, we each took a good, long drink.

Chapter Twenty-three

I told Frank, who thought I should pursue it. He said it would clear my name, undo the rumors about me and my role. I didn't care about that, I said. No one could believe I had anything to do with the actual murder. And no one was questioning me. Let the town have its hero, and let the murder remain a mystery, give people something to conjecture about now and then. None of it changed what I did. Nothing could save my reputation as the guy who left the scene.

There was one time, though, that I was tempted to tell what I knew. We were all at my parents' house. It was an unusually warm day in October, Indian summer. My mom had made her famous potato salad and bought brats for one last cookout before it got cold. I've always loved October in Minnesota, with its odd mix of promise and closure. "The boys of October," that's what they call the World Series teams. I love that. Closing out with a big win, somehow rallying the strength for a series of big games, wearing long sleeves under baseball jerseys.

For me, things were going well. It did seem like people might forget about Chris Miller eventually. In any event, his death didn't color my interactions with people in public places like it had a year earlier. There would be the anniversary in a few weeks, but I was hoping we could just move on. Knowing what happened, even after deciding not to expose Chris, made me feel better. People could say what they wanted, but I knew what I knew. And Kelsey, and Frank, they knew the truth, too. That was all that mattered to me, really.

At the cookout, my dad was in good form. From the moment we arrived, he started telling stories about guys from the granite company, about the old days. He even complimented my mother on her potato salad. We were all just happy to be together.

The boys were right at home. I helped Zach get out an old model John Deere set my mother had brought down from an upstairs closet. He was playing harvest in the gravel along the side of the drive. Clare joined him and they were having fun. Like cousins. Shane was allowed to play one video game on my mother's computer before dinner, and was inside while my mother finished up the meal.

Patty really liked Kelsey. She helped her get the table set with an old tablecloth and plastic plates. Kyle didn't like anyone moving in on his mother like that, and so was making a big show of getting the plastic cups.

"Why don't you and Patty write everyone's names on the cups," Kelsey said. She retrieved the Sharpies my mother used for that.

"I'll write my family's names," Kyle said. "You can write yours."

"Who's gonna write Gramma and Grampa's names?" Patty asked.

"I'll do Grampa and you do Gramma," Kyle instructed.

"I'll write Uncle Paul's name," Patty said.

"No!" yelled Kyle. *"No you won't!"*

My dad looked over from the grill, and Kelsey spoke up sharply. "Kyle! Don't be bossy."

"But she wants to write Paul's name," Kyle whined.

"That's OK," Kelsey said.

"She's supposed to write her own family, not mine," Kyle said.

Kelsey looked at me. Everyone was focused on the kids now, even Frank and Joanie, sitting on lawn chairs drinking beer with me.

"Uncle Paul's *my* family," Patty said, meanly. "*Not* yours."

Kyle's face crumpled up, hearing that. He started to cry.

"I need two cups," I said, "for my beer and my iced tea." But it was too late. Kyle was entering a full-blown meltdown.

Kelsey went to him, and he raised his arms to be lifted up. He was too big for that, but she helped him off the bench and turned to go inside. I stood up.

"Patty, why can't you be nice to Kyle?" Joanie said.

My dad, though, didn't look pleased. I could just hear him muttering, "Mama's boy." He'd made a comment here and there about the boys being oversensitive, though really it was just Kyle. The defense that they'd lost their father just made him more sour. Kelsey and Kyle disappeared inside, and I could hear my mother asking what happened, inviting him to tell her all about it.

"When Kyle comes back," Frank said to Patty, "I want you to say you're sorry."

Patty just dropped her head to one side. She traded her blue Sharpie for Kyle's green one and kept writing names on cups.

"You better not be writing his family's names," Joanie said.

"I'm *not*," said Patty. "But can I write Gramma *and* Grampa's?"

In the end I got two cups, "Paul" and "Uncle Paul." They were decorated, one with flowers and one with baseball bats and balls. I highly praised both. And though I prefer beer from the can, I used Kyle's for my beer, at his request.

My father's good mood had been broken, though. He was quiet during dinner. Afterward, Shane offered to help my mother serve the ice cream. She took his hand and they walked inside together, and I saw my father frown. He said, low but clear, "He's a little old for holding hands, don't you think?" I felt a wave of embarrassment for Shane. I felt protective, too.

After apple pie and ice cream, the kids ran around the yard playing flashlight tag. It was cooler, and we adults put on sweatshirts and jackets, but the kids couldn't be convinced to put on even socks and shoes. Minnesota kids, I thought. There's no such thing as cold.

My parents' yard was small, but the kids used the trees and garages, the neighbor's fence, hiding and flashing. Patty and Clare squealed with excitement whenever they were caught in the light.

Eventually, as was inevitable, someone got hurt. It was Shane, who fell or maybe was pushed, and skidded in the gravel of the driveway, scraping his palms. As his hands started to burn, he wailed. Kelsey and I both jumped up, and I went to get him. That's when my father lost it.

"Jesus Christ," he said. "What the hell is it now?"

"The boy's hurt," my mother said.

"The boy is a sissy," my father said. I stopped and turned around.

"Dad, that's enough," I said.

But my dad wouldn't be stopped. He stood up and slammed his bottle of beer down on the arm of his chair. It hit sideways and fell to the cement patio, breaking into a thousand shards of glass. We all froze. Frank stood up now, too, and Joanie put her hand to her mouth.

Shane wasn't crying anymore. His mother had reached him, but just stood there. The crash of the bottle, my father's fury, shocked us all. My father stepped toward me. "God damn it, what the hell, Paul," he said. I had no idea what he was talking about.

"Dad, that's enough," I said.

"No, let me say it," he said. "It's about time someone does."

My mouth went dry. I knew exactly what he was going to say, and I would have done anything to stop him. Behind me, my mother was talking. "Don't, Bruce. Don't."

"Paul, I didn't raise you to be a coward. And I am not going to sit by and watch you turn Chris Miller's kids into sissies either. Maybe we were too soft with you. We thought we were encouraging you, that maybe because you were good at school—
"

"Stop it," Kelsey said. "Stop it now." But I held my hand up.

"Look at you. You've disgraced our family, our name. I can't show my face—"

Frank was up now, too, moving over and putting his arm on my dad's shoulder. But my dad waved him off.

"No, Frank. No. We all act like everything's all right. But it is not right, what Paul did. And nothing can make it right."

"It's not his fault," Kelsey said. "Chris—"

I cut her off right there. I turned to face her, where she was holding a pale and confused Shane to her side at the edge of the driveway. I recognized Shane's expression from the day Chris threw the baseball away. "No, Kelsey," I said. "N. O."

This was between me and my father. And this was it, the ultimate consequence for what I did. This was what I deserved— for leaving the scene, for deluding myself into giving a false description of the killer, for betraying the chief and my fellow officers. I had wanted to feel it keenly, and up until then I didn't.

Oh, sure, the town blamed me. The town shunned me. But I lived in the half protection of my family. They let me hold on to the sense that I, too, was a victim, and others were treating me unfairly. In a way, I got away with it. Except of course I didn't.

The broken bottle and my father standing there in the square of light shining from the kitchen onto the patio told me so. The glint of yellow light off the puddle of beer, the shards of amber glass, let me know where I stood. My father's words were my punishment, the ultimate judgment. And once it was said, I was relieved. I could handle it. I knew it. Now it was out there. I was going to have to leave Maurus. Now it was certain. And in a way I was free.

My dad had said what he wanted to say. He didn't have anything more. Frank stood with his head down, rubbing his forehead. No one spoke a word. And then, as I had held everything in that alley when Chris Miller was shot before I passed control of the scene along to the chief, I needed to be the first one to move, to reanimate the scene.

"Let's go," I said to Kelsey. We didn't even bother finding the boys' shoes or getting our dirty casserole dish. We gathered the boys together and into the car. My mother and Joanie started quietly cleaning up, though no one yet found a broom for the bottle. My father skulked off somewhere inside. We abandoned the scene of that family party and were silent the short drive home.

After Kelsey put the kids to bed, I went up to reassure Shane that the evening wasn't his fault. I looked into his pale face against the Minnesota Twins pillowcase, but I couldn't bring myself to touch him, to put my hand on his forehead or arm.

"Are you going to be my dad?" he asked. It took me by surprise. I had thought I'd have to apologize to him, explain something, but he didn't care about any of that.

"Is that something you want?"

He nodded his head. "Yes."

"Me too."

"I love you," he said.

Tears filled my eyes and my voice cracked when I said, "Me too."

Things ended. Things were beginning, too.

Chapter Twenty-four

A friend from college hooked me up with a job at the parks and rec department in Fargo. My experience as a police officer and a landscaper made me an attractive candidate. It might have helped that I was a baseball player with a business degree. I was a little worried about what Chief Kramer might say when they called him for a reference. I figured he would understand as much as anyone the desire to get on with life. In my interview with the rec department, the Chris Miller case never came up.

At home, in good Minnesota fashion, we moved on from that horrible night. We let it go. We didn't forget, but we knew that we were family, no matter what. All families had pain and disappointment. They didn't stop being families. We could live with it. No one apologized. We just couldn't. My dad and I shook hands the next time I saw him, making sure the rest of the family saw it, too. My mother hugged me.

Kelsey and I were married by a Will County judge in a courtroom in Castor. My mother cried and kissed the bride. Kelsey's mother cried and kissed the bride, too. Joanie liked that it was a woman who married us, but my mother did not. There would be a church wedding later, in Fargo, when we were established in a parish.

We sold the houses below market value just to get them off the market quickly. I lost money on mine, but Kelsey did OK. It was a wedding present from Chris, she said, which made me uncomfortable. When we left town, my dad and Frank helped us load the moving van. My mother cried and kissed the boys. Kelsey's mother cried and kissed the boys, too.

I am in charge of the West Fargo sports facilities, the baseball diamonds, soccer fields, and two swimming pools. In winter we maintain the outdoor ice rinks and coordinate indoor gym programs with the schools. I get to be outside a fair amount, but my job is mostly managing staff.

When I'm driving around, checking on the various facilities, I remember the old days on patrol. I'm getting to know the neighborhoods, though I'll never know this place like I know Maurus. There is more diversity here in Fargo, and there is a lot more going on in the parks than baseball and basketball. We get the kids involved with cultural things, Native American heritage and ecological activities. It has been good for Shane, Kyle, and Zach to live in a bigger place. Kelsey is in school in elementary ed. We miss family, but the move has been good for all of us.

We come back to Minnesota often, on long weekends and for vacations. Kelsey takes the boys to see their dad's grave and put flowers on it. They visit Chris's parents, too. Nicole has remarried and has a baby, and everyone's happy for her. She's moved to Castor and works for County Services.

Shane likes to go see the sign on Highway 41, the Chris Miller Memorial Highway. Zach, who doesn't really remember his father, calls it "Daddy's highway." Kelsey's told them that I don't like to go see the sign because it's too painful. She's told them that I was there when their dad died and even though I couldn't do anything, I feel bad about not being able to save him. I know the truth—I don't feel bad about not saving their father. That was never a possibility. I feel bad about saving myself. That's a different thing entirely.

I wonder what will happen when the boys are older and hear the stories about me. Someday they will, from cousins or online, reading stories about their father's death. I try to keep their heads clear of stories about heroes, though in this culture it is hard. Zach is in a superhero phase and wears a cape most of the time. I tell him he doesn't need the cape, that he is strong and fast and good enough without it. He says everyone could use a little extra. I can't argue with that.

Our part of town has gone a little nuts over the World Series this year. A graduate of the local high school is a home-run hitter for the Anaheim Angels, whose chances are good. He has the same lean, wholesome features of Cooper Krekling, my college roommate, who only got as far as the minor leagues. This guy has another great baseball name, Ryan Favaro.

I was in the Walmart Supercenter and one of the clerks, a teenager, was wearing a jersey with his name and number.

I said it was great to see all the support for him, and she said, "I love Ryan. He's my hero."

I just nodded my head. For a moment I felt sorry for Ryan Favaro. It is a lot to live up to, being people's hero. It doesn't usually work out the way you imagine.

Back at home, I told Kelsey the story. She put her arms around my chest and said, "You're my hero." I shook my head. That wasn't what I meant.

We were at a barbecue in June, for the families of some of Kyle's classmates. One of the moms came up to me and said, "You have such great boys."

"Thank you," I said, "but they're not mine. They're Kelsey's kids from her first marriage."

"Oh! I didn't know," she said. "Well, you certainly are good with them. Do you have full custody?"

"Their father died," I said.

"Oh, so Kelsey is a widow," she said. "How long have you been married?"

"Two years," I said.

"Wow, that's brave," she said. "To take on a wife and three kids."

I just looked at her. I didn't know what to say. I looked across the yard at Shane, who was tossing a whiffle ball to a younger boy, very gently, so he could hit it with the giant bat. "They're great kids," I said.

"Still," she said. "Raising another man's three boys. It's a brave thing to do."

I shook my head. "I'm not brave," I said. "I got lucky." And I walked over to where Kelsey was standing and talking to some other parents. I put my hand on her hair and lightly kissed her head. I knew what I said was true. I am the luckiest man alive.

About the Author

Susan Sink is a poet and writer living on 80
acres in Central Minnesota with her husband
Steve Heymans. She has an MFA from Sarah
Lawrence College and was a Wallace Stegner
Fellow in Poetry at Stanford University. Her
website is susansinkblog.com and she posts
essays and poems on medium.com

She has published two volumes of poetry,
The Way of All the Earth and *H is for Harry*
(Northstar Press) and a book of 100-word
stories, *Habits.* This is her first novel.

Deep thanks to the St. Joseph, Minnesota,
police department for answering my
questions about small town policing,
particularly to MaryBeth Munden for reading
a draft and offering valuable feedback. Also
those who read and talked me through
multiple drafts, including Connie Carlson,
Garnett Kilberg Cohen and, of course, Steve.